MARY ROSE

MARY ROSE

GEOFFREY GIRARD

ⓐ ADAPTIVE BOOKS

AN IMPRINT OF ADAPTIVE STUDIOS
CULVER CITY, CA

Lyrics from the song "The Hearse Song" on pages 25, 113, 114, 179 and 197 are
used with permission. Words and Music by Harley Poe © 2012 Harley Poe.
All Rights Reserved. Used with permission of Harley Poe.

"An Old Master's Unheard *Cri de Coeur:* Alfred Hitchcock's
Mary Rose" courtesy of Joseph McBride is used with his permission.
© 2001 Joseph McBride. All Rights Reserved. The essay
was originally published as "Alfred Hitchcock's *Mary
Rose:* An Old Master's Unheard *Cri de Coeur,*" in
Cineaste, Spring 2001.

Visit us on the web at www.adaptivestudios.com

Library of Congress Cataloging in Publication Number: 2017941209
B&N ISBN 978-1-945293-36-8
Ebook ISBN 978-1-945293-45-0

Printed in United States of America.
Interior design by Elyse Strongin, Neuwirth Associates, Inc.

Adaptive Books
3578 Hayden Avenue, Suite 6
Culver City, CA 90232

10 9 8 7 6 5 4 3 2 1

dedicated to
Barbara Pinzka
who haunts my efforts still
(in a good way)

Yes, very sad. Because the real theme is:
If the dead were to come back, what would you do with them?

**—Alfred Hitchcock,
discussing his plans for a movie adaptation of
J. M. Barrie's play *Mary Rose***

Ghosts were here.

Everyone said so. That you could hear them wailing like banshees underneath the winds and surf. Or might even see one slipping between shadow and gray moonlight and the tall dark grasses, lurking just outside the protective beam of a quivering flashlight.

From where the ghosts had come, no one knew for sure.

He'd heard they were the spirits of unbaptized babies.

Or, also, of water spirits who instigated drownings and shipwrecks and lived beneath the island in deep underwater caves. Maybe of forsaken Nazis or pirates who'd drowned here years before and now shambled together along empty dark shorelines for eternity. Or rail-thin wraiths floating on unearthly winds, phantoms with iron claws and grotesque crimson faces dipped in their victims' blood.

Or, these ghosts were simply those who'd heard the island's call. Those who'd chased after it and never returned again.

Ronny trudged ahead even more slowly now.

Straying farther away from the others, probably. Away from his father, too. The sting of the man's hand—or at least the memory of—was still fresh upon his cheek, from when he'd objected to searching without his father by his side. His father embarrassed, disappointed. Yet, Ronny's whole life, the man had expressly said to keep away from the small island. His whole life, he'd only ever known it as "A Forbidden Place." He'd been told its most ancient name, an evil name, a name for a land of few animals but many strange sounds and strange lights, even portals to other worlds and, yes, ghosts.

The few people who ever came out here were devil worshippers and perverts, dared teenagers, and—as proven again for all—foolish tourists.

Tonight, however, the island was overrun with locals. Twenty men, including his father and the village constable, had already combed it from one end to the other. Now the men were dragging the small lake on its southern side, and he and a few of the other boys had been sent off together to look again through the tall grass. No longer forbidden, it seemed.

Oh, how he'd jumped at the chance to join his father and help find the girl. Now he knew better.

He couldn't remember how he'd gotten separated from the other two boys. That was the island, did that. Not its supposed ghosts. Not its brownies, fae, doonies, selkies, or river sprites. All the things various people claimed walked here. No. It was the island itself. A living thing that breathed and hungered. Or, more likely, Ronny suspected, a thing long dead that was only feigning life. Yet still carried old desires, older appetites.

Ronny turned back around, thought he heard the others' voices. Only ten minutes before, he'd been beside Aaron McDuffy and "Mousey" Costello, the three of them finding strength of sorts in numbers. Now there was no one there with him. His schoolmates somehow lost to the night. Each mound and hill in the distance appeared as enormous roiling waves, waves which even moved, so that it was impossible to know where the island ended and the sea began.

He thought of running once more but feared stepping into a hidden hollow, a cave, never to be seen again. No different from the English girl.

He wanted to cry out to the guys. Call their names, call for help.

But what if he wasn't truly alone?

If he cried out to them, what might hear him first?

Behind him, birch trees wavered dimly in the silhouette of night. Like dozens of long crooked witch fingers breaking free from the black earth, stretching to touch an even blacker sky.

He'd already doubled back twice, every turn somehow taking him farther away from where he'd thought his mates had last been. The willowy moon was lost behind massive black clouds, hovering like some prehistoric god above the whole island. Watching him, watching them all, look for the girl. Watching another tragedy unfold. For this was not the first time something like this had happened. There'd been other more horrible stories than the one playing out here tonight.

This time it was an English tourist and his daughter.

Six years old. Gone missing the whole day.

His father and the other local men cursed the English family under their breath. It was more than customary dislike of the outsiders, though. It was something else. His father and the others didn't like being here, either. Old enough to not need a good slap to force them into it but still wary.

"Best hope she's drowned," his father had said, and the other men agreed as if he'd said something kind.

The ground was ragged and uneven suddenly, the grass giving way to rough clusters of rock. Beyond, an outcropping and short hummock. The sound of a narrow stream trickled in the darkness between. Brilliant! He could follow the stream back to the lake where his father would be, or to the shore. In either case, he had his bearings again.

Ronny struggled more carefully, hands to rock, flashlight looking for hidden crevices and jagged edges.

What if he found her?

Out here among the rocks, her body twisted and limp like a discarded toy doll. Would her eyes be open? Would they be glassy too, like a doll's eyes? Shining in the dark.

Or would they be dull and empty? Dead was dead.

Last spring, he'd seen his grandpa laid flat in the casket, all waxy and frozen like a big candle wrapped in a man's suit.

What if the English girl was lying there dead like that?

She might be right here beside him in the dark and he wouldn't even know it. Faceup in the unseen stream. Swollen and blue from the cold. Or worse, alive and sitting in the dark on one of the adjacent rocks. Knees up to her chin. Just sitting there in the dark and waiting for someone else to come along. Would she grab him or, much worse, gently take his hand?

A sound floated past him on the cool night wind, shifting across his face. He told himself it had not been the sound of a little girl.

Ronny's foot slipped, something ripped into his ankle. Fangs! Claws! He screamed and shone his light down. It was not the sharp teeth of a doonie or the ghost of a Nazi. It was not the claws of some dead little girl. It was only a rock.

He moved quicker now, following along the lip of the stream, jogging even, now running, praying his choice led to the lake and his father and not to some mysterious cave where horrible things mostly crawled but sometimes walked.

Then something winked to life, over the next hummock. Glittering, whatever it was. His friends' flashlights, he told himself. Another searcher, maybe. But the light was not one he'd ever seen before.

It was too blue, almost neon. And too . . . *shifting*? More like a cloud of smoke. Unnatural.

He stopped. The weird light now swelled, the glow seeping over the top of the approaching hill and casting dark shadows down toward him. The rocks between mimicked dozens of tiny tombstones. The sound in the wind had pursued him and grown more specific. It had become words.

Many little voices, becoming one voice. Two words, he thought. Over and over and over. Clearly imagining the name he'd first learned only hours before.

Getting up his guts, he started toward the light, the sound, the next mount. The stories were true. The strange lights, the witches' gathering. Rows of black candles, no doubt. Surely the girl was there. Being sliced open, still alive, on a stone altar before an enormous man with thick goat legs and a book with pages written in blood. Or being transformed into something by old naked women smeared in filth and prancing over their black robes.

But he would . . . he would find her, yes, and save her from that and be the hero of this night! And everyone would know, and they'd tell the story for a hundred years about the time he'd found the missing English girl. How his father would look at him then. He could do it—he would do it!

The blue glow hung, lingered, waiting for him. Goading him. Penetrating. One instant promising a lover's slick caress. The next, the warm protective embrace of the Virgin Mary herself. It was like someone trying to pick a lock somewhere deep inside him, fumbling for the precise combination.

The next step forward was somehow more difficult. And the next after that, didn't even happen. He stood shivering in the night. Alone. Except for whatever was behind that hill.

The whispers escalated. Then something almost like music began. High and pulsating as if a hundred tiny fingers were slowly circling the rims of a hundred unseen drinking glasses.

After that, whether it was some kind of Will-o'-the-Wisp or spunkies or only a lost little girl—or maybe something far, far worse—he didn't discover that night.

Instead, he finally turned back and ran. And ran.

Behind him, the island became still and dark again, and any screams he'd cried were lost beneath the violent break of black water against hidden shorelines.

I

For nothing is secret, that shall not be made manifest;
neither anything hid, that shall not be known and come abroad.

—The Gospel of Luke

1

Mary Rose had vanished.

Simon scanned the room again for her—its lolling dark waves of sleeveless silk and tailored summer wool, the buzzing staff, the four-piece ensemble in the corner—half of Philly seemingly gathered tonight in this single penthouse loft. But she was no longer among them.

He moved toward the terrace, hoping for the best. He should have known. Earlier, she'd seemed—

"Simon Blake!" One of the guys from Swaine, Dunn & Crutcher stretched out a hand. "Congratulations, man. Hey, want you to meet some new friends of mine. These fine folk are in from Tenet Healthcare, in Dallas." He'd turned to make the introductions over something by maybe Vivaldi. "We gotta be extra nice to Simon tonight, everyone. He just won a big one against the city this week, and there are a few people in this very room who, well . . ."

"The case against the Housing Authority?" one of the women in the group asked. "Mobility impairments."

"That's the one." Simon skimmed the crowd politely enough behind them, looking. Nope. *Damn.* "How are you all enjoying our city so far?"

"Fabulous!" Another visiting attorney held up his drink to toast one of the truly sterling, and newest, highlights of Philly realty; its double-height ceiling, the five-thousand square feet, the floor-to-ceiling windows. "All we need is to find one of those legendary cheesesteaks before we go, and it'll be a perfect visit."

Simon smiled politely. It was a smile that did well in rooms like this; one that did even better in front of juries and judges. Somehow revealing confidence *and* humility at the same time. If the last five years with the Penn Law Collaborative were any indication, there was no telling how far that smile might take him. The big lead-pipe contamination lawsuit was only last year, and now this one, and up next: lead counsel on his first international case; a little something against one of the world's largest chocolate manufacturers for slave and child labor. Also, the dreaded word "politics" was starting to rear its ugly head for him, hinted at by more than a few people in this very room. Shudder. A path he'd never considered before. And yet . . .

"You were on CNN a week or so ago," the first woman said. "Or was it *Fox & Friends?*"

Simon shrugged. "Is there *really* a difference?"

They laughed.

"Oh yeah," the Swaine, Dunn & Crutcher guy explained: "Simon's turning into a regular national celebrity. Cable news' patron saint of human rights law."

"Well, now . . ." Simon brushed his knuckles on his jacket. "I wouldn't say that. Couple of producers got my name is all. Guess they like me for some reason."

"Producers tend to like good-looking men," the woman said, arching an eyebrow playfully. Perhaps hoping to make her visit east more memorable than a cheesesteak.

"They should meet this guy, then." Simon squeezed Swaine, Dunn & Crutcher's shoulder. "Someone I need to speak with . . . Nice meeting you all." He bowed slightly, then continued quickly to the terrace. Their discussion of him continued, he could hear, in his wake.

Still no sign of Mary Rose, but he'd seen Keith outside chatting up the new local ABC news anchor. It would help to get a second pair of trusted eyes. He'd hoped it would be a good night. Most were. But, too many people, damn it, and this was on him. He hadn't realized it'd be such a zoo.

"Well done, Simon." He felt the pat on the back, turned briefly to see the president of Temple University. He'd done his undergraduate work there, even been cocaptain of the wrestling team; his accomplishments since had not gone unnoticed by the school.

"Thank you, ma'am." Simon saluted, made a mental note to follow up with her later, but pressed ahead. Outside, the heavily ferned terrace overlooked the Schuylkill River from ten stories up. Beyond, the lights of southwest Philadelphia. Home more than ten years ago, though it seemed like a hundred years from there to here, a whole lot of hustle and luck—and, yes, smiles—between.

"There he is!" Keith reached to tap Simon's arm. "Fuckin' Robin Hood."

"Yeah, that's me." Simon checked the terrace. More nope. "Hey, Keith—"

But Keith had turned to the news anchor. "This is the guy who made fifty million for the disabled homeless this week."

"I saw that," she said. "That's very cool."

"Hope so. Could be." Simon looked at Keith. "Not an insurance thing. So, the city will need to find real money somewhere. Just means someone else, someone who probably needs it as much, will get screwed instead."

Keith laughed. "Simon's always a ray of sunshine. Where's Mary, huh? She's the fun one."

"As a matter of fact, I was hoping *you'd* seen her."

Keith shook his head, laughter closing down though his smile remained easy. "Everything okay?" He'd gotten serious quickly, a genuine friend who Simon had confided in before. The only one who knew about Mary Rose, about her bad days.

"No, no . . ." Simon shook off his friend's concern. "Everything's good." *Was it?* Simon finished the drink he'd been nursing. "Thanks."

Keith nodded, changed gears again. "The danger of dating a truly beautiful woman. . . ." He lifted his hand to include the anchor. "Probably stolen by a troll or something."

"Happens all the time," she agreed.

Keith winked at her, turned back to Simon. "So, when's the engagement?"

"Subtle. You're in a merry mood tonight, pal."

"'Mary'? 'Marry'? See, what you did there?" His friend made stupid faces at the news girl, easing the moment even more. He was good at it. "He's had the damned ring for months."

"As a matter of fact"—Simon waved for him to stop—"in two weeks, we're traveling to her parents' home in England. Place called Alderley Edge."

"Oh my God." Keith blinked. "You're asking their permission?"

"We're visiting her parents. Who knows what'll happen?"

"I think it's sweet," the anchor offered.

"Thank you." Simon bowed his head.

"To Simon"—Keith held up his glass—"who wants to change the world, but still loves old-ass traditions."

"Only the good ones," Simon countered. "But all of that won't matter if she's fled the country. Or something about a troll. I'm going to make another round of the apartment."

"Try not to get lost." The anchor laughed.

"No kidding. Keith . . . ?"

His friend had casually pulled out his phone and waved it at him, letting Simon know he'd text if he found her. That Keith carried a little crush for Mary Rose wouldn't hurt.

Simon lifted his hand in goodbye and thanks, then grinned at the woman. "Take care of him for me, will you?"

"Maybe." The news reporter winked coyly.

Simon ditched his empty glass with a passing waiter, dodged back through the room, offered several more quick hellos, and pressed on to the two bathrooms. Still nothing. He stepped out into the hallway. Nodded at the couple commiserating there together, thought briefly of asking if they'd seen her pass but kept his head down and walked past the elevator and down to the steps.

He opened the door. The stairwell within was dark, only two small emergency lights glowing above the door and in the corner of the landing below.

"Mary Rose?" he called down into the darkness.

He could picture her sitting there, below. Knees up, arms pulled tightly around them. Wrapped in silence and shadow. "Mary?"

Simon stepped into the stairwell, bent to wedge his pen at the bottom of the door in case it was one of those that locked. Maybe she'd come here for some peace and quiet, gotten locked out, and had had to make her way all the way down ten stories in the dark to get out. Maybe even now, she was on her way back on the elevator. He checked his cell. Nothing yet from Keith, or her. Simon took the next few steps. Sounds from the party above filtered down, deep toned and otherworldly.

"Mary Rose . . ."

He kept his voice kind, soft. Didn't want to startle her if she was down here. Didn't want to appear angry. She always blamed herself so harshly after one of her . . . incidents. Consumed with guilt that she'd somehow ruined everything again. Hell, the days *after* times like this, when she was quietly beating herself up, always seemed more trying than the actual freak-outs.

Simon turned the corner and took the next row of stairs down to the ninth floor. Chilly air lifted from the darkness and floors far below traced gently across his face. The glow of faint light appeared. Here, the door gaped open. Propped open with some workman's bucket of plaster. Done earlier today or minutes before, he couldn't say.

He pushed past it and stepped into the ninth floor.

They were still doing construction. Scaffolding everywhere. Neat stacks of drywall and Sheetrock, half shrouded in tarps. The frames of two separate condos, clearly marked with poly sheeting; some plastic sheeting fluttered gently in unfelt wind. Blue light cast from the window at the end of the hall, framed in original century-old brick. The building, an old textile shop in the 1860s, then a woman's shelter from the 1940s until about 2008, was now getting the full gentrification treatment: condos for multimillionaires. Simon knew the women's shelter had moved another twenty miles upriver, had actually studied the legal proceedings that'd led to the land grab. Knew he'd have lost the case also, but at least given them better odds. He lay his arm against the fluttering sheet and pushed it aside.

"Mary Rose?"

The sound, her name, vanished into the dark half-formed rooms within. Simon stepped past the sheeting and followed it.

The whole apartment was lustrous with the unique colors and shadow of night—like something Mary Rose would have shown him from Picasso's Blue Period—the enormous windows opening to the moonlight, and light escaping from the party above.

She stood silhouetted at the windows looking out into the night. Or, perhaps, the ghost of her own reflection.

The first time he'd found her this way, they'd been staying at a bed-and-breakfast down in Maryland, Saint Michaels, and there he'd woken to find her perched at the end of the bed, kneeling back on her heels, staring at the mirror opposite the bed. She'd been naked and strangely vibrant in the darkness, as if born to the shadows. He'd watched her, and if she'd known he was observing her or even still in the room, she gave no notice. Finally he'd called to her and she'd slowly turned to look back at him.

Then, she'd appeared like some kind of vampire, he supposed. Or, perhaps something out of Greek mythology. In either case, a creature who'd walked the earth a thousand years before man, made from the night. Feral, dangerous. He'd seen her sad and quiet, sure, seen her go to a place he tenderly dubbed "October Country." But never before this way. Her shoulders, the black hair down her back, the curve of her hips, her bare ass settled tight against her legs, and those eyes looking back at him. Eyes that glistened like the mirror looming behind her.

It had been a side of her he'd never seen, would only barely glimpse another half dozen times over the next two years. Mostly, it was diluted times like this: sneaking off for some alone time in a dark room. And from the day they'd met, he'd always wanted to care for her, protect her. But that night, he only wanted to possess her—or, maybe be possessed *by* her—and he'd crossed the bed to her, and they'd made love, and it *had* been being with an entirely different woman. If he were being honest, it was the night he'd first decided to marry her.

What, he wondered breathing deeply, would her eyes show when she turned tonight?

"Excuse me, ma'am'," he spoke gently. "We've received reports of a burglar in the neighborhood."

"Is that so?" Mary Rose's voice was soft, throaty. Her typically restrained English accent somehow always more pronounced when she spoke so hushed. Her shoulders were bare, taut slim marble in the moonlight. "Any leads, Officer?"

"Something about a spectacular ass."

She snorted a faint laugh. "I think I should call my attorney."

"Perfect. I'm your attorney."

"A man of many hats, it seems."

He slid his arms around her waist, pressed up against her back. Her hair smelled like honeysuckle tonight and tickled his chin. She'd surrendered against his weight. Seeming to dance for all that she was standing still. "I'd like to wear one more," he said.

Maybe some jasmine, too, he decided. He'd gotten better at learning her relentless array of sprays and lotions: coconut and tropical spices, violet and jasmine, frankincense, patchouli, cinnamon, and—of course—rose. Her favorite, he knew, however, was a combination of vanilla and sandalwood.

He looked at her face in the window's reflection; so, she had been looking at herself again.

Her gaze finally lifted to meet his, her expression breathtakingly refined, like a spring flower opened too early, dismayed the rains could be so bitter, yet still lifting its face defiantly toward the sun. Her wide eyes weren't glaring like something untamed, either; they were simply . . . terribly resigned. Almost regal. "Oh, Simon . . ." She'd grown rigid in his arms. "I'm so sorry."

"For what?"

"I ruined your party."

He turned her to see her real face. "First, you haven't 'ruined' anything." His hand caressed her chin. "Second, it's not my party. It's just some people I know. *You're* my party. Got it?"

In reply, she rested her head against his chest.

"You okay?"

"I am indeed," she said.

"Needed a break?"

"Apparently." She blew out an angry breath. "I was thinking about England too much, I guess. About my parents."

"I can imagine. My mom? I get anxious when I have to *call* her."

Her chuckle was soft, reassuring. "Silly Simon."

"You still want to do the trip?"

"I should. It's been six, seven years. They've always come here."

"Look, if it's—"

"No, I'm fine." She smiled then, that smile that worked even better than his, for all she wasn't trying. "It's just what I was thinking about. I suspect it had more to do with all those people. So many . . ." He felt her breathing deeply against him. They stood together awhile, swaying to the faraway music lovers alone always seem to fabricate together. It took a few bars, but eventually her movements grew slower, more languorous, her sighs longer and sweeter, curling in the air, setting everything alight with possibility the way she always did. All the tensions of the week, of his whole life, falling away.

He ran his hand up her hip onto her waist. "So, maybe we could . . ."

"But, Mr. Blake, there are important guests upstairs," she murmured. "Think about your reputation if we were caught."

"It'd improve."

"Uh-huh. Take it easy, sailor." She squeezed his hand.

"Okay. Maybe we'll just hang a bit."

Holding her close again, he looked around and inspected the unfinished loft more intently. Wondered how many more years it would be before he could afford such a place. To be able to give Mary Rose something like this. By forty-five, he decided; a little more than ten years. It was entirely up to him.

"You know," he said, "I think I prefer it down here, too."

"No fair teasing."

"Seriously. Look, you can see everything better." He pointed outside, and she turned back to look out the window with him across the river. "There's Saint Gertrude's. See the steeple? Got my ass kicked on the church basketball court. That scar on my lip you think is so cute? Tommy Watson. Could see my teeth with my mouth closed. And there . . . all the trees . . . that's Kingsessing Park. Billy Spanelli fell off the gazebo roof there one night and broke his back. When it happened, he couldn't stop laughing."

"Your stories of youth are always so horrid."

"Okay, then how about this: so, there's Kingsessing Park. I saw John Legend play a free concert there when he was still in college."

"And he was brilliant." She'd pulled his arms more tightly around her, somehow enfolding herself in his memories. "And you had fun."

"You know, I don't remember. I was, like, fourteen. There to drink lousy beer and hit on lousier girls. I probably had fun."

"Ah, the perfect scoundrel."

"I like when you say things like that. Feels like I'm dating Queen Elizabeth."

"The First, I hope." She turned again completely in his arms, staring up at him. "Do you miss it?"

"Not really. Had to grow up somewhere." He looked over her and across the black river, across all the years between there and tonight. "Learned a lot."

She grimaced. "Tonight, I fear, you've learned only that you're dating a weirdo."

"Learned that long before tonight, love. Besides, that's how I like 'em."

"I'm sorry. I wanted us—"

"Enough, already." He'd taken her hand. "*Terminamos*. Apologize again and I'll . . ."

"You'll what?"

"I'll think of something."

Mary Rose leaned up to kiss his neck. "Why do you put up with me?"

"Because I love you."

She smiled. "How do you know?"

"Come on." He held out both hands, shrugging. "'Doubt thou the stars are fire . . .'"

"I may swoon. Seriously, how do you know?"

"'Seriously'? Jesus, Mary Rose, I just do. I don't know. Same way I know when I'm going to win a case. You just . . . okay, here's how I know. Every time I see you, I . . . well, I still basically feel like I've been punched in the stomach."

She laughed. "That sounds dreadful. Or delightfully cliché."

"Sorry, I'm not very Hallmark. But that's what came to mind." He grinned down at her, put his hands on her hips again. "See, *I'm* the weirdo."

She reached up to flatten a tuft of his hair. "What am I going to do with you?"

"Just love me back. And, let's get out of here. Call it a night."

"But Keith and—"

"Keith's focused on making the nightly news. Come on." He stepped from the window and pulled her by the hand. "Let's get you home."

"Yes," Mary Rose said, glancing back toward the window. "Home."

2

Home . . .

A simple word. One syllable, four little letters. A word toddlers used. And yet it conjured a thousand different meanings. Emotions. Memories. How many had come to her these last weeks and minutes? Too many to count. How many more would come four days from now after they'd actually arrived? She feared to even imagine an answer.

Mary Rose half closed her laptop, crossed her hands atop the screen, and leaned forward to lay her chin there. Beyond was the short bank and then the Delaware River passing in long meandering ribbons of slate blue and gray as ducks bobbed peacefully along its shore.

She loved it here, the perfect place to work, to draw, to think.

Farther downriver, several men sat in lawn chairs or on upside-down buckets, fishing from the riverside. Two women glided past together on kayaks, and her gaze and thoughts drifted beside their black sinuous wakes.

It'd already been more than five years since she'd been home. Almost seven years, actually. *Could it truly have been so long? No, that was impossible.* Anytime she'd been off to one boarding school or another or some college, she'd somehow always returned again in months. Inexplicably drawn back to a place where she'd always felt like an outsider. An impostor. Finally escaping to America had been the longest she'd managed to keep away, and she now felt like a recovered alcoholic considering "one more drink" after so many years of sobriety.

Mary Rose tried evoking all that time passing, hoping to create a montage of such milestones and memories—things she'd done, all the remarkable people she'd met, places visited, and so forth—but nothing came to mind. Throwing herself completely at her grades first, then her work, at getting As and scholarships, at finishing projects and keeping clients happy. Most all day, seven days a week. And she'd gotten all the As and more clients, yes, but the residual consequence was that seven years had seemingly passed in minutes. Been nicked from her without her even knowing it'd happened.

She almost feared blinking and waking in her late forties.

The age her parents had been when she'd last been home. How different would they look now? She'd seen them since, of course, during their few visits to the States, but that was not the same at all. She tried envisioning them taking breakfast together in the back patio, or moving through the house's dim hallways, or asleep at night in their rooms. What new art had her father acquired? What new flowers to be found, if any, in Mother's back garden? Or were they and the house the same as she left it seven years before? A dollhouse waiting for her eventual return.

How haughty to believe so, yet that's what she believed entirely.

The house would be exactly the same. And so would they.

And so, she dreaded, *will I.*

No, not possible. She concentrated harder to come up with something tangible to prove she'd grown beyond her long-ago self. If not specific memories, then at least a personal résumé she could cling to beyond the grades and accounts. She'd earned *two* degrees in art, worked for a top agency, made diverse American friends, vacationed in Mexico, volunteered at community arts programs, bought her own condo, ran a bloody half marathon, gone freelance.

And, fallen in love with Simon.

Simon. Beautiful Simon.

Mary Rose allowed her lips to curve into a smile, tilted her head, her thoughts turning from the shadows of the past to the mirror-bright possibilities of her future.

She would marry Simon. Yes. And in four, maybe five, days, he would ask her parents for her hand. Or, rather, for their blessing. An outdated custom, surely even offensive to many these days, but she didn't care one bit. It somehow made all of it seem more like something from a fairy tale.

She closed her eyes and felt the early September sun warm against her face. Not, perhaps, the best idea to work by the river today. The metaphor too exact, her mind too easily carried downstream into the bay and then out to the ocean and yes, back home again.

Mary Rose leaned back and set her laptop aside. If she could get at least one assignment delivered—the rough sketches for the new vodka company logo, perhaps, the revised treatment of the cranberry juice carton—she could call today a success with a straight face.

She retrieved her sketchbook and began working again. Each swipe of her pen, each decision, slower than the last. But twenty minutes later, she'd managed to force out two genuine possibilities for the logo. Maybe. She drew a line through the first image. *One* genuine possibility now.

"Well, aren't you the sweetest thing?"

Mary Rose turned to the voice.

An older woman stood behind her. Early eighties, at least. Entirely frozen but no more than ten feet away. Hovering, almost. Her gray hair buzzed close and tight. Only the dark shawl across her back fluttered behind her in a lifting breeze. "Like a little angel," the woman added.

Mary Rose glanced around to see who the woman was talking to, realized it could only be her. "Good afternoon," she said to her. "Isn't it a gorgeous day?"

The woman now tottered forward, each step cautious and labored. She muttered as she walked, eventually reaching Mary Rose's bench. She laid a hand on its curved metal back and asked: "What you working on?" Her voice held a gentle childlike quality. Closer, Mary Rose saw the near-hollow look in the woman's brown eyes. Homeless? No, the clothes were meticulous. The onset of some form of dementia, for sure.

"Oh, nothing." Mary Rose looked again to see where she'd come from. "Just something for . . . It's nothing."

"Can I see?" the woman asked.

Mary Rose held out the book with the picture she'd been drawing: a rough abstract of a woman's calf, ankles and high-heeled shoes, ending in the top of a bottle.

"Oh, that's a nice one," the woman said, smiling. "You gonna be an artist, I bet."

"Well, as a matter fact, that's what I am." Mary Rose closed the book and smiled broadly.

The woman studied her. Silent, confused.

"Where your mama at?" she asked suddenly.

Mary Rose blinked. "My—?"

"Your mother."

Oh . . . kay. "Probably in her garden, I suspect. I'm afraid she lives far away now. In England, actually. But, funny you should mention her. I'll be seeing her in a few days now."

"You going to England?"

"Yes, ma'am."

"Who take care of you?" the woman asked, paused, her muted eyes going wide. "You playing with that boy? I've seen *him* before, but never you. Who you stayin' with?"

"I'm sorry?" Mary Rose couldn't follow. "I'm not sure what you mean."

The woman stared ahead. "The white boy," she explained, flapping a craggy dark hand.

Mary Rose followed her gaze, saw nothing. Only the river, pleated in inky and dimming furrows.

"His mama . . . She did the bad thing. How come you—"

"Deena!" A man's voice interrupted whatever the woman might have said next. He'd jogged up toward them from the path, hustling behind the benches. "I'm so sorry," he said quickly to Mary Rose.

Good, she thought, someone who could take her away. As soon as she thought it, shame snapped through her, and she smiled brightly to dispel her uneasiness, the strange touch of melancholy that limned the golden air with the coolest shades of fall. "Not at all," she offered. "We were just talking."

He took the old woman's arm. "Aunt Deena, you had me scared half to death."

"Oh, Jaylen." She turned to him. "Isn't she the sweetest thing?"

"Oh, yes, ma'am," he said. Mouthed the word "sorry" again.

Mary Rose lifted a hand. "It was very nice meeting you, Deena," she said.

"And so polite." The woman waved back at her. "You be careful now, darling."

"Enjoy your day," she said to them both.

The man turned his aunt and started leading her back toward the path. "Thanks," he said, looking back, his relief mirroring her own.

Mary Rose waved civilly and watched them go, then returned her gaze back to the river and thought about what the woman had said but not for long. She'd reopened her sketchbook to get working again. To get something down—anything. This logo wouldn't create itself.

A half hour later, she'd filled several pages.

And when she saw what she'd drawn, she blinked. Torn out and then folded the pages over. Then over again. Then a third time, boxing and pressing, flattening and forgetting. *What a silly thing to have drawn.*

Irritated, Mary Rose refocused on the Delaware, her mind skittering over the buildings, the water, the slow indolent current. Farther downriver, the summer before, a mother had plunged with her infant into the water. She'd wrapped bricks to his chest, the tape going around and around. Neither of them had survived. A little white boy, she remembered now.

Words from her childhood, a silly song, again came to mind:

> *They wrap you up in a big white sheet*
> *and cover you from head to feet.*
> *They put you in a big black box*
> *And cover you with dirt and rocks.*

Mary Rose straightened carefully on the bench. Started to collect her belongings. Perhaps this wasn't the best place to work after all.

Perhaps many things.

3

At Heathrow, Simon rented a Mercedes-Benz for the week, for less than a Maxima would have cost back in the States. Remarkable: 550 horsepower, pearl white, immaculate. He'd met Mary Rose's parents only twice before, lunch in Philadelphia and an afternoon spent in New Hope, and—considering his intentions—it was important he secure a more permanent and inspiring impression this visit. He hoped the car would help.

Something had to.

Because the closer they got to her childhood home, the tenser he'd become. Nervous, almost. Surprisingly so. He wasn't one too easily shaken.

At first, he'd simply written off the clenched fingers around the steering wheel to the strangeness of driving on the wrong side of the road, but each mile closer to Alderley Edge, he'd grown more anxious. While the reaction had been disconcerting, he'd sorted it out well enough: it was, after all, the first—and last—time he'd ask someone for their daughter's hand in marriage.

Mary Rose stared out the window beside him, head resting against the glass. She'd been quiet for almost the entire trip. Lost to her own thoughts, memories, and sentiments, unshared though they were, of seeing her parents. Perhaps he was just feeding off *her* overstimulated energy.

"Strange being back?" he asked to break the silence, to focus their now-shared angst.

"I suppose. I don't know what to feel. I . . ."

"Yes?" He studied the next highway sign.

"It's almost as if I've never left."

Simon smiled. "I think that sometimes when I'm back in South Philly—maybe more than sometimes—that all that time, all those years passed mean very little."

She murmured in agreement, closed her eyes again.

An hour later, he'd pulled off the main road and was working his way through the southern half of Alderley Edge. A lot of cafés and high-end designer shops. Mary Rose awake once more, watching them pass.

"That's Congleton, yes?" He squinted at the street sign ahead.

"Yes," she replied quietly. "Just down the road now."

He followed the street past mostly hidden residences, lost behind lush tree lines and privacy fences of stone and/or iron. The few glimpses he'd gathered suggested homes starting in the low millions; though several were easily eight-figure estates. He kept his surprise to himself. He'd always suspected Mary Rose had come from money—the way she carried herself, the way she paid no attention to its necessity—but he hadn't really given much thought to her parents' wealth. Her father was a retired magistrate in his midfifties, taught a single course at a local university, but he didn't know much about the family beyond that.

"Macclesfield Road," he announced, turning the car as Mary Rose perched more in her seat, focused on the properties they passed. A stone wall about four feet high ran the length of the next property. The GPS on the dashboard flashed arrival, and Simon slowed the car to a crawl as he scanned the stone wall and its open gate for an address of some kind. "This is it, yes?"

Mary Rose nodded, the joy on her face indisputable as he pulled slowly into the narrow opening and proceeded up to the house.

An enormous Tudor with several steeply pitched roofs and prominent cross gables stood majestically on manicured grounds, half stone with gingerbread timbering and shakes weathered to a mellow gray. A luxurious black shadow stretched from the house, and verdant lush ivy ran across most of the front yard like an ocean, creeping up to the porch and over its railings. A fountain was surrounded by neatly cropped bushes that formed a low wall in the center of the wide paved driveway. Larger bushes, equally trimmed into a natural wall blocked the back lawn.

He remembered Mary Rose saying something about it being some sort of gentlemen's club more than a century before: a home where various local judges and doctors, admired politicians and professors, gathered to drink, smoke cigars, and trade in fossils and exotic pornography amid enthralled discussions of everything from world exploration and science to prostitution and cannibalism. The left corner of the house was all stone, a three-story tower; the time-eaten rock, patched unevenly with black ivy and dripstone concretion. Its few windows were bare slits of dull light framed in thick lumber that pocked the sides of the mansion like narrow ebony scars.

Simon drove to the top of the driveway. Breathed out deeply.

"We made it." He smiled, turning.

But Mary Rose was already half out of the car. Springing from her seat and leaving the door swinging open behind.

Simon sat dumfounded and watched her bound up the steps to the double doors. "Okay," he drawled to himself as she vanished into the home.

He climbed from the car, stretched his back, and took several more deep breaths, looking over the property and house. In one of the windows above, a dark figure stood to the side, half-lost behind obscure reflections in the glass. Simon squinted up into the sun peeking over the house, gave a chest-high wave of hello to whichever parent it was.

Deciding to save their bags for later, he followed slowly after Mary Rose while crunching up the gravel path and onto the broad porch steps.

Mary Rose had left one of the double doors wide open, and Simon stepped within. He shivered, his first thought that the old house was unusually cold—then again, everywhere in England felt cold to him. His next thought was that his future in-laws' home, for all its external grandeur, was cluttered and somewhat, if being polite, out-of-date.

The walls paneled in dark walnut, the entry hall crowded on either side with huge antique furniture; a pair of marble statues on pedestals and the high-backed chairs with burgundy velvet lining. Cascading rows of dark-colored paintings and black-and-white photographs. A curved staircase led up into shadow where a second-floor corridor overlooked the entryway. Above it all, an ornate chandelier and a paneled ceiling crisscrossed in late-afternoon sunlight.

Closer, most of the paintings turned out to be portraits. Family members, he assumed from the clothing, muttonchops, and sour expressions, from another century ago or more. One, clearly a newer painting, was of an attractive and refined woman who looked like Mary Rose might look in another twenty years: the mother. Francine Morland. Certainly one of the colder fishes he'd yet run into in this world.

Farther down, a painting of Mary Rose herself. Mid- to late teens, he assumed. Seated before a window but turned sideways and looking back at the artist. Her delicate hands folded neatly in her lap. Eyes wide and almost surprised at the intrusion. Challenging.

Simon smiled. It was a look he knew well.

He passed the other photos and paintings, the eyes of young Mary Rose and several generations of her bloodline following each step, and chased after the warm low voices in the next room beyond where the hall opened to an adjoining sitting room or, he now saw fully, a study. At the end of the hall, something glinted back at him from the shadows.

"Ah, here's our lad now!" Mary Rose's father, standing at a table beside another man, waved Simon into the study. "Welcome, welcome," he greeted warmly.

Simon crossed the room to shake hands. "James," he said, carefully using her father's Christian name. "Mr. Morland" was respectful but somehow seemed too boyish for the business at hand this visit; besides, her father had several times before corrected him, asking to be called James.

Her father was taller than Simon remembered, and thinner, too, his cheeks hollow, his hair a thatch of brown turning silver. His body gave the unsettling impression of being at war with itself, his lips dipping down at the edges even as he smiled broadly at Simon, his head canted and shoulders sloped as if to make up for his height, the thick sweater a bit too heavy on his thin frame, his stylish trousers baggy.

Even his voice boomed too loud in the quiet room, a man most comfortable being at odds. "A pleasant trip, she told us," he said. His eyes as gray as the shakes on the house.

"Oh, yes." Simon turned about the room, looking for Mary Rose.

"Already dashed out to the back garden to fetch Franny. The dear girl burst in like a cyclone. Simon Blake." Morland turned. "This is George Amy, a local busybody and a family friend for a hundred years."

Simon smiled, shook hands with the other man. Unlike Morland, Amy was what he expected in a Northern Englishman—sturdy, red faced, and wrapped in tweed. And older. Early sixties, he supposed. "Pleasure," he said.

"How *are* you holding up in the colonies these days?" Mr. Amy asked, his voice strained. His playful remark a mere feign at levity.

Simon shrugged, playing back the humor carefully. "I'm from Philly and can see Independence Hall from my office window. We're hanging in there as always before, sir."

Mr. Amy grunted, then turned and winked at Morland, who chuckled curtly. Meanwhile, Simon noticed, the man had started edging away, making his exit. "Well, I best be leaving you all now," he said, confirming Simon's read. "You'll be wanting to catch up and—"

"Nonsense!" Morland huffed. "You only got here! And Mary Rose hasn't seen you in ten years, or more."

"Yes, well . . ." Mr. Amy looked out into the hall and toward the front door. Planning more than an exit, more of an escape. "I'll unearth the time later this week for a proper visit. You should be allowed more privacy to suitably welcome your guests."

"First, perhaps, we resolve this matter of the art you've brought me." Morland turned to Simon, smiling. He'd stepped back to the table. "You're not going to forget and leave it here, are you?"

"James . . ." Mr. Amy shook his head crossly. "You're a shameful—"

"Do you know much about collectible art, Simon?" Morland asked.

"No, sir. Despite the efforts of Mary Rose and our trips to many museums. Still working on the difference between Renoir and Seuss, I'm afraid."

Morland chuckled. "I suspect otherwise. She was always . . .

always *loved* art. Well, take a look at this." He waved Simon closer. "Mr. Amy has evidently found a genuine Guy Peellaert. An unsigned original supposedly found hanging in some dusty record shop in London."

Simon stepped up to the table to see what Morland was looking at so intently. "It's quite nice," he commented carefully. "This is 'pop art' style. Yes?" Not knowing what else to say about a painting of a half-nude girl speeding on a motorcycle in the shape of a panther. "Not familiar with the name."

"He painted one of David Bowie's most famous album covers," Mr. Amy explained. "So there's great collector interest again. James, and always has, begrudges my having found a prize." This time, he winked at Simon. Clearly, his go-to gesture.

"Not much of a prize." Morland smirked. "As I was explaining when Mary Rose burst into the room . . . *this*"—he stabbed his finger down—"is the work of a clever amateur."

"It's Peellaert," Amy argued.

"Definitely *not*."

Simon laughed, hoping first to deflate an argument that'd already deconstructed to its simplest two-sentence form and, so, might go on for the whole week or, more predictably, *years*. His next instinct, however, was to perceivably end the argument with facts. While not his business, it was a curse of his trade. "Why do you suspect it's not?" he asked.

Morland pointed. "See the lines? Heavy and labored, yes? And look at the colors, for goodness' sake."

"What's wrong with the colors?" Amy asked, returning to the table.

"The green here . . . and *here* against orange. It should be pink, like the bike. And here, these lines would be white, not black. Destroys the entire balance of the composition. There's no true 'Pow!' Not the way Peellaert does it."

"You sound just like Mary Rose." Simon grinned.

"Well, it's in her blood, after all. Also"—he turned again on Amy—"look at the ink." He picked the print off the table, held it flat and at eye-level, where all three men could look at it evenly. "After fifty years, there should be a slight discoloration on the back from the

India ink. It's clearly synthetic ink someone's used here."

"Is that bad?" Simon asked, genuinely interested now. The look on Amy's face suggested it was.

"It's unlikely Peellaert used synthetic ink in 1964," Morland concluded for them both. "And don't look so dejected, George."

"Congratulations on hurting an old friend." He took hold of the print and lay it over others on the table.

"Oh, stop, 'old friend.' I could easily have made the same mistake myself."

Amy brought the bundle up beneath his arms. "Enjoy your week, Mr. Blake." He bowed slightly.

"I'm sure we will, sir."

"James chasing you off again?" A new voice from the hall.

Simon and the other men turned to find Francine Morland. Mary Rose stood behind her.

Francine was as Simon remembered. Attractive. Alluring even, he admitted, despite her frosty demeanor. Perhaps it was her similarity to Mary Rose, he thought. The two of them of a height, the mother merely a slightly faded version of her daughter still in the full blush of her youth. Nonetheless, Francine Morland still clearly possessed the form of her former beauty—the large eyes and dark hair, the high cheekbones and firm chin, her figure a soft hourglass now compared to Mary Rose's sylph-like form. It was nice, he confessed, being able to see firsthand and quote clearly what Mary Rose might well look like in another thirty years. If it was anything like her mother, Simon was in full approval.

But Francine Morland didn't have Mary Rose's almost electric and oft-intimidating energy. Her smile was soft and pleasant enough, but whatever fire she might have once carried there was gone now. No fire and surprisingly little warmth.

"No, no." Mr. Amy angled past Simon to meet the two women in the entranceway. "Lots to do today is all."

"Goodbye, Mr. Amy," Mary Rose said. Her voice had gone almost lyrical. "I hope we'll see you again before we go?"

"Yes, yes," he agreed, moving past them into the hall. "It was . . .

It's nice to see you again, Mary Rose. Simon, a pleasure." He looked back, dipped his head, and then hurried to the front doors.

"What's wrong with Mr. Amy, Daddy?" Mary Rose asked, stepping back into the room. She reached out to squeeze Simon's arm in hello.

"Dubious ink." Morland grinned at Simon, who smiled back.

Francine Morland shook her head slowly, sagely. Reproving. Her whole bearing rendering: *Obviously*, it had been something stupid like that.

"George is the local vicar." James added an ominous look. "Better we stay in his good graces, I suspect."

"No doubt." Simon laughed, trying to gauge the unspoken words between husband and wife. "Mrs. Morland." Simon stepped closer to shake her hand. Sensed, as always, a kiss on the cheek—or calling her by her first name—was not her style.

"How long has it been?" Francine asked somberly. "Mary Rose and I couldn't remember."

"Oh." Simon thought. "It was August. Last. A while."

"Yes, well . . ."

He smiled again to take the sting out of the moment. Best to play nice with future mothers-in-law. "Thank you, both, for the invitation. What a beautiful area."

She grumbled something in reply.

Morland scoffed. "She's always troubled by all the flush footballers come to town. Tearing down the older houses to build— What *are* you doing, Mary Rose?" he continued, looking past Simon.

Simon turned with the man's confused gaze. Then stared also.

Mary Rose stood behind one of the long drapes. Only her elfin shape remained visible behind, her fingers curving around the blue edges.

"Mary Rose," her mother's voice snapped, more demanding.

"I'm hiding," the blue curtain said.

"From Simon, no doubt?"

Simon looked back at James Morland, who shrugged with a grin.

"No, I'm not sure why," her small voice replied.

"Mary Rose . . ." Simon started for the drapes.

Confused. Embarrassed. Not sure what his role was suddenly.

Was this some kind of old family game, he wondered. How many days, years had these three carried on so before he'd ever entered her life? No wonder she was often a little . . . *eccentric*. Was this supposed to be funny? An inside joke they shared? Maybe even some sort of test?

"Maybe hiding from myself," she said.

"Not an easy undertaking." James Morland laughed.

"Mary . . ." Simon stepped closer, teeth clenched more than he liked, and pulled back the curtain to reveal her.

She blinked up at him, an enormous tooth-filled grin. "Boo!" she laughed, and James Morland laughed also behind Simon.

"Mother!" Mary Rose gasped as if seeing her mother for the first time, and pushed past Simon to get back across the room. "We should all play a game. Wouldn't that be fun?" She wrapped her arms around Francine Morland, who civilly patted Mary Rose's back, even as she rolled her eyes at her husband in shared good humor. Simon couldn't help but notice the awkwardness of the embrace. He'd always suspected a strained relationship between the two—no different, he confessed, than he and his own father would have likely turned out.

"I want Simon to see everything. To know how much fun we once had here." Mary Rose looked intensely about the room. Her eyes large like a character in one of those Japanese cartoons, eyes filled with too much life. She laughed.

"What's so funny now?" her father asked, playing along.

She shook her head, another secret. Simon had seen this played out a hundred times before. Mary Rose often giggled darkly, briefly, for no discernible reason and then clammed up when asked what she was thinking.

"But first, Simon and I have a big secret," she said. "And I'm frightened to tell you." She'd stage-whispered the last to her mother. Her voice was deep and husky.

"Mary . . ." Simon went for good humor as well, forcing himself to chuckle. There'd been no discussion of how or when they might broach the marriage subject. Surely, this was not the way he'd—

"I think he wants to take me away," she said.

"Is that so?" James Morland gasped theatrically, then exchanged a brief look with Francine. "We suspected as much."

Simon put his hand against Mary Rose's back. This was not how he'd pictured the conversation going. At all. Best to get out of the room, and moment, as quickly as possible. "It's been a long trip for both of us," he started. "There's nothing that can't wait until—"

"He's taking me somewhere very special," Mary Rose blurted.

"Oh?" James Morland looked at Simon, keeping jocular.

Simon held out his hands. Still no clue where she was going with this and a bit bemused over how easily she'd seized full control of the room.

"Somewhere I haven't been for too long." She looked at her father. "You took us there before, Daddy. But now Simon can."

"This is . . ." Francine Morland waggled her head exactly like a pitcher shaking off his catcher's pitch call. Hoping to move on, also. "I don't think—"

"Mhoire's Point," Mary Rose said.

"Dear God . . ." Francine Morland had covered her mouth with both hands, lowered them again slowly to her chest.

"Mhoire's Point?" James Morland laughed. A forced laugh, Simon noted. "Why, in Heaven's name . . . You never said anything about visiting . . ."

"Scotland," her mother finished for him.

Simon braced for whatever family squabble would come. Obviously, not a popular idea with the Morlands. Moreover, there'd been no mention of visiting this place, or even Scotland, before this very moment. He squinted at Mary Rose curiously.

"I suppose I just thought of it," Mary Rose explained to all three, first taking Simon's arm, then sliding down to hold his hand. "And, well, anyway, why wouldn't we? It's wonderful there and only a few hours away. I want to show Simon everything."

"There's plenty to see *here*, darling. Take a trip into London, of course. But, if you . . . It's hardly a 'few' hours away, closer to five, and you'll waste the whole day in the car for an hour in a rundown village. I've heard it's fallen to absolute ruin. You're here for less than a week and—"

"This is absurd." Francine Morland crossed her arms, puffed

angrily. "We didn't realize you two were using our home as some sort of hostel this week."

"Oh, Francine . . ." James Morland scowled. "Let's not make too big a thing of it." She flashed her husband a look that implied he'd offended her and also that the conversation would continue privately. "They won't even go, I suspect." Morland pressed on, finding a warm smile. "If they must see Scotland—and why not?—there are several wonderful towns merely *two* hours away."

Simon lowered his gaze uneasily, not sure how to play peacemaker here. "Two hours sounds a whole lot better than five," he agreed. Siding with the parents seemed the better course tonight; it'd be easier to make amends with Mary Rose later than with them.

Mary Rose squeezed his hand. He wasn't sure if it'd been in acquiescence or forewarning.

"You're in love with Simon, aren't you?" her father asked. His voice had changed, gotten peculiarly grave.

She grinned slyly, looking between them. "Daddy. Mother. What could I do? He's my big brave American man. My knight in shining armor."

"Yes, well." Francine Morland scrutinized Simon more sharply. As if this outburst was somehow his doing. "Enough of all that. Mary Rose, why don't you show your American 'knight' to his room? You should both rest. We'll have dinner at seven, if that's agreeable."

"Sounds great," Simon said quickly, the clearest path to an escape at last revealed. "Mary Rose?"

"Yes, sounds great," she echoed, her frantic energy seemingly spent. "Come along, Sir Simon." But then she laughed again and taking his hand, pulled him from the room.

4

Mary Rose had stopped dead center in the upstairs bedroom, looking this way and that, eager to verify her bearings. A room she'd surely walked into more than a thousand times in her life now felt somehow unfamiliar.

She traced her fingers along the edge of the bed. The furniture was comparable to her original pieces but still new, she decided. Yes, that was part of it. And the walls had been painted over several years before, a once-deep chocolate, today somewhat faded. She could almost make out the ghosted lines on the wall from where a mirror had once hung. The room smelled perfumed, anise-like, a fresh bouquet of purple fox-glove set in a vase on the smaller bureau, a welcoming touch no doubt added by some biweekly housekeeper.

Between the pleated black drapes, she could see a single knotted branch of the old tree that'd stood sentinel outside her bedroom for a hundred years, a hundred unspeakable nights.

"You good?" Simon asked.

"Yes, I . . ." Her thoughts came back to the now, and she turned to him. She remembered dragging him upstairs, pulling him down to this room. And then, everything before. "Sorry. I'm not sure what got into me."

He made a face. "I gotta admit, you seemed a little . . ."

"I know, I know." She closed her eyes, pushed hair back from her face. When she opened them again, Simon was peeking into the ad-joining bathroom. "I feel like an idiot," she said.

"I wouldn't go that far. Been a long day of travel, is all. Your dad's right. A little rest and—"

"Being here again." She blurted out the words, wanting, needing to cut him off, though she couldn't say why. "I'd told myself it wouldn't be a big deal, but it is. It's, well . . . odd being back home. *Really* odd. Being here, being with them, I suppose. It happens every time I'm around them. It's like I never left, somehow." She shook her head, nervously clenching and unclenching her hands. "I fear someday I'll be fifty years old and still behave like a child anytime I'm in the room with one of them. I feel so pathetic."

"Why?" He kept his gaze on her, steady and sweet, the way he always was steady and sweet even when—especially when—she didn't deserve it. "I suspect most people feel the same about their parents. The vast majority of our time with them is spent *as* children, when you think of it. Our adult years are all lived mostly offscreen to them. As were their younger years for us. Bet they feel unreasonably older somehow whenever *they're* around *you*. But we have bigger concerns."

"Yes?" She smiled.

He indicated the room's single twin-size bed. "They expect us to fit in this?"

She snorted, half laughing. "You're adorable. Not even a true fiancé would be so bold. Or boorish."

He rolled his eyes. "Let me guess . . ."

"Down the hallway with you, my dear friend."

"I assumed you were joking. Not even the room next door?"

She looked to the wall where such a room might be. Shook her head.

"Fine," he said drily. "How traditional."

"Eternally."

"Was this your room? Growing up, I mean."

She shook her head.

"Okay." He looked around with less interest. "How about I run down and grab our luggage and then you can show me to my cell. A nap before dinner sounds grand, as a matter of fact."

"As you wish, sir." She took hold of his hand.

He didn't move. "Your parents didn't seem so thrilled when you hinted at the . . . well . . ."

"Our *marriage?*" She said the word overloud on purpose, eyes widened and playfully daring. Though daring *what*, she couldn't say.

Simon grimaced. "Right. That."

"I wouldn't read too much into it. I was being silly down there, caught them off guard. My mother has never been a fan of silly."

"Shocked, I am."

She smiled into his beautiful, steady, sweet face. "You'll talk to them tonight."

"If the opportunity comes up."

"Tonight." She squeezed his hand.

"Yes, ma'am."

She pulled in against him, let his arms fold around her, vanishing into his embrace.

"It'll be fine," he said, perhaps more to himself than her. "I'm pretty good at this talking shit."

"Yes," she agreed.

He kissed the top of her head and stepped back. "I'll be right back," he promised.

She nodded and he left the room. When he'd gone, she glided to the window and moved the curtain aside with the back of her hand to see more of the tree and lawn beyond. She had vague memories of climbing that tree many nights, sitting cradled in her favorite bough to watch the setting sun, or the deer that braved the yard at sunset. Once, two bucks had—

Mary Rose stopped.

For there, oh right there, beyond the yard, within the edge of the thicket was . . . someone. Yes, she was sure of it. Not a deer. Not a shadow. Nor trunks and branches bended so. Instead there was a head, and there, yes, she was sure of it! Tiny shoulders. A tilted face looking up toward the house. A neighbor's child. Who would—

She'd retreated from the window. Leaned back enough so the figure—this trick of eventide gloom—vanished again.

She could only see the ancient tree again now, and that was fine. She withdrew her shaking hand from the drape, allowing the heavy fabric to drop back into place, hiding even the tree.

A chill, or whisper, directly behind her.

Whirling, Mary Rose turned to the room's doorway looming dark and empty. All that terrible unclaimed space. All these pent-up years. She half expected to see someone standing there, waiting for her, angry at her. She'd stayed away for so long, and now she was back, and it was here, the imagined figure from the woods, somehow brought to life in this room.

Here with her.

The moment passed, and she shivered, put the flight of fancy from her mind. What was it Simon had said? We were all still children in our parents' home.

Simon. What was taking him so long, anyway? Or had he been gone only a minute? She wasn't sure and breathed deeply. *One, two . . .*

Hoping to chase away the childish thoughts, the anxious thoughts. To step away and let them pass, like brittle leaves on a flowing stream. Not her thoughts at all, but someone else's, nothing that could hurt her.

Three . . . Counting each breath, she looked back to the window. Mary Rose screamed.

"Better?"

She handed Simon back the glass of water and nodded. "I thought . . ." She had no real memory of what she'd seen. Only the haunting outline, fading like a quickly ebbing dream. "It was nothing."

"Didn't sound like nothing. I almost broke my ankle running up the stairs."

"The tree startled me, I think."

"Uh-huh. You've low blood sugar, is what *I* think. Bet I can find something in the kitchen for you. Biscuits and tea, yes?" He waggled his brows.

Despite herself, she laughed. "Oh, no. Crumpets for me, luv. Or 'ow 'bout some bangers and mash." She rolled her eyes. "A nap is enough," she said. "Like you said: after, I'll be fine."

"Okay, rest. Guess I'm down the hall."

"Oh, I should show you."

"I can find it." He smiled. "I should probably check in at work real fast anyway. I'll wake you before dinner."

"Okay."

He leaned down to kiss her cheek. "See you soon."

"Um-hum."

He pointed to her bags beside the dresser, then left her again, shutting the door this time, as she listened to his heavy steps retreating back down the hallway.

Mary Rose sat on the edge of the bed, hands folded in her lap.

For several minutes, she stared at the wall where the mirror had once hung. The outline that wasn't even there anymore, long since covered over. You'd never know there'd even been a mirror, if you hadn't sat in this room, faced that wall a thousand times.

One . . . two . . . three. Deep breaths in and out, letting it go, letting it all go.

She laughed, almost experimentally, and the voice sounded right. Soft and deep and settled, not a child's laugh but a woman's. A woman all grown up who'd come home to see her parents with her fiancé, nothing more. A long trip back to a house full of memories.

She smiled. They were good memories, too.

Most of them. She was sure of it. Though few of *any* kind came to mind this afternoon. She was just tired.

Standing then, resolute, she crossed back to the window to pull the drapes shut all the way. She noticed where she must have pressed her fingers against the pane, fresh tiny handprints etched against the glass.

She pulled her sleeve down over the base of her palm to wipe the prints away. The effort had no effect.

She tried again, and studied the now-waning handprints more closely, furrowing her brow as she brought her face almost to the window, her breath fogging the glass.

She froze.

A moment later, Mary Rose stepped sharply away from the window again, snapped the drapes shut.

The prints, she understood, had been on the outside of the glass.

5

The creepy mirror was full-size and seemed unnaturally enormous hanging on the wall that way and reflecting only darkness. Framed in antique scrollwork, the glass within was pitch-black, and there was no image beyond the impression of hundreds of dark clouds clumped together in a bleak, lifeless night sky.

Simon tried several different angles. Nothing. Perhaps there simply wasn't enough light where it hung at the far end of the first floor, down the hall and past numerous rooms and shut doors. He'd just ascertained this had been the mysterious glint that caught his eye when they'd first arrived; he'd rediscovered the thing again as he killed some time studying the family portraits and landscapes hanging in the main hallway.

Odd. Some kind of minimalist modern art, he supposed.

"It's a scrying mirror," James Morland explained behind him, and Simon turned to his voice. "Belonged to my grandmother."

"It's very striking," Simon said, leaving out the "creepy" part. "But, forgive my ignorance, what's a 'scrying' mirror?"

Morland smiled. "It was used to see the dead."

Simon looked back at the black glass. "Does it work?"

Morland breathed out heavily before answering, something between a chuckle and a moan. "My grandmother thought so."

"Really?"

"She was into all of that. Special gems, tarot cards, and such. But, she also attended Mass at least twice a week, so . . ." He held up his hands as if to say "go figure" and waved for Simon to follow him into the study where they'd met earlier. "Let's find a drink."

In Morland's old-school "man cave" again, Simon inspected several more framed works of art and concert posters on the walls. Bowie, Sex Pistols, Fleetwood Mac. Original artwork by Gerald Scarfe, SKETCHES FOR *THE WALL* the copper plaque on the frame read, a watercolor by Jerry Garcia, and something that reminded him of Johnny Depp for some reason.

"That's an original painting by Ralph Steadman," Morland said, crossing the room. "The artist who worked with Hunter S. Thompson. Lives an hour away from here. Here you go." He handed over the glass. "Cheers."

"Thank you, cheers." Simon raised the drink for a quick clink. Then they both drank, and Simon looked back at the painting, nodding appreciatively.

"But let's not let Franny catch us looking at it," Morland said. "It was, I admit, a selfish purchase." He motioned his head for Simon to join him in two waiting chairs. "What are your selfish diversions, Simon?"

Simon sat, thought before answering. His focus on work was 24-7. Always had been. He and Mary Rose were very similar that way; it was part of why they got along so well. Started shortly after his father had died and his mom informed her four teenaged children, in no uncertain terms, that they were now broke and any hopes for college would be entirely on them. He'd had his nose to the grindstone ever since, fighting to win and keep scholarships, internships, partnerships. He supposed Mary Rose counted as a genuine diversion, his one respite from the day-to-day hustle, but wasn't sure how her father would take that as his answer. "Not too sure I have any yet."

"Find one," James said, sipping his drink. "At *least* one. Work can too easily become all consuming, and before you know it . . . Well, any number of things. Another decade has passed, for one. Three of those and you're done. And don't think I don't know it."

"Yes, sir."

Mr. Morland eyed him. "Mary Rose told me you accomplished quite the victory recently."

Simon put on a humble face, but was pleased she'd told him. In a house like this, surrounded by so much old money, the guy surely wanted to know his only daughter hadn't fallen for some American white trash. "Yes, that's right. A mobility-impairments argument against the city's Housing Authority."

"That's good, Simon. Very good."

Simon didn't know what to say to that so nodded again. His mom only half understood what he did at work, so it was nice having someone around who, perhaps, did appreciate his efforts and achievements. "Anything interesting on *your* docket, sir?"

"Very little. Mostly just teach now. I *am* mediating a pitiful estate squabble next week. The black sheep of the family, a total wretch with a criminal record four pages long, made off with millions. The mother had brain tumors, and he'd withheld morphine as 'they' rewrote her will. Sound mind and body, my arse. But, as he had power of attorney . . . all perfectly bloody legal."

Simon held up his glass and quoted one of Hamlet's specific gripes: "The 'law's delay.'"

"Indeed." Morland chuckled, finished his own drink. "Wish there was more I could do for this family."

"That horrible man"—Francine Morland swept into the room— "will receive his true judgment one day."

Simon stood politely.

"In 'hellfire,' my dear?" James Morland asked, smiling from his chair.

Francine Morland glanced quickly at Simon, her gaze piercing, her face flushing slightly. She was clearly embarrassed at having been teased in front of a guest, a "stranger." Simon wasn't sure how seriously to take this whole exchange, but James Morland's face hinted it was common, and amusing.

"Another drink?" James asked, finally getting up as Francine stepped back, keeping the distance between them. The movements almost choreographed, Simon thought. A perfect pas de deux between a couple grown too old, too soon.

"Allow me," Simon said, reaching for Morland's empty glass. "Mrs. Morland?"

She shook her head.

Simon set the two glasses, poured. Felt the pointed intimacy of the moment and tensed. "Should we wait for Mary Rose?"

Mrs. Morland was shutting the room's double doors. "She went for a walk," she said crisply. Of course, *everything* about her seemed crisp, he thought. Her dress and hair perfectly pressed, her face carefully set. Even her movements were precise, her turn back to him almost a pivot, as if she'd been practicing. "She thought it'd be nice for the 'three of us to catch up.'"

Simon held his laugh. Mary Rose hadn't been kidding. Her agenda for tonight was clearly full steam ahead. Fine. Best to get this truly awkward moment out of the way, and then maybe enjoy the rest of the week without having to fret. He passed the freshened drink to Morland. "Yes, well . . . James, Francine . . ." He'd prepared words and wondered if his proposal to Mary Rose would go as pathetically. "I'd wanted, *we've* wanted, to—"

"Before you go any further"—Morland stopped him and then waited for Simon to process the interruption and to look him in the eye—"Mary Rose was quite right to put the three of us together privately for a spell. Before we give you the floor, however, there's something *we* need to talk to you about first."

"Of course." He pondered her two parents, trying to deduce what it might be about. A hundred possibilities entered his now-anxious mind—from revelations of previous engagements she might have had to questions about his religion or finances, or perhaps, God forbid, even specific sexual inclinations. "Please, go on."

"It's about Mary Rose," Francine said.

"Okay." That was a start. Narrowed it down by half.

Morland looked again at his wife, who'd crossed the room to perch on the edge of the sofa. Her head canted down slightly, her gaze on the floor as she clasped her hands on her lap. No help there, Simon decided as he collected his thoughts. This was getting more interesting by the moment. And if he was honest, slightly more unsettling, too.

"How 'bout we all sit again," Morland continued.

Simon's nerves jangled at the request, though he didn't know why. "Look, Mr. and Mrs. Morland," he started, realizing too late he'd reverted to formal address. "Maybe now is not—"

"We need to talk with you about Mary Rose."

"About her past," her mother clarified, or, perhaps, corrected.

Simon frowned, sat. "Then shouldn't she be part of this conversation? I wouldn't feel right talking about her. Behind her back, I mean."

"Were she here, she wouldn't understand what we were talking about," Morland said, his tone turning wistful. "It would be to her as if we were talking about a complete stranger."

Simon tensed. "How's that?"

"Perhaps—perhaps Simon is right, dear." Francine stood, took a few steps, then seemed trapped in the middle of the living room, unmoored. "This is unnecessary," she said. "To go about it this way. Mary Rose seems happy. Simon here, so happy." She smiled at him, but the expression was almost forced, desperate as Simon stared.

"We agreed," Morland said quietly, reaching out to take his wife's arm and stop her. Caught like a fluttering bird in his grasp, she stilled. Then she turned and looked down at Simon.

He gave her a reassuring smile. "This sounds . . . important."

James Morland was the one who answered, however. "Something happened when Mary Rose was young," he said brusquely.

Simon refocused on him, his hackles lifting. "Again, if there's something in Mary's Rose's past, I believe strongly I should learn it from her." It was certainly nothing she'd brought up yet. "I appreciate that you—"

"She doesn't remember," Francine blurted.

Simon blinked. "How do you mean?"

The father again: "This happened when she was six years old, and she's never appeared to have any memory of what exactly happened to her."

"Okay . . . then why tell me?" Simon asked.

"Because, one day, she *will* remember," Morland said. "A year from now or, maybe, twenty. But we always agreed that if she—"

"If she were ever to marry," Francine clarified.

"If she were ever to marry—which, seems to be where this is heading, dear Simon—then we would share with her husband everything. So that he would understand, and be able to . . . *help* her. If needed. Do you understand?"

Simon leaned back in his chair and breathed out deeply. "Mr. and Mrs. Morland. This is . . . look, I appreciate your trust. It means a lot." His years of legal wrangling paying off, he'd already turned to imagining what the big family secret was. Adoption? Dead sibling? Some sort of sexual molestation? Part of Mary Rose's allure had always been this amazing sense of mystery about her, this something he could never quite put his finger on. Would whatever her parents were about to say enhance that feeling, or destroy it forever? Would they, in the next few minutes, transform her into an ordinary girl again?

Yet, he couldn't quite find the words to tell them no, to say no more. And the silence held its breath between them, savoring its secrets, making them bigger, rounder, more salacious than surely they were.

"What happened?" Simon asked, shattering the anticipation. His heart was beating too fast, his nerves pricking the way they did when he met opposing counsel for the first time, everything hyperaware.

"Mhoire's Point," James started.

"Okay, I could tell you two weren't thrilled with the idea of us going."

"Little seaport town, where we used to holiday," James continued. Francine was still beside him, but there seemed more distance between them now, her attention and gaze looking out one of the windows into the dusk. "One morning, I'd taken Mary Rose out in the boat to one of our favorite spots. This little speck of an island off the coast where I could fish and she'd play for hours. Never a soul around. 'The Little Island That Likes to Be Visited,' that's what they call it."

Simon kept focused on James but noticed Francine's subtle reaction, a slight narrowing of the eyes. Morland had clearly touched on a hurt—or, perhaps and more interesting, a dispute—that went back twenty years.

James Morland huffed a harsh breath, a man forcing the words out. "Well, the short of it: she went missing that morning."

"Got lost, you mean?" Simon asked. "Or . . ."

"She vanished," Francine Morland said.

Morland nodded, finally glancing at his wife. "One minute there, painting . . . the next, our little girl was gone."

"That must have been very frightening for both of you," offered

Simon cautiously. He wasn't sure what else to say, where Morland's next revelation might lead.

"It was, it was," Morland said. "I couldn't begin to describe that feeling. I . . ."

"But you clearly found her."

"We did. I did, in fact. Sitting in the exact same spot I'd left her. Painting again. And looking at me as if she had no idea why I was crying, why I was shaking so."

Simon looked between the Morlands. How many parents in how many campgrounds, shopping malls, metro stations—losing a child and finding her again happened a thousand times a day. "I don't understand," he said. "What am I missing?"

"She was gone for a full month," Francine Morland said, her voice oddly loud in the quiet house.

Simon's eyes sharpened. "A *month*?"

"Thirty-three days, to be precise," James Morland amended. "And a hundred people must have looked for her the first two weeks. The police. Volunteers. Coast guard. We searched every inch of that island a dozen times. We . . . They even dragged the bloody lake. And found nothing. Then she appeared thirty-three days later in the exact bloody spot where I'd last seen her. No explanation for her disappearance or return was ever determined. She was gone . . . and then she came back."

"But *someone* must have taken her," Simon protested. "Then returned her." His mind began to pull at that thread and the horrible realities it might lead to. *Who* had taken her? Why? In all likelihood, she'd been molested, raped. He knew well enough how these stories went. "That's the only explanation."

"There was no one else on the island," said James.

"There must have been." Simon's voice, deep and alarmed, betrayed his developing thoughts. How bad had it been? How did *he* feel knowing that Mary Rose, his beautiful, ethereal Mary Rose, had likely been sexually abused? Was that the "October Country" she carried? The touch of some other man's perversion. "I'm sorry, but how else can you explain it?"

Francine Morland huffed out a small cry, staring at him in outrage before turning away.

Simon hastened to bridge the gap his shock had widened between them. Keep them talking, keep them talking . . . "My apologies. I didn't mean to offend." He paused, but they both stood frozen now, a tableau of a terrorized past. "What do you think happened?"

"We don't know," James said. "But, you can see, I hope, why we were so startled when she brought up the idea of going to Mhoire's Point. We haven't been back since that time. And she's never mentioned it before today."

"Never before," Francine Morland echoed, as if to imply Simon had something to do with it. A place he'd never heard of until four hours ago.

"No, I understand totally. That must have been . . ." He paused, still thinking. "And Mary Rose remembers nothing."

"Nothing." Morland's assurance was absolute. "We had her in therapy for several years and . . . nothing came of it."

"Was she . . ."

"Violated?" her mother finished his question, snapping the word off bitterly. "Is that what you want to know, Simon. Did some terrible monster spoil her? 'Penetrate' her? Take lewd photographs for his friends to share?"

Simon's hands came up reflexively. "Hey, easy. Look, I'm sorry. I said up front this was none of my business. You're right. I think I'd prefer if Mary Rose—"

"She doesn't remember a thing," Francine stopped him. "And we've never told her."

"The police wanted to, wanted to do an . . . examination. It didn't seem necessary," James Morland explained. "She was perfectly fine. You could tell nothing, nothing like *that*, had happened. She was our Mary Rose. The exact same as when we'd last seen her."

Simon noticed immediately that Francine thought otherwise. The woman's face turned sour, pinched. Even her eyes seemed darker. She crossed her arms and looked away from both of them.

James reached out, took his wife's arm again. "You've spent enough time with Mary Rose to know she has . . . well, blue days."

"Yes."

"And some days are worse than others."

"Yes, sir. I've seen that, too. I want you to know that—"

"Some days are . . ." He sought the word, then let it go. "Over the years, she's seen several counselors. Psychiatrists. We've learned all about psychological trauma, traumatic grief. It explained the panic attacks, insomnia, even hallucinations. We can only assume these are some terrible reflection on what may have happened to her. In any case, we wanted you to know lest she ever does remember. For years, we were told she would. That she'd blocked the whole experience from her mind, trapped it somewhere inside as some sort of defense mechanism, and that, someday, it would return. All of it. The doctors, several, warned us that would not be a good day. Or a good year. It's important to me, to both of us, that whoever—"

"And *you* are caring for her now," Francine Morland said. "She lives five thousand miles away now. If this thing happens, you're the one she will need. Not us anymore."

Fair enough. "I understand."

"Do you?" Her gaze challenged him.

"I'll do whatever I can for her. Always. I want you both to know that." Simon found he'd risen from his chair. "Mr. and Mrs. Morland —Francine, James—I love your daughter. Whatever our future, or her past, may bring . . . I'll do everything necessary to make sure Mary Rose never knows fear or pain again."

"Show him the book," Francine said, and Simon stared between them. Up to now, James had been the one in control. That'd changed.

James Morland lowered his head. "I don't think that's necessary."

"Go ahead," his wife demanded. "If he must know this, he should know all of it."

"What book?" asked Simon.

Morland took a hard-backed notebook off the desk beside him. One that'd been lying there, Simon realized now, the entire conversation. "This is one of Mary Rose's sketchbooks. One she used the year after her disappearance." He held it out to Simon. "There are others, from different years. The last in high school. But . . ."

Simon took the book from him, the cover rough in his hand, the paper within yellowed with age. He started randomly in the middle, flipped through the pages.

A passing blur of colors and black ink. Childish drawings but good ones: the sketches of a future artist. At first, little caught his eye. Simple landscapes, animals, suns. Then the repeating pictures.

Every third, fifth, page.

In equally splashed colors. Reds and golds and vibrant greens and tropical blues. But once he ignored the colors, he realized the trees and animals and suns were all in black and that only this one picture—this one picture repeated every third or fifth page, in different sizes, slightly different. But really the same, all the same.

"What is this?" he asked again, looking up.

The Morlands stared back, their gazes filled with sadness and loss.

"Who but she would know?" James said.

The pictures were of a child. A child with no face.

Any eyes, nose or mouth were covered over completely with a hundred shades of the Crayola, heavy lines streaked downward, like hair, stopped at the shoulders. And beside the girl . . . three times her size:

"Is that a dog?" Simon asked.

One standing beside her on two legs. A dog only because of its button nose and two loping Snoopy-like ears hanging on its side.

"Did the police see these?" he asked.

"Yes."

"And?"

"Nothing." Francine snapped. "There's . . . what's to be done with *those*? It's all the same. All through her childhood. Then, even after. The same."

"Maybe ask Mary Rose what it means?"

"Counselors have. Many times. She says they're only pictures. Things she's imagined."

"You said 'even after'—what do you mean by that?"

James Morland handed over another folder filled with drawings. "Some of these she did as a teenager. In college, even. When sent to an expert for psychological evaluation, he believed they were drawn by a girl no more than eight. Have you ever actually seen her draw a human face? Not in twenty years that we've ever seen. Only this one girl, done just so."

Simon held up one of the drawings more tightly. "Split personality of some kind?" he dared ask, and couldn't help but think of her behavior hours before. Another part of his mind focused on visualizing portraits she'd drawn, or illustrations of faces for her work. He couldn't recall any. "Perhaps brought on by the trauma, or . . ."

"They looked into that, too." Her mother sighed, clearly frustrated. "Nothing. Another waste of time, and money."

"I guess," he pacified. "At least you can cross it off the list."

To escape the expected frown from Mrs. Morland, Simon looked at another illustration Mary Rose had done—a terrifying doodle she'd drawn almost twenty years before—or perhaps, more troubling, only a few years ago. The dog's purple eyes, round dots, stared back at him. He shuddered.

"I think I'd like to see Mary Rose now," he said.

"Think you can help us avoid Scotland this week?"

"Seems a good idea. I'll try."

"Thank you, Simon. And you *mustn't* tell her about any of this," James added quickly. "We needed you to understand. Simply to understand."

"I do. Perfectly." Simon handed the book and folder back to James. "I won't say anything."

James and Francine exchanged looks.

"However," Simon continued, "if I ever feel I *should*, that that's in Mary Rose's best interest, I should tell you . . . know that I will bring it up, without hesitation."

"That's fair," Mr. Morland said, nodding quickly. "And we appreciate your discretion until that day, Simon. Know we've successfully protected her from this nightmare for some twenty years."

"Well, that's a task for both of us now, isn't it."

"As we'd hoped." James reached out to shake Simon's hand. "Now that that's out of the way, was there anything else you'd like to discuss?" A smile. As if everything was normal again, everything was right.

"Ah, well, I'm not sure this is the time, but—"

"Mary Rose is out back," Francine announced abruptly, her voice too sharp. She stared back at both men, almost belligerently. "You'd said you wanted to see her right away?"

Simon smiled. "Yes, ma'am. Well . . . thank you, both. Again, for your trust on this. I . . . I'm going to find Mary Rose."

Her parents watched him leave, no doubt waiting to debrief as soon as he was out of range. How many discussions between the two, he wondered, had led to that little bizarre meeting?

Simon stepped from the room, rubbed his face. Studied the wall of family portraits and gothic landscapes.

But he didn't really see any of it. Instead he could only recall the little faceless girl and the dog man, the image etched deeply into his mind. Too deeply. One particular detail more horrifying than all the rest combined.

In almost every picture, the two hideous figures were holding hands.

6

Mary Rose couldn't sleep.

She sat up in the bed, knees to chin, a blanket over her head and shoulders like something out of Deuteronomy. The house's various creaks and knocks floated through the walls and ceiling toward her, each night sound more familiar than the last. Nothing like those worming through her studio in Philadelphia; these sounds were older, more reconciled, welcoming her home while vainly attempting to lull her into slumber. Which wasn't going to happen. Not with her mind chasing a dozen different reflections.

Simon hadn't spoken to her parents about engagements or weddings or falling in love or any of it; he said it hadn't been the right time. So they were no closer to engagement than they'd been yesterday, and also she'd tromped through acres of wet garden alone for nothing. No, not for nothing, she revised. Her mother's garden had never looked more exquisite: the careful clusters of notched pink hollyhocks petals, the catmint and peonies, large domed blue phlox, the wisteria twining in long cascades of violet off the garden trellis. She could almost smell them all now. Always better than the other smell. And it was nice that she could later comment on her mother's work, to have something personal to say. Anything truly intimate. Otherwise, their conversations thus far had been formal, awkward, even strained. No different from before, she admitted now in the dark. Moving away for seven years couldn't possibly change that. It could only make the distance between them worse: a distance that had, she knew, been there since she was a teen. Maybe before there'd been something different, but she wasn't willing to remember back that far. Had her mother always been so cold to her? So difficult to get close to? Had she merely imagined a different childhood?

Mary Rose tugged playfully at her own toes in the dark, tried to remember times her parents had been more affectionate, more natural with her. Even with each other. Yet the years before were always a bit of a blur. She couldn't tell one Christmas morning from the next, one closed door, one worried discussion, one slurred criticism from any other.

She'd always envied those who could hold on to such memories, regaling friends and loved ones with wonderful detailed stories from years before. Where hers had crept off to, she couldn't say. Perhaps they'd become too entangled in her fancies and creativity. The overcharged imagination that'd plagued, and saved, her for her whole life.

Like the fingerprints on the outside of the window. Wholly invented. Five minutes after she'd seen them, they were gone. A smudge, maybe. Or tiny shadows from the adjacent tree.

She looked at the same window in the dark, the drapes pulled tightly together. Behind, the tree limb sometimes scratched gently at the side of the house, up along the shutter. And every time she heard only long fingernails clotted with dirt.

So silly.

To banish such fears, she'd thought of opening the curtains, letting the moonlight filter through her room as she used to, but couldn't bring herself to leave the safety of the bed, let alone touch those sagging drapes.

Her eyes shifted finally to where the mirror had once been.

In the daylight, she could visualize the mirror's frame still etched on the wall. Tonight she could almost imagine its actual reflection. Yes, there in the darkness, sitting directly across from her and her own shrouded face staring back from the illusory cassiterite surface.

So silly, she thought again. Silly, silly Mary Rose.

A new sound echoed in the dark.

Mary Rose jerked her head toward the door. This wasn't the usual pop or creak, she thought, but familiar still. In the hallway. Like a television on someplace far away. Voices, maybe, or rather wind passing from some half-cracked window through the dark hallways.

Yes, a voice. Whispering. Sharing delicious secrets.

So quiet and airy, she could barely hear the sound, let alone make out who it was. Yes, there again. Seemingly right outside the bedroom doorway, beyond the utter gloom that lurked in the slim space beneath the door.

Almost without realizing she'd done so, Mary Rose climbed from her bed. The wood floor was cold beneath her feet. Behind her, faint scratchings pressed at the window again. She ignored that sound for better ones and continued to the door.

As she cracked it, a rush of cold air from the hallway blew across her whole body.

No one was there.

She stepped into the darkened hallway and looked first down toward Simon's room, where dim moonlight flushed that end of the hall, and confirmed his door was shut. She crept to the banister, clutching the railing, leaning to peer down into the lower levels, to see who might still be up. Had Simon snuck down for something? One of her mother's late-night rambles, assuming she still did such things?

Downstairs, however, was dark and empty.

She saw only the black edges of various-sized frames, the paintings and photos within lost to night, her ancestors going back five generations. Well into high school, she'd too often imagined them reaching out of the frames for her. Their lifeless claws gripping her shoulders, wrenching her away. Tonight, their faces, and hands, were hidden, and even the bordering that held them had grown darker.

Mary Rose stood perfectly still, holding her breath, eyes drifting closed to help her focus, hoping to hear the sound again, to pinpoint its origin. Ten seconds, thirty. Silence. The whole house, too, seemed to be holding its breath. But there was nothing there.

She opened her eyes again, ran her fingers along the railing, watching them trace the snaking lines of polished wood. Here was something real, something corporeal. Her fingers, the banister. Her soft, pale gown and bare cold feet. All objective, all right and true. Everything else was . . .

Nothing at all. Nothing but fantasy. Silly, silly Mary Rose.

She turned back toward her room. And froze.

At the end of the hall was something large.

Someone. A person. Standing there quietly in the dark.

No, not standing. *Swaying* almost, as if caught in faint wind.

And it was enormous. Too enormous. Its head almost reached the ceiling. So, not a person—that was impossible—but formed almost like one, shoulders bowed out, arms dangling to its sides, and the smaller ovoid where a head should be. A misshapen head, yet somehow familiar . . .

"Simon?" she called out, but wasn't sure the word had even passed her lips. Had she called for him to come out of his room, or because it was him standing at the end of the hall? Who else could it be? It was no one. It couldn't be . . .

"Who is that?" she asked, more loudly. "What do you want?"

Each word issued forth with more power but also more fear.

Her mind fighting to rationalize the shape of what she was seeing. Maybe it was some dresser she hadn't noticed before, a grandfather clock. Yes, the shape of a grandfather clock was *exactly* what she was seeing . . .

A grandfather clock that had just stepped closer.

The sound of her breathing, rapid and uneven, filled her ears with its strange and terrible panic. Her own shadow cast terrifying images along the wall beside her, though the light hadn't changed. She thought again of screaming, waking the whole house. Simon would come and help her. Her parents would come and . . .

She didn't scream, though. She didn't. She wouldn't.

Instead she paced forward, accepting whatever fate awaited down the hall. Each step was quicker, heavier. Mary Rose's teeth gritted, hands clenched into balls, and her panic fell away, morphing into a surge of desperate, eager certainty. She would fight, yes! She would face this creature, meet it head-on, tackle it. She'd already crossed half the distance between them, and at any moment it would—

She blinked, stopping short.

No one stood at the end of the hall. Not even a grandfather clock.

Instead, there was . . . a painting. Gold hued and busy and very seventeenth-century Dutch. But the frame was square, not tall and wide. The half table beneath barely a meter high, and it held only two short unlit candles and a crystal bowl filled with cerise potpourri.

Is this all she'd seen? How could this . . . how could she . . . ?

Her body still trembling, Mary Rose scurried back for bed. But another door stood between her and that sanctuary.

A closed door, also familiar and terrible and—

And the source, she knew, of the sound she'd first followed into the hall. She was sure of it now, more certain than anything. So she took hold of the door's handle, turned it slowly, and the door cracked and she—

"Mary Rose."

This whisper was hissed. Urgent.

So very different from the sound from before.

She'd stopped, turned to where Simon stood in the hallway, dressed only in those dreadful gym clothes. His hands were held out, his eyes wide, confused. Concerned.

"You okay?" he asked.

With a snick she pulled the door closed once more.

"Yes," she said, moving toward him. "I thought . . . Yes, I'm fine."

She smiled brightly up at him. He looked so handsome and, in the dark, even deliciously roguish.

"What are you doing out here?" he asked quietly, a grin coming to his lips, too, his expression wry. "It's after two."

"Couldn't sleep."

"Suppose it's only ten back in Philly." He'd put his arms around her, pulled her close. "You should have woken me."

She shook her head against his bare chest. "Uh-uh."

He hugged tightly, stepped back. "What's in there?"

"Oh," she said, peering at the door. "Just another room."

He grabbed the handle. "Locked," he concluded.

"I guess so."

"Okay." He smiled. "How about you get back to yours and try and get some sleep?"

She took his hand. "I have a better idea."

Mary Rose led Simon past her room and down the hall to his.

He chuckled in the darkness, the sound full and alive and certain, chasing away everything she thought she'd seen, everything she'd heard. "You gonna tuck me in?" he asked.

"Oh, yes." She sighed, grateful for the feel of him, the force, strength, and truth of him—more grateful than she'd been for anything in a long while. Without another word, she pulled him into the room.

Later he breathed heavily beside her while she cuddled against his arm and chest. She'd spent the past hour drifting in and out of sleep herself, thinking night thoughts again. Strange notions she couldn't quite shake.

"Simon . . ." She whispered his name, half hoped he'd stay sleeping, because then she could drop this and might finally sleep, too.

But he lifted one eyelid, pulled her closer to kiss her forehead. "What?"

"There's something I want to do tomorrow," she said.

He grunted, the torpor of night pulling him back as quickly as it had released him. "Fine, yes. Whatever. Tell me about it tomorrow . . . That's in, like, two hours."

"I want to go somewhere," she said. Yes, that's what she wanted more than anything. Above all the rest. Where the idea had first come from, she couldn't recall. Didn't care. "Somewhere special."

He sighed heavily and looked down at her, both eyes open. Focused. "Okay," he said. His voice sounded odd. "And where's that?"

"Mhoire's Point," she said.

He pushed himself up to his elbows, staring at her in the dark. "I have no desire to drive ten hours for a couple minutes in some run-down tourist trap."

"We'll take turns driving."

"Mary Rose . . ."

"Yes, love."

"Your parents. They didn't seem too happy about that plan."

"Good thing, then, they aren't invited."

He laughed hoarsely. "Let's drive to London. Or, like your dad said, somewhere close in Scotland."

"Mhoire's Point," she insisted, closing her eyes.

"Why?"

"Because I want to go there. And then . . ." Mary Rose kept going, the words formed decades ago, but only now being truly heard. "Then to a little place I used to visit when I was a girl."

Simon's whole body had grown firm and somehow cold against her.

"A special island," she said.

7

Christ, Scotland was cold.

Simon dipped his chin and mouth into the top of the borrowed rain jacket, then cinched it tightly. His ski cap was already pulled down all the way. Out of the harbor, the ocean winds had easily tripled, and his whole face now numb and also wet. Mist sprayed off the sides of the boat as it sped in its uneven advance across the North Channel.

He again debated pulling up the coat's hood but didn't want to give the ship's pilot, safely inside, the satisfaction. To take his mind off the cold, Simon focused on the waves, the small whitecaps, wishing he'd picked up the motion-sickness pills as Mary Rose suggested back in town.

She stood beside but a step ahead of him, hooded and scarved, though a wisp of black hair had endearingly slipped free to waver in the wind behind her jacketed form. Seemingly oblivious to the rocking boat or driving winds, gloved hands rested casually against the railings as she half turned to face the open water ahead. The coastline ran along their left, gray sea-blanched buildings giving way to a dark tangle of craggy seaboard and spotty woodland.

He tried imagining Mary Rose and her father following this same course twenty years before. Some small power boat they kept at one of the docks for the summers, the fishing tackle and bait, a carry bag of art supplies, a lunch packed, or, rather, bought in town before they'd left. Mary Rose no doubt lost in whatever book six-year-old

Mary Roses read, the same sea winds blowing her hair the same way as today. *What had they talked about during the ride out? What, if anything, had hinted at what the day would bring them both?* Did such things really ever just happen, or weren't there always clues, hints, forewarnings of what surely must come next?

If that were true, he thought for the hundredth time, what might the next few hours bring them today? He'd agreed to Mary Rose's moonlit request without any real argument. Even the next morning, when he discovered she'd snuck back to her own room while he slept, when he lay alone thinking about what he'd promised to do, completely dismissing her parents' wishes, the almost "forbidden" place he'd promised to take her, he found he still couldn't quite carry the debate too far into his mind.

This was more of a gut decision. If she wanted to visit the little town again, the damned island, then so be it. Why the fuck not? Whatever came of it, whether some form of breakdown or trauma, he would—and could—deal with then. Wasn't it always best to handle such things straight on instead of living some damned lie for *another* twenty years?

And it had 100 percent been her idea. She clearly remembered more about her disappearance than her parents had admitted.

Simon studied Mary Rose again—the side of her face, the back of her still form—watching for any sign there was something new she'd realized or wanted to share. There was nothing, though. She simply stared ahead, looking out to sea.

They'd already passed several smaller islets, uninhabited specks of rock no bigger than a few acres floating in the black undulating water. He'd given up guessing which one might be "her" island, and had also convinced himself she was also freezing and only genetic pride kept her unmoved without complaint. Several dark shaggy seabirds drifted beside the boat, no doubt come out to root her on and laugh at his dumb ass. Simon lifted up a gloved middle finger at one of them, then refocused beyond the birds to the coastline.

"It's quite beautiful," he said, behind her.

She made no reply. Not even a polite mutter.

"Don't you think so?" he tried again. "Mary Rose?"

She turned this time. But her eyes were wide, empty, as if she were looking through him altogether. Her mind a thousand miles away. Or, he speculated, twenty years. Perhaps something really *was* coming back to her.

"Does it look the same as you remember?" he asked, he led.

Yet her eyes, and thoughts, were still not with him. As if she were no longer even on the boat.

"Merz?" He tried his pet name for her.

Then, finally, her gaze pulled to his, her head tilted. Recognition filled her face, and then, even, a smile. "You're freezing, aren't you?" she asked as her eyes danced impishly above the scarf.

"Me? No, this is fantastic. Why anyone would ever choose the Caribbean over . . . *this*." He lifted one eyebrow. "My balls are absolutely enchanted."

"They should put that on postcards." She looked up at the boat's cabin looming above them and started for the steps. "Okay, tough guy, let's get you inside."

"Hey . . ." He shouldered her gently as she passed. "Not on *my* account. My balls and I have been cold before. And, seriously, you can't knock the view."

"Cabin's got windows." She nodded toward the top of the boat. "Come on." She climbed the narrow teak steps easily, as if she'd been on boats her whole life. Simon followed more slowly, clinging to the handrail a bit too tightly.

The boat's pilot glanced at him as he entered the cabin, and there was no mistaking the humorous scorn in the Scottish guy's quick look. *Whatever*, Simon accepted, *so I haven't spent forty years yanking out fish guts in the North Pole. If that makes me a pussy, laugh all you want, pal.* He took the raincoat off and hung it back on the peg it'd come from. "How much further?" he asked.

"Depends," the man replied.

Simon studied the pilot again. The guy was similar age, he assumed, maybe late thirties, but the weather no doubt took its toll out here, so who knew. Thick dark beard and short wavy hair. Tattoos, colorful art Mary Rose had fawned over, visible on his forearms. At least, Simon reconciled, he was on the smaller side, and female thin.

Simon stopped himself. Groaned inwardly. Seemed that even in spite of impending engagement and the obvious love of a beautiful, intelligent sexy woman, he still carried a competitive, jealous streak. Still sized up the other roosters.

"On what does it depend?" Simon asked, walking to stand behind him.

"Margawse Loch is up the left." The man pointed through the window down the coast. "Could take ye both into that for the day. Plenty of nice pictures and so forth. You could take the dinghy onto half a dozen beaches or isles. Most scenic place for a hundred miles. Everyone who comes here says so."

Simon looked back toward Mary Rose, who sat on the bench in her raincoat staring across the cabin at nothing, no doubt secretly focused on getting warm. "That's not *the* island, though," Simon confirmed, and realized he'd used a quieter voice than usual. "The Likes to Be—"

"No."

Simon knew the guy hadn't been too keen on taking them out to Mary Rose's childhood stomping grounds. Rather, he'd hemmed and hawed like a schoolboy when Simon had mentioned the island by name, and if they hadn't already been on the man's boat when their specific request was given, Simon suspected the guy wouldn't even have taken them aboard. Fortunately, three hundred English pounds had sealed the deal long before any specifics beyond time. "Thanks," he said, "but I think we had our hearts set on seeing that one."

"It's only another island, mate." The pilot looked back at Simon. "Whole lot of rocks and gull shit, mostly. *This* up here is the place to see."

"Maybe another day."

The man tapped his hands gently on the wheel. "Aye, Captain."

"'The Little Island That Likes to be Visited.'" Simon restated, without interruption this time, their destination's strange name out loud. "What's the deal with the name?"

"How do you mean?"

"Just seems odd. Not very Scottish, first of all. And a bit misleading if it's, as you say, mostly rocks and gull shit."

The Scotsman turned, smiled with a crooked grin. "Guess it's like Greenland, then, eh? And the original Gaelic name is too hard for most folk to get out. Even for locals."

This sounded interesting. "Try me."

The pilot shook his head. *"Thaeilean-beag'toighleisa'bhith a'gabhail luchd-tadhail."* He'd purposefully thickened his already difficult-to-understand mumbly accent.

"You messing with me?"

The man smirked. "Not yet, mate."

"So, what's the deal with this place?" Simon decided to pursue openly. "I get the sense you aren't too thrilled about bringing us out here."

"No 'deal.' Tricky shores is all. Rocks there can sneak up if you don't know what you're doing. I do, but plenty of boats sprung a leak when they've gotten too close. Lots of shipwrecks over the years. Pirate ships, they say. Nazi scouts, even, in the war."

"Anything else out there? Anything, I don't know, 'strange'?"

The pilot quirked him a glance, and Simon realized Mary Rose had risen again. She stood close beside him now, her gaze open. Happy almost. The Scotsman looked between them. "You two looking for the haunted island tour, then? Is that it?"

Mary Rose shook her head. "Not even remotely."

"*Is* it a haunted island?" Simon chased.

"Has a reputation these parts, I suppose." The boat captain kept his eyes on Mary Rose a moment too long for Simon's comfort. "Various legends, but every island out here does. You might say we Scots have a way of putting stories on things. Ghosts, witches, little green men."

"You don't seem convinced."

"Not something I think about."

"Yeah, but—"

"Not something I think about."

Irritation skated across Simon's determined good cheer. The man was being deliberately vague, obnoxiously so. How hard to answer a direct question? "So, tricky shores," Simon summarized for them both.

"As I said, lots of places to run aground, to fall, get turned 'bout. People have drowned out there, OD'd. Only last spring, one lad nearly froze to death when his drunken mates forgot 'im. Lost a couple toes and fingers. But it's . . . There's nothing there worth seeing, mate."

"Maybe a couple of witches."

He shrugged again. "Halloween horseshit. Wicca. Druuuuuiids." He drew out the word ominously. "Like I said, mostly it's kids muckin' about. Rat-arsed drinking, playing with homemade Ouija boards, trying to talk the girls into getting naked."

"You said 'mostly' kids."

"Gettin' naked's a goal for adults also, I hear. There's a history there, sure. If rumors are history. But no human sacrifices I ever heard of." He turned. "Not yet, anyway."

Simon smiled as he was expected to do. "Why there?" he asked. "I mean, if it's only another island. Why all the local attention and, as you say, half-assed occult stuff?"

The man shrugged, returned his gaze to the water. "Oh, hell, mate. I don't know. Local folklore is all. The yarn that it hasn't always been there, I suppose. The rest of the coast, and islands, you can look at 'em and know they've stood fifty thousand years, longer. But folk claim this one just appeared one day, not that anyone remembers when. Though, some of the oldest folk in town swear it wasn't there when they was wean, kids. That it moves closer to the mainland some nights, *or* further away depending on its mood. That its size constantly changes. Or, even that it still comes and goes. There one minute and then . . ."

"How very *Brigadoon*."

The pilot groaned. "You asked."

"I did." Simon smiled, apologetically. "And no one lives out there?"

"Civic property. Vacant. Like a thousand other islands up and down this coast. But kids still sneak out there to get high, screw, and scare one another."

"I'd always heard it was enchanted." Mary Rose had spoken suddenly, and her voice startled both men. "That it has portals to other worlds."

"Can't tell you anything about that, miss."

"That people *vanish* there," Mary Rose pressed.

Simon stiffened, a thread of panic worming through him. He stepped toward her. "Maybe we could go outside again," he suggested. "I've warmed up, and we must be getting close. Why—"

"Have people vanished here?" she asked, ignoring him. Her manner had swung intent, feverishly so, and Simon's panic twisted in his gut.

To his credit, the pilot seemed to give Mary Rose's question due consideration. "I don't know about that," he said finally. "Stories built around poor souls who been lost at sea, I suppose. Or folk who never even set foot on the island. For years, everyone claimed Old Man Harris vanished out there, and turned out he'd just moved in with a niece in Framlingham." He looked directly at Mary Rose. Deciding something. "There *is* one story . . ."

Simon felt trapped, knew exactly the words that would surely come next from that damn bearded mouth.

"Girl got lost once."

Simon felt the phantom tug of his whole body collapsing but only for an instant. As quickly, he recovered, remembered Mary Rose had brought the topic up. Mary Rose was driving the conversation here. There remained the real possibility she'd been playing her parents for years, only pretending to have no memory.

And, so, been playing *him* for hours. Or worse, maybe all three of them were simply fucking with him, and this was some elaborate hoax that even the bearded guy was in on. He couldn't begin to imagine *why* that would be a possibility.

"It was an English girl," the pilot continued ponderously. "On holiday with her—"

"Oh, we're so close." Mary Rose's low declaration cut under the man's words, and she clapped her hands together. "I'm going back on deck."

Before Simon could even respond, she was out the door and working down the steps. He and the boat pilot exchanged "go-figure" looks that men, universally it seemed, shared at such times. But there was definitely something else in the captain's look. . . .

"The English girl?" Simon asked. "What's the rest of the story?"

"Tourists," the man said brusquely. Too brusquely, his whole face shutting down. "Got lost. Happens all the time. The only weird part was she was back again a month later. Found no worse for the wear, apparently."

"Oh! Well, that's good," Simon said, trying to draw the man out. "Was there ever an explanation for her coming back? The way she did, I mean. Out of the blue like that."

"None." He stared out at the water, not meeting Simon's eye. "Most folk round here simply blamed the father. He's the one who lost her *and* then found her, too. That's suspicious enough, yeah? Most of the local chin-wag was about him. The weeks she was gone, most assumed he'd killed her. There was something about an uncle, too. But then"— he smirked—"there always is. And any blather at the expense of the English, gossip I mean, is much enjoyed in these parts. But this was twenty years ago, so . . ."

"Understood." Simon had never heard mention of an uncle before. "Anything else you can remember? About the story. The gossip?"

"Nah." The Scotsman's gaze had shifted slightly from the bleak, watery view to focus unmistakably on Mary Rose. "Nothing comes to mind. Up to the right, y'see? We're nearly there."

Simon looked out over the bow and saw the hint of an approaching island. "Doesn't look too scary," he said.

The boat captain grunted again.

"Better head back down myself." Simon started for the door, leaving his raincoat behind. "Thanks for the info."

"Feel free to use the coat again, mate," the captain said.

"I'll be fine."

"Suit yourself."

Simon escaped from the cabin and made his way gradually down the slick steps. Mary Rose had already reached the front of the boat, getting as close to their destination as she could without climbing over the lines and random boat shit piled up front. Her mood was once again bright, open—she nearly trembled with excitement. Too much so? he wondered.

Then: *Did she truly not remember?*

As he wrestled with those ramifications, he watched the island grow in size and complexity. The small tumble of ashen rock and green shadows became a good-sized bit of land, large enough that

Simon couldn't make out its full shape. It was clearly remote, though. Uninhabited. Green became a thick forest of trees, gray split and rambled between dirt and rock and beach. He could make out the strip of sand and rocks that reminded him of the kind of place that a Scottish King Kong might live.

Something wild and dangerous. And very, very old.

Something waiting for them.

Simon shuddered.

"Isn't it just perfect?" Mary Rose beamed.

8

Mary Rose perched in the bow while Simon operated the outboard motor from a cushioned bench in back. Holding the steering handle like that, hunched forward against the wind and chill, he looked exactly like her father. Her elusive memories of him. How many afternoons she'd spent together with him exploring the neighboring lochs and islets, and how many of those afternoons they'd come to this same island.

She couldn't quite remember but well recalled the feeling of the undulant boat skating forward to the empty shoreline, the wind smoothing her face as she dipped tiny fingers over the side. Like an uninhibited seabird gliding above the Prussian-blue water.

This time, they both wore thick uncomfortable life preservers. Icy water sprayed over the sides of the dinghy, splashing the empty seat between them. The boat captain, Cameron, had not come with them. Rather, his hoary vessel bobbed gently at the head of the cove, anchored and waiting for their return.

Which she was very glad of. She'd wanted to introduce and share the island with Simon alone, the way her father had once shared it with her. No strangers were needed for that. That would ruin the magic of the experience for sure.

And, also, she didn't care for the captain's stories. Suspected he was talking about another island altogether and had gotten his stories crossed. More likely that he trotted out the same local twaddle, canned for the tourists, every time he brought someone out. A pity, really. Each of these islands certainly had their own history and personality; it would be nice if visitors learned the true stories. Nothing he'd said of this island, other than its name, rang a bell at all with her. When she and her father came here, there was no talk of such things. Such dark things.

She sucked in the sea air in deep gulps.

They'd always come alone. Her mother had rarely gotten on the boat at all, in fact. And when they'd gone, it was always sunny and warm and exquisite. Every time. Or, that's what she told herself now; no memories included gray clouds and blue fingers and rain. Which seemed impossible, she admitted, considering Scottish weather, but, even so, they were her memories to change. And in them, they would beach the boat, then her father would fish and she would read or paint or play along the shoreline and among the Scottish firs and scattered rowans still gleaming with red berries. And whole days would go by like this, wonderful days, days she'd chased after her whole life it seemed, until she'd almost believed they'd only ever been imagined.

But now that she was back, she knew it had always been real.

All of it.

"Isn't this perfect?" she asked Simon again.

"What?"

She cupped her hands. "You look good back there! Very pirate!"

He grimaced. "I'm probably going to hit a whale."

She laughed, thoroughly, unreasonably delighted with him, with herself, with all of *this*, and he pointed behind her. "I was heading over there. Good?"

"Yes!" She nodded. It did look like a good place to land, and turned her back to him again to relish their approach. Her return. *Twenty years . . .*

Funny, the awareness she felt was even stronger here than when she'd returned to her childhood home. She supposed it was the amount of time. It'd been almost seven years since visiting home. Another thirteen since here. And yet, as with many such things, it might as well have been only a few weekends ago. Time had a way of stretching back interminably until suddenly it—simply disappeared, the past memory becoming as vivid as her last indrawn breath.

Simon eased the engine back, its dogged rumble giving way to a low puttering and the sounds of groaning wood and water lapping and the wind. Closer still, like he'd been doing it his whole life. Mary Rose grinned to herself, warm with pride at her capable Simon.

When he finally cut the engine completely, a small wake lifted the boat softly, then carried it the final few feet onto the beach. "Hold on," he warned, and then the boat struck the shore, sliding up another foot. The tip of the bow offered a fine step onto wet sand, and Mary Rose was already out the boat.

The feel of the sand under her boots, the inimitable crunch and sink, was perfect. The Jersey Shore had been too loose and new, too soft. *This* sand had rested here forever, a fine pebbled surface awaiting the birth of man. Mild waves turned the boat sideways behind as Simon started crawling forward. "Tilt the engine up," she coached him, and he scrambled back for that step before joining her ashore.

"Not bad, newbie." She smiled at him.

"Hey, 'newbie' my ass. I was a Boy Scout, I'll have you know, and canoed my fair share of lakes and rivers."

She grabbed along the bow, indicated he should do the same. "Do you still have the uniform?"

"Maybe . . ." He grabbed the other side. "Interested?"

"Maybe." Together, they tugged the dinghy backward so that it was almost half onshore. Simon reached within and removed the anchor—a paint bucket filled with cement—and walked it another ten feet onto the beach.

"I don't think it's going anywhere." She laughed.

"Well, you never know. I want to keep all my toes and fingers."

She held out her hand, wiggling hers. "Come here."

Simon took her hand and started down the beach.

"We got the right place?" he asked.

Mary Rose squeezed his hand in reply and kept walking.

It *was* the "right place."

She didn't know for sure, no, not yet. But she felt it all the same; every nerve in her body that *could* feel tingled with familiarity, even intimacy. Yes, she'd been here before. And both she and the island knew it.

"You said your dad came out here as a kid?"

"For years," she said. The swash of a breaking wave chased them both back a step from the water. "Both my parents did, actually. My mother stayed with friends when she was a teen, but Daddy had spent every summer up here with his family. His parents owned a little cottage retreat near the village."

"Same place you three would stay?"

"Yes, but we sold it many years ago."

"You've never mentioned any aunts, uncles. Do your parents—"

"My mother is an only child, like me. Daddy has an older brother."

"Yeah? What's he do?"

"Oh!" Mary Rose shrugged, laughed. "I'm not really sure. Odd jobs, I think. They don't talk now. There was a falling-out of some kind years ago."

He humphed. "Any idea what about?"

She shook her head.

"That's a shame."

"Yes." Then: "I want to show you something."

What, exactly, she had no idea. But she suddenly felt *it*, whatever *it* was, must be right down this same beach and up that next hummock. Something she would recognize completely. Waiting there, for her, for twenty years.

She'd pulled him away from the water's edge up into the tall wild grass.

"What a wonderful place for a child," Simon said beside her.

"Yes. You could hear them sometimes."

"Hear who?"

But she'd stopped listening. To him, anyway. "I think we're close."

Then, sure enough . . .

Back away from the shoreline of patchy emerald grass besprent with tiny white anemone, which her father had always called windflowers. "Look!" she cried, and ran toward it, Simon trailing closely behind. "They're still here."

"What are those?" he asked, breathing hard.

"Cairns!"

There were dozens of various shapes and heights built across the same wide patch. Handmade towers of rock, most no higher than her knees. She and Simon weaved together carefully through them. This one was only five bigger rocks carefully balanced in a single leaning tower, each rising level smaller than the rock beneath. The one beside it more balanced and planned, with a single larger rock nested in the center. But hers was the biggest. Twenty good-sized rocks carefully stacked into a pyramidal tower, a marker to last twenty years.

"They're very special markers you make yourself. A guarantee of sorts you'll return again someday." She gently touched the top stone. "And I did, see? I did."

"Yes," he agreed quietly behind her.

"And to think, I made this twenty years ago. So fantastic."

"You think? Mary Rose . . ." He tilted his head, smiling. "Come on, there's no way that's your same rock pile. A good storm would knock that down in half a minute. It looks like—"

"It's the same," she decided, and ran her finger along several of the center stones. "They say if you take a stone from the pile and put it under your pillow at night, in the first light of morning, an angel will appear for an instant, then will change back into a stone and magically return to the pile."

"An angel, huh?"

"Or . . ." Mary Rose scrunched her lips in thought, smiled. "Maybe it was a soldier." She retrieved a free rock from the ground, then laid it carefully upon the topmost rock. "I want to come back again."

"Well, I can understand why." He cleared his throat. "You must have lots of great memories about this place."

"Oh, yes." She smiled warmly. But there was, again, no specific memory she could call to mind. She couldn't even picture herself building the cairn that particular day or anything exactly she and Father had ever done. Only vague assumptions. In fact, until she'd seen the cairn field, she hadn't even remembered making one. So, to imagine, then, that this one was hers—"Let's make our own," she said. "You and me."

"So I'll come back, also."

She reached up to brush back his windblown hair. "*We*," she corrected him.

"Done," he said, and started moving about looking for solitary rocks spread about the ground.

Mary Rose helped gather some, too, and they built a simple nine-stone tower, alternating turns, and moving up from biggest to smallest.

"How's it look?" he asked.

Mary Rose grinned down at their little stone spire. It already looked, like the others, like it had stood there for centuries. "It's perfect." She reached around his jacket and hugged him. "I remember this place," she said, quietly into his coat. "It's the funniest thing."

"What about it?" he asked. His voice sounded uneasy.

Mary Rose looked up at him.

"Over the next hill," she said. "If I remember right . . ."

She laced through the cairn field and kept marching forward toward a short hill with Simon coming after.

Beyond it, she had sight of a second hill and there, there was the tree. *Yes.* Exactly where she expected it to be. Where she remembered.

Alone, the nearest neighboring tree a quarter mile away or more. Exactly as she, only now, recalled. The one large trunk splitting into two, which then wrapped around each other twice before splintering off again into separate boughs, the branches that sprung throughout full and green and splashed in red berries but too often too far away from one another, giving the tree an autumn-bare lonesome appearance.

They trudged together toward it. If it had grown any—it must have, yes?—she didn't know, for it'd seemed enormous all those years ago, but she'd since grown, too. Beside the tree, she recalled, floating in a sea of pillowy moss, would be the tree stump of a second tree cut down a hundred, or five hundred, years before. A stump where she'd sat and waited happily for hours in the sun, drawing or reading or simply being, while Father fished.

Closer, she couldn't believe the stump was still there, expecting that years and the harsh elements to have rotted it away. But there it waited, for her, as always long before. From this spot, she could turn and take in miles of the island on all sides, framed on two sides by the black ocean. To see her father's boat drifting closely offshore. She stepped in a slow circle beneath the half-barren tree.

"Look, Simon." She crouched down, rested both hands on the top of the stump. Not one more ring added or lost in all those years. As if all that time had meant nothing at all. "I would sit here for hours and hours and draw. Or . . ." she looked up at the tree looming above them. "Sit in one of the boughs and read like Alice."

"Anyone we know?" He crouched also and fingered the weather-worn graffiti carved into the side of the trunk:

mRm

"Mary Rose Morland," she said aloud. Her voice trembled, the slightest bit. "I . . . Yes, I remember now. My father carved that."

"Yeah?" Simon studied her. Without even looking at him, she could *feel* his exanimation.

"Yes . . ." She grinned and touched her hands to the deep, yet faded etching. "I sat right here, for hours, truly. Or . . ."

Simon had reached up to grab one of the branches. The berries so thick and red, it looked like he was holding a flaming torch.

"Stop!" She jumped up.

"What's the matter?" He loosened his hold on the branch.

"The rowan is an incredibly sacred tree," she explained. "You have to be utterly careful with how you treat one."

He grimaced. "Sorry."

She reached up to run her fingers through the same branch.

"The Romans believed the red comes from the bloodshed of an eagle who fought demons for the gods." She held her fingers behind the green leaves. "And *these* are its lost feathers. And the Norse said the first woman was created from the rowan tree."

"Where'd you learn all this?"

"I don't know. My father, I suppose. The Scottish say the branches provide protection from evil spirits and that fairies have ceremonies beneath them. They're carried as wards against evil and still planted in churchyards. You're never to cut one down."

"And who do you believe? Which legend?"

Mary Rose grinned. "All of them," she said.

"We should get a picture," he said, freeing his phone, usurping her next thoughts. "With you sitting on—"

She shook her head. Then looked up again at the lonesome tree above them, suddenly feeling, well, a bit overcome by the enormity of it all. "I wonder if . . ."

"Yes?"

"Could I . . . I'm sorry, would you mind if . . ."

Simon smiled. Her capable, understanding, beautiful Simon, anticipating her every need. "Want some alone time?"

"I'm sorry."

"Why? Perfectly understood." He pointed down the hill to the right. "How 'bout I walk down to the beach right down there, and you can come and get me whenever you're done. Gonna build you a sand castle in the meantime."

"I'll only be a minute," she assured.

He leaned forward to kiss her forehead. "Take as much time as you'd like, Mary Rose. I'll be fine. It's been too long since my last sand castle."

She closed her eyes in thanks, in love. By the time she'd opened them again, he was already turned away and started down the hill. She watched his retreating back and stroked her fingers down the half-dead tree, eventually looking up through its desolate branches to the flawlessly blue sky.

Alone finally, Mary Rose sat on her old stump. Knees pulled up tight to her chest, arms wrapped around her legs as once long before. She could see down to the beach, and Simon, and when he turned her way, could look back to the cairn field. It was all so familiar now.

She wished she'd brought a sketchbook. To draw what she saw today, or maybe try and capture the little girl from twenty years before. She'd risen and was moving away from the shore. Toward the foothills and denser forest. Where she was heading, she had no idea. But these steps were as sure as those that'd led her to the cairns, the tree. More so.

Suddenly she blinked. She stood at the edge of the wood already.

Whirling, she looked back to the lone tree on the hill, a quarter mile away somehow. Mary Rose spun around, then around again, confused. She hadn't remembered walking so far, she didn't remember. Her mind clearly somewhere else, no doubt some*when* else.

She needed to get back, though. She needed to . . .

The sea breeze whistled past her and through the stand of trees into the darkness waiting within. It almost sounded like music. Or a whisper.

And Mary Rose, wanting to hear more, longing to hear again, followed.

In the dark, all women are the same.

—Ovid, *Metamorphoses*

9

She'd covered her eyes, and Simon first supposed she might be crying, which made no sense at all because Mary Rose was many things, but a crier wasn't one of them and also for most of the day she'd been in such high spirits. Having a blast, even. Relaxed and content, in fact, despite the chill, her whole face absolutely glowing with the serenity of an entire afternoon on her childhood island—*never mind that the experience had damn near gutted him*—with no indication or mention of recollections connected to her disappearance.

But then she'd devolved into the hidden eyes, and he realized the day of Memory Lane *had*, finally, been too much, too long. Or, rather, that some kind of emotional breakthrough, the purging of dredged-up memories, was, as her parents had warned him, actually happening. Only a few hours ago, he'd been congratulating himself for agreeing to bring her. But now . . .

Where would such a breakdown lead? What had he been thinking?

Then suddenly, like a curtain being torn away, Simon understood.

Mary Rose wasn't covering her eyes, exactly, but was *peeking* from within those interlaced fingers, like a child watching the scarier parts of a horror film, trying to create the barest slit from which to see the world. He looked from her to where she was staring, and only at the last instant did he grasp she was peeking at something specific.

A particular bluff between Margawse Loch and the village of Mhoire's Point. A house there, maybe. A small gray structure, half-lost within the scrub and rocks. Obviously, he figured, it was somewhere she knew. Another memory. Maybe even, presumably, one having something to do with her disappearance.

"What do you see?" he asked. Might as well go straight at it; how he usually handled everything that wasn't connected to Mary Rose. Problems didn't get solved by pussyfooting around.

She dropped her hands. "What?" Then smiled at him, and her face was peaceful again, though almost vacant. The fine line between relaxed and withdrawn, which she'd been dancing along for the better part of an hour. Ever since he'd lost and then refound her, which was not an experience he'd want to relive again anytime soon, thank you very much.

When he'd first looked up to the tree and not seen her there, he took several steps back up the hill before another thought entered his mind. He'd stopped, hands on hips, looking up and down the shoreline for her. But, he'd told himself, there was no danger here. The entire island was empty except for the two of them, and Mary Rose likely knew her way around here better than she did around South Street, back in Philly.

What was there to worry about? To fear?

Above all of these thoughts, however, was one more: Her father must have believed the exact same things twenty years before—out of ignorance or recklessness, he couldn't say. Which of the two would it be if she somehow vanished on *his* watch? Standing beneath the vacant ridge, Simon had checked his watch. He'd give her fifteen more minutes and then head back up. Or, better: ten more minutes. Seven minutes later, he'd reached the tree where he'd left her. She, of course, wasn't there.

And he laughed at first. Karma playing its part so faithfully.

Mary Rose had somehow figured out exactly what her parents had told him and was now teaching him—and maybe them, too—a lesson. She'd snuck off to some secret location and was watching him from afar. He'd reassured himself this, made jokes out loud, but even as he said the words he could taste the bitter lie in them. Because he'd been terrified. Absolutely frozen solid with the shock of Mary Rose simply . . . simply being gone. His body no longer skin and bones but a shell encasing a cold, hollow ache of confusion, of wrongness. The logic of where she *should* be suddenly had no relation to where she apparently was. It'd been maddening, infuriating; as if reality, which he'd trusted for thirty-odd years, no longer counted.

For the first time, Simon could truly begin to imagine the terror James Morland must have felt that day all those years ago.

"Mary Rose!" He'd cupped his hands and shouted against the wind in seven different directions. Nothing . . . nothing . . . nothing. And then staggered up and down and back and over the ridge and hillocks and dunes and sand and even into a small wood some, and there had only been—more nothing.

An hour later, she came strolling up to him, back down by the beach, claiming she'd been looking for him all along. Simon had gone beyond fear. Barely an hour, and his carefully constructed world had been on the brink of genuine terror, of falling apart. Then up Mary Rose had popped like a jack-in-the-box with no hint as to who'd been turning the crank. Her claims of trying to find him had been utter bullshit, of course, the first time Mary Rose had ever clearly lied to him, and his panic had shifted to anger easily enough. His instincts were to blast her some, to finally question this impulsive frivolity and tell her to grow the fuck up a little. But he'd hidden all that well, he thought, kept his mouth shut, acted like he'd had a grand time making sand castles the whole time instead of completely freaking out, and for that he deserved a medal.

Mary Rose hadn't been much for talking on their walk back to the dinghy, and still wasn't back on the fishing boat. She gave him only that contented smile, and they spent the rest of the boat ride in silence, her entire contribution to any more questions given in distracted one-word answers.

At the docks, another man helped fend off the boat, then shouted and pointed at one of the ropes for Simon to toss to him. He offered an arm to Mary Rose, who'd begun stepping off the boat before it had even completely settled. She then waited at the end of the dock, while Simon thanked the boat captain.

Simon found a £20 note and handed it as a tip.

The man waved it away. "We're square, mate," he grumbled.

Simon began to protest but caught the look the pilot shot the man on the dock as he stood with Mary Rose—a look that said "what a knob"—and let it pass, slipping the bill back into his pocket. "Okay. . . . Well, thanks for the tour."

The fisherman saluted, holding the gesture long enough to make the other man laugh.

Simon stepped off the boat and found Mary Rose waiting at the end of the dock. "How about some coffee?" he asked. "Or whiskey. Or both?"

She shook her head, her eyes once more bright. "I'm going shopping," she announced.

"Shopping?" He hadn't expected that, stopped focusing on the splash of red florets from the tiny rowan branch she'd tucked in her hair. "I was hoping to get the personal tour of the town. Isn't that why we drove five hours?"

"I'm buying a secret gift for my fiancé." She smiled still, but her words seemed curiously intense. "You can't come."

The idea of letting her out of his sight again, after this afternoon, seemed insane. He wasn't too sure he could handle another disappearing act. But nor was he going to spend a lifetime being one of those clingy douches he knew. Individuals deserved their own lives beyond the couple; she no less than he. "Hey, you okay?"

"I'm fine." She checked her watch. "Meet back here at five?"

"Five," he agreed, swallowing his real response. Fine. He'd have to kill more than an hour, but he sure as hell needed that drink. It was clear Mary Rose needed more alone time, and would probably crash hard tonight back at the house. Seek the comfort of a dark room. This would help all of that. "See you in a little bit. Be safe."

"Thank you." With a lingering kiss to his cheek, she stepped back, then turned and started off down the street alone.

He watched her vanish down a side street before moving himself. The wind gusted off the harbor across his back. He started up the street himself, heading away from where Mary Rose had gone.

A pub on some corner appeared quickly enough, and he took the steps down to its front door. The heads of a black and white ram painted over the entryway. This would do perfectly. Warmth, a drink, and maybe even an answer to one of a hundred new questions.

Inside was exactly what he'd hoped for. Shadowy, tables and stools crowded together, the floor-to-ceiling wall of bottles behind the bar, ale mugs of various shapes and sizes hanging above the stools, dark wood–paneled walls covered in framed photos and newspaper clippings covering a hundred years or more. The place was mostly empty, but there were still a dozen men and a few women gathered at several tables and at the bar. Most turned to eye his entrance.

He took a seat toward the center of the bar, folded his jacket over the stool beside it. The bartender, nearly bald with full grayed muttonchops, stepped forward. "Didn't you see the sign out front?" he asked.

"What's that?" Simon turned to the front door, then back to the bartender.

"'All Americans must be accompanied by an adult,'" the man said, without any hint of joking.

Simon nodded. "That obvious, huh?"

The man put his stony hands on the bar. "What you want?"

"Pint of local stout, thanks."

"Tennent's or Foster's?"

Simon smiled back, not playing to the joke.

The bartender nodded, his eyes finally revealing the universal joy of fucking with tourists, then stepped away to fetch the pint. Simon had already laid his crumpled £20 on the counter by the time he'd returned with the drink. "Beautiful country," he said. "Took a boat down past Margawse Loch."

The bartender looked around the room, clearly unimpressed.

"Guy took us to this island," Simon continued. "The, ah . . . what was that, *Thaeilean-bea* . . ." He took a swig of beer, put the glass back down. "Oh hell, 'The Little Island That Likes to be Visited.'"

"Let me know if you need anything else," the man said gruffly, but he wasn't moving any farther away, either.

"Guy said a little girl vanished out there once. Found her again a month later or something?"

The bartender shrugged, eyes narrowing. "Don't know any ghost stories for you, friend."

"Who said anything about a ghost story?"

The Scotsman truly smiled for the first time, then retreated to the far end of the bar, where a rugby game waited in the corner TV.

Simon looked directly at the guy on his left, sitting between him and the bartender. "What about you?" he said. "Know anything about this "Little Island That—'"

The man chuckled, turned his head away to also watch the game.

Strike two, and Simon decided he didn't need a third. Instead, he turned to stare at the bottles behind the bar. He worked quietly, and leisurely, at his beer. He'd have time for a second one, he decided. He deserved at least that, after a day of freezing his ass off and feeling like a lost eight-year-old.

"It's devil worshippers," a voice muttered behind him and to the right.

Simon turned, peering at the older woman sitting three stools down from him, beside another man. "What's that?" he asked, knowing exactly what she'd said but hoping to draw her out.

She didn't disappoint.

"Devil worshippers go there," she said, and the combination of a thick accent and what had no doubt been a long afternoon of drinking made each word harder to understand than the last. "Sacrifices to the devil. And"—she leaned closer, her breath warm and sour—"*sex* orgies. To sate their lust with demons."

"Was out there this afternoon," Simon said. "Certainly no signs of that."

She waved away his attempt at a joke, grunted angrily. Clearly, she suspected she was being made fun of.

Damn. He'd thought "light and fun" would work with her—he needed to stick with straight at it: "You know anything about this girl who vanished? Guess it was about twenty years ago now . . ."

She scowled, but she didn't pull back. "Lots of people vanish out there."

"So I've heard. But, this one came back."

She waved a finger. "That there's the devil's business."

"Why do you think so?"

She shrugged again, withdrew to her drink.

Simon took a swallow himself. Decided to try a curveball. "Passed a bit of land out there," he said as casually as he could muster. "An old farmhouse. On one of the higher hills directly past the Loch . . . Any idea if it's for sale?"

She shook her head. "Nah. Don't know it."

"Little small gray house? Looked vacant."

"That's a hundred houses like that around here, pal." It was the bartender, returned.

"Sure, well this one—"

"What's the name, Yank?"

"*My* name?" He noticed in the mirror behind the bartender that much of the room now watched their interaction. "Simon Blake." He offered his hand across the bar. "And you . . ."

"You need another pint, Simon Blake?"

Simon lowered his hand, looked down at his half-finished beer. "Definitely, thanks."

The bartender withdrew to pull another draft. By the time he returned and laid the glass down, the older woman and the man at Simon's right had crept away to a table across the room.

Simon lifted his first glass to the barkeep. "Cheers," he said.

James and Franny Morland were not happy.

It had been a four-hour-plus drive, and Simon and Mary Rose had also stopped for dinner, and it was moving on midnight before they'd gotten back to the house in Alderley Edge. Texts from Mary Rose regarding their imminent return and that "everything was fine" had apparently not been enough.

Simon couldn't believe it. He'd wanted to enjoy this interlude with Mary Rose, and even with her parents—tell them what a great time she'd had, that *nothing* sinister had happened—only they were treating her like she was thirteen and had missed curfew. All magically without openly discussing their concerns about Mhoire's Point. Everything had to be done under the guise of taking-too-much-time and not being forthcoming regarding their plans for the day.

He'd tried to run interference, first offering up the idea that they really had planned to go only an hour into Scotland but then were having such a lovely time seeing the countryside and just kept going; then to take the full blame for running late, and for agreeing to take her there, going so far as to claim it had been *his* idea, that he'd wanted to see Mhoire's Point more than she did.

"Did you . . . did you go to the island?" James Morland asked in a voice that barely crossed the room. "The little island."

"Yes," Simon answered for them both. "And it was a lovely day, and everything was fine. I can see why you and Mary Rose loved it so."

But his attempts had been in vain. Her parents were interested in Mary Rose's explanation, her defense and apology, and hers alone.

Even now, the three of them were in the study, where she was no doubt being lectured like a teen. Deferring to her little-girl self to appease her parents' unreasonable irritation.

He'd wandered down the hall, giving them privacy, recognizing his place in this family dynamic. Still the outsider. And so he'd defer.

For now.

If the angst and finger wrangling continued much longer, however, he might have to start setting some boundaries with these two well-meaning loons. Mary Rose deserved that. They both did. He wasn't going to spend the next twenty years being pushed around by folk who didn't know when to let go.

Simon found himself standing again before the large black mirror.

It wasn't as if he had much choice, candidly. He could either exit out the front door or stand here waiting for the lecture to conclude. He looked back down the darkened hallway past the pictures and several generations of Mary Rose's family. Soon to be *his* family . . .

Absently, he touched the dark glass, the mirror icy and hard against his fingers. It reminded him of the ocean water surrounding the island.

Simon gazed into the utter blackness, clearing his mind of the portraits watching behind him, the day's discussions and questions. He suspected the true power of such mirrors rested not in faraway spirits, but in the ability to relax the viewer. To provide a truly vacant space to seek—

A face appeared in the mirror.

Simon lurched.

Right behind where his own reflection should be was a gray pear-shaped oval. Point down, like an alien head. Or, rather, an empty skull. Like the pictures in Mary Rose's bizarre drawings, he realized with sudden clarity.

It lifted then, and he could almost pick out new features. Two wide eyes and the thin slash of a black mouth . . .

Simon spun around.

Mary Rose stood there, head tilted at him curiously.

"What's the matter?" she asked, clearly startled.

Simon shuddered, looked back at the mirror.

It, of course, was completely dark again. No reflection of any kind.

He waved his hand in front of it, trying to make the image come back.

"They think the house is haunted," Mary Rose said behind him.

Simon turned again slowly. "Your parents?"

She looked past him at the mirror and nodded.

"Do you?" he asked.

She kept staring.

"Mary Rose . . ." He rested a hand on her hip.

She looked up at him as if surprised he was there. "Yes?"

"Why do they think that?" He'd changed his question.

"Oh. Why, I don't know."

"Do *you* believe in ghosts?"

She looked away, thinking. "I don't know," she said again.

He tried surmising what *his* answer might be when she asked him the same. But she never did.

That night, Simon woke to the persistent slow wash of dark waves breaking against a craggy shore. For the past four hours, in fact, his whole body still felt like it was on the fishing boat, or in the dinghy, being rocked this way and that, lifted and pulled.

He slid out from bed and stood to feel the fixed floor beneath his bare feet, more grateful than he'd ever remembered for the fact that he was standing on firm, dry hardwood. In the dark, the swish of Scottish breakers still lingering in his ears, he half expected his feet to sink into damp sand.

Simon checked his phone, saw it was barely past two. Had only been asleep an hour at most. He started for the window when he heard a new sound.

High-pitched whispering. Giggling, even.

Before he could convince himself otherwise, he crossed the dark bedroom and opened the door to the hallway.

Nothing. The whole house was quiet and dim. Everyone appeared sound asleep. The hallway itself was illuminated by only one softly lit lamp, far at its end, and everything seemed hushed and still, though at the far end of the hall, one of the curtains wavered gently in an unfelt draft.

Simon stepped from his room, decided the voice—if he'd truly heard it—had come down from the other end of the hall. Exactly where he'd found Mary Rose the night before.

He stopped at her door, stood motionless, listening. Nothing stirred within. He thought of opening her door and checking but didn't want to wake her. It'd been a long day, and quite possibly a traumatic one for her. God knew it'd been borderline traumatic for him. At least she and her parents had managed, it seemed, to call a civilized quite-British truce prior to going to bed. Best to let her sleep in peace.

He stepped slowly farther down the hall to the next room and the door he'd tried the night before.

Tonight, however, the door was open.

A crack only. A shadow from the room within spilled out into the dimly lit hallway in one long line of black that cut across the floor and lapped against the opposite wall.

Simon rested his hand against the door.

Something within the darkness growled.

Panic rooted him, disorientation, but he hadn't imagined it—hadn't. Something in the dark room had *growled* at him.

An animal of some kind. A large animal.

Swallowing back his fear, Simon thrust the door open, and—

Found only more darkness.

He reached into the room, blundered along the wall for the light switch. Found none. Something darker than night stood in the center of the room. Like a small child standing there alone in the dark.

He stepped fully into the room's doorway, his eyes growing more accustomed to the dark, and pushed the door open wide. Behind the small dark shape, several walls within the room shimmered. And as the light from the hallway spread into the room, he saw more.

Crosses. Dozens hanged on the one wall. Fifty.

Various shapes and sizes. Celtic style. Gothic. Bronze, wood, polished brass. Rustic wood. Wrought iron. Silver, gold, two-tone. Dark oak, etched, beveled, painted.

He tossed on the light and stepped fully into the small room.

All four walls were covered in crosses.

And the mysterious shape in the center of the room proved to be some kind of prayer station. A "kneeler," he thought they were called. A prayer-book shelf and cushioned knee rest for one. He stepped toward it and studied the subtle carved crosses in the wood and the prayer book resting beneath the top panel.

Looking about the room, he noted that most of the crosses were equally subtle. Unadorned. Plain. It was too small for a bedroom, he decided, and wondered if they'd built the room solely for this purpose. He even finally detected a short triangular closet built into the one wall, painted the same color at the rest of room, covered in several crosses. Simon hadn't ever been much of a cross guy. Not like his Catholic friends who often sported a gold cross around the neck like Mary Rose's mother. But even *they* would find this ridiculous. Overdone. Honestly, a little unnerving. He could only assume which Morland had—

"What are you doing?"

Simon recoiled, then, steeling himself, turned to the grave voice behind him.

A black figure stood in the doorway.

Francine Morland. Wrapped in a heavy bathrobe.

"Oh, hey . . ." Simon felt trapped, caught in some terrible transgression when all he was doing was standing in a room. "Sorry, I heard . . . Doesn't matter. The door was open and . . ." He managed a smile, redirected. "What a perfect room for a personal, ah, chapel. Prayer space."

"It was her playroom," she said. "Before."

Francine Morland glanced around, taking the dark room in from one shadowed corner to the next. "After she came back . . ." It seemed she spoke mostly to herself. "She never entered this room again." She stepped back to imply he should join her in the hallway.

Simon followed and tried another line of discussion. "What a beautiful collection. It must have taken years to—"

"They're not there to be beautiful," she managed, her tone officious, ignoring his second attempt at a genuine discussion.

Simon switched off the light and pulled the door shut behind him.

The lines in her face were drawn again into a disappointed scowl. Still, standing before Simon so closely in the newly darkened hall, he couldn't help but notice how much like Mary Rose she was. Her build. Her challenging eyes. Even the tiny freckles at the top of her exposed pale collarbone. An inimitable warmth coming off her body. She was only in her late fifties, but Simon couldn't help but imagine what she'd been like before marriage and motherhood and family secrets and all the regrets that surely must come with real life. Before the room of crosses.

"Sorry about poking my head in without asking," he said to defuse the tension, to end the line of thought, adding a polite chuckle. "Last night, it was locked and—"

"It's never locked," Francine Morland cut him off, then looked past him at the closed door. "It's held," she said.

10

In the morning, Mary Rose and Simon drove into town together.

It'd been her idea, for she needed to be away from the house. For a while, at least. There, she suddenly felt trapped. As if, she decided, quite melodramatically, someone were trying to entomb her deep in the ground. She knew full well it had everything to do with her parents' ludicrous tantrum the night before; still, what a terrible thing even to imagine about your home.

Out here, however, the streets were wide open and bursting with unambiguous life. People flowing in every direction between the rows of quaint storefronts as they shopped and met friends or found a bite to eat. The local business crowd and white-hairs and other handsome young couples, and even children, too. And, all the trees running alongside and, sometimes, stretching over them, blushed with the first roseate hints of fall, several boughs slashed charmingly with long, incipient streaks of slaughterous red and ginger. Almost like driving into one of her own paintings, she thought now.

It also reminded her, disquietingly so, of the dreams she'd had the night before. Something about a door, not being able to open a door, and someone more powerful pushing on the other side. Nightmares, in truth. Fortunately, they were of the variety she couldn't quite hold on to, those which so often slithered back away beneath the edge of daybreak, where they would linger to attack her some other fell, lugubrious eve.

Mary Rose breathed deeply as Simon parked the car.

No wonder she'd had a terrible night of sleep—despite all her hopes. She'd been in an extraordinary mood all day. The boat trip, time on the island, the darling little village after their return. All of it. More at peace than she could remember being in weeks, months. Years, maybe.

Only to return to her mother's questions and warnings and frosty stares and mumbles. What difference did it make that she'd gone to Mhoire's Point? Both parents, truly. Blatantly concerned. Overly prying. As if it had become some kind of terrible mistake but they couldn't quite get around to telling her *why*. Which would all have been perfectly fine, she supposed, if she were still a six-year-old girl. But she wasn't. She'd changed.

Mary Rose stood outside the car, arms crossed. Hers wasn't the only transformation, either. The shops she'd remembered so vividly, so lovingly, had all changed also.

Driving through the village before, she'd noticed many boutiques and some new high-end shops—and her father had made some cracks regarding the evolving downtown—but she hadn't truly grasped the depth of the changes until now. Any thoughts of showing Simon her childhood hometown were shattered. Where Mhoire's Point had proven exactly the same as she'd always remembered—not a cobble-stone or storefront shingle out of place—downtown Alderley Edge had somehow become an unfamiliar city she today barely knew better than her American guest.

She took Simon's arm and started down the street with him.

There were hazy memories of a small bookstore where a designer sunglasses store now stood, and her artist's mind could easily overlay the new store with the ephemeral outline of her own careful memories. Yes, there, the shoe store, Peter Lord, where she'd gone each fall at the start of school. And a Woolworths between the Coral Betting Shop and, she thought, a tailor (all three replaced). Down there, the Our Price record store where she'd bought her first CDs: Spice Girls, Oasis, Peter Andre. The Pick 'N' Mix candy shop, where she'd always find her favorite chocolates.

Now, they were all gone. Replaced with faceless sidewalk stops that tendered no personal recollections. Still, she allowed the new buildings to surface from behind her own remembrances and tried, instead, evoking the last time *she'd* walked the same footway. If she couldn't make the buildings materialize again, perhaps she could, at least, conjure the Mary Rose of all those years ago.

Simon gently tugged her hand, breaking whatever spell she'd started down. "Careful," he warned.

She looked up at him, confused.

He grinned and used his other hand to indicate the crossway she'd started over. And then the red light flashing on the other side.

"Oh! I wasn't even—" she said, finally becoming aware of several other people standing around them, waiting to cross. When he squeezed her hand in response, apology accepted, she nestled against him. She closed her eyes, selfishly hoping that when she opened them again, the town would be returned to the way it had been before. Twenty years before. Then it would display itself exactly as it had been on that most perfect of days.

She opened her eyes, seeing nothing had changed back and laughed suddenly.

"What's so funny?" Simon asked.

She couldn't say. Nothing, truly. She'd been tense before, now she was merely sad. Thinking of something terrible, violent: throwing herself in front of the last car that passed. Imagining the shocked reaction of those around her, and of Simon, too, the sensation of the car's terrible weight passing over her. Silly. A laugh was simply what had come out.

The light changed, and they crossed, window-shopping the block of boutiques together. Simon kept asking if she wanted to "check out" any of the stores, encouraging her to take as much time as she wanted. But she couldn't bring herself to it. She preferred the fresh air, the musty smell of wet leaves, the wind on her face.

Mary Rose examined her watch. If they drove right away, they could be back at Mhoire's Point by three. Spend the whole day and night there, maybe. No more sneaking back at midnight. Instead, she'd fall asleep to the steady slurp and swish of the ocean, as familiar as her own breath. Still, she could hear its imagined echo in her ear, louder again than in many years. The day-old memory so much fresher, more corporeal. All through the night, even after showering, she'd still felt the gritty hints of sand on her skin, the trace of sea salt still in her hair.

She wondered what Simon would say if she asked him to take her again. Only once more, of course. No more than that, sincerely. To say: Goodbye, little island that likes too much to be visited. Would he think her insane? Would he take her again joyfully? Would it, she wondered with the seed of another unexpected laugh, matter what *he* did?

"Look who it is," Simon said beside her, and Mary Rose chased away her next thoughts. "Your old pal."

Mr. Amy, her father's friend, stood two doors down, having just come out of a tea and coffee shop. He looked directly their way, then froze, half caught in a bungled, and somewhat charming, attempt to pretend he hadn't seen them.

"Mr. Amy!" Simon shouted, sealing the man's decision, and Mary Rose couldn't help but giggle. Darkly.

George Amy smiled widely and waved back, then waited as Simon and Mary Rose walked toward him. "Having a lovely visit?"

"For sure," Simon answered. "What a wonderful town this is," he continued on, as he always could with strangers. "Is one of these yours?" He pointed between the two visible churches on the street.

Amy stabbed a finger behind them. "Saint Philip's," he explained. "About two blocks that way. Those"—he looked back to where Simon had indicated—"are the Methodists." He held his coffee cup up at the other. "And Saint Pius, the Roman Catholics."

"Modest church, for Catholics. Smaller following here, then?" Simon commented, overdoing, she thought, his interest.

"We can blame Old Henry and the Acts of Supremacy for that."

"Mother attends Saint Pius," she added to Amy's reply.

Mr. Amy turned, looking at her directly for the first time. "Indeed she does."

She'd never given the man much thought, she realized. For twenty-some years, he was merely one more of her father's milquetoast friends. Nothing particularly noteworthy physically or intellectually. Nor even, sadly considering his vocation, spiritually. He was just another adult who'd swirled at the peripheries of her childhood without notice or consequence. A minor character in the ensemble of those who'd stood, sipped drinks and gibbered in her father's study or under party tents in the backyard. Seeing him today—a little rounder, lighter of hair, surrendered to life—made him seem even more banal.

What, she wondered, did he see when looking at her after all these years? An older woman now. Traveled. More educated. Sexually active. In love, even. Could he tell merely by looking at her how much she'd changed? Would he only see that she was *less* bone thin. Because he clearly saw *something.* Why the evident nervousness? One, she realized now, he'd always kind of carried with her. Why, he was practically gaping at her, as if staring at a dead rat lying on his pillow.

"You've lived here how long?" Simon asked.

Mr. Amy turned back to Simon. "M' whole life." He sipped at his coffee. "Except for schooling and some service work overseas when I was younger." He went on with a brief résumé, politely only, for Simon.

Mary Rose had stopped listening. She'd tilted her head to indicate she still was, but her eyes looked beyond the man talking at the rest of the street. There, the people seemed to move more slowly. More silently.

The whole street had somehow grown hushed. Even the passing traffic had faded, morphed all too easily into the deeper sounds of rumbling surf hitting a rock-lined shore, the wet drag of glimmering shingle.

There was movement at the corner of her eye, something stepping faster and sharper than all the rest seemed to, and she rocked toward it as her mind fought to register what she'd seen but gone as quickly as it had first appeared. Still, she'd seen—if she'd seen anything at all—where it had gone and was already taking her first and definite strides toward it.

"Guess that's our sign to go." Simon chuckled nervously behind her. He put a friendly hand on Mr. Amy's shoulder.

"Oh." Mary Rose blinked. "I'm sorry. I thought I saw . . . It's nothing."

Simon smiled. "All good." He turned back to Amy. "It was nice—"

"No, you two chat." She stopped him. "I'll run ahead some, maybe even do some real shopping. You know how us girls can be."

"I *was* hoping to talk with Simon, actually," said Mr. Amy, a bit too quickly, but she didn't care. She wanted to be off on her own.

"Oh?" Simon smirked at Mr. Amy, confused.

"Planning a trip to New York and Philadelphia next spring. Was looking for advice on where to stay, eat, and the like."

"Talk." She gently grabbed one arm each of both men. "Simon knows the East Coast as well as you know Alderley Edge. I'll be half a block that way." She'd squeezed Simon's arm as she said the last.

"Sure," Simon agreed. "I'll catch up in a minute."

Mr. Amy had retreated to his coffee.

"It was nice seeing you again. Mr. Amy," she offered.

"Yes," he agreed as before, and nodded curtly. "Brilliant to see how well you're doing in America, dearest child. Continued blessings."

She smiled in thanks and turned her back to both men, heading down the street, chasing after whatever she'd seen. Whether a passing shadow or merely some figment escaped from her own uneasy thoughts, she was determined to see it again.

A block farther away, she did.

11

Simon half watched Mary Rose retreat slowly down the street away from them, then turned his full attention to Mr. Amy, who looked up with judging, narrowed eyes. Simon was okay with that. He'd spent ten years looking at such faces. More to the point, he'd *also* wanted to talk to the old family friend, and was thrilled when Amy'd asked to chat. Privately now, too. Simon couldn't have planned it better himself if he'd tried. There was one question in particular he'd been dying to ask since the day they'd first met.

"So," he said, playing his part first, deciding how to best approach the man. "When were you looking at heading east?"

Amy smiled a little self-consciously. "We'll see. I, honestly, was hoping to talk with you about . . ."

"Mary Rose," Simon finished the thought. Couldn't believe what he was hearing. This was too good to be true. But also a touch disconcerting. "And why so?" he asked, and found he'd crossed his arms. Unfair, considering he'd wanted to talk about the exact same thing. However, a man protecting his future bride was one thing; this was some family friend she hadn't seen in almost ten years.

"Her parents worry about her," Amy replied.

"Parents do that." A definite edge had snuck into Simon's voice, warning. He relaxed, hoping to keep agreeable until he got his own questions, all of them, out. "Was there anything in particular?"

Amy stepped past Simon and dropped his mostly untouched coffee into a trash can, then jammed both hands into his coat pockets. "I've been a family friend for many years, Simon," he explained. "And even a spiritual advisor when called upon."

Simon nodded, waited.

"I was with them when she vanished, and I know James and Francine have already told you about it."

Simon lifted his brows. "And how do you know that?"

"Because you're afraid, son."

Simon flinched, insulted almost, then realized the man was likely transferring his own emotions onto Simon. "Afraid?" He laughed when he said it. "Interesting. Of what?"

"It's in your eyes. And wasn't when we met. Especially when you look at her."

Simon looked away, rubbed his mouth before speaking again. "You didn't answer the question, Mr. Amy. How about we both stop playing 'how-much-does-*he*-know' because I've got some questions for you, too. Here's what they told me: Mary Rose vanished from that island when she was six, sans explanation. She then returned thirty-three days later—"

"'Sans explanation.'"

"With no memory of where she'd been, or that the event had even happened. A memory lapse, which has allegedly continued for the succeeding nineteen years."

"You don't believe that's the case."

Simon shook his head. "I found out about all of this only two days ago, Mr. Amy. I'm not sure what to believe. So, what can you tell me? What do *you* think happened?"

Another shrug. "I haven't a clue."

"I imagine the Morlands were terrified."

"I'm not sure that word's enough. I've never before or since seen Francine Morland that broken. Or James that strong. Isn't that funny? James's unfamiliar fortitude was the more chilling, and most dreadful, expression of the whole ordeal. He and I spoke on the phone almost every night that month. And he drove in to see Franny several times."

"She didn't stay in Scotland? Francine was here in Alderley?"

"She hadn't gone up that summer. When it happened, they decided it was best if she stay here until . . . well, we didn't know what to think. James asked me to help at the house here with Franny while he dealt with matters in Mhoire's Point."

"Search parties. The police."

"Of course. It was bedlam for the first forty-eight hours. Dragging the lake. The SCD swept in, the Scottish FBI, if you will. Then England's Missing Persons Bureau. Scotland Yard got involved, even. Their Child Investigation team. 'Morland' is an important name here. *And* in Mhoire's Point. It was news. After a few days, everyone assumed the worst."

"That she'd drowned."

Amy nodded. "That's what the police thought. How else to explain it? A hundred people had gone over the whole island two dozen times by then. By the end of the second week, it was only James, and some locals he'd paid, who were looking for her. By the end of the third, it was mostly only James and his brother. Some nights, I shudder to think how long he'd have *kept* looking for her. 'Obsessive' isn't word enough for where he'd gone, I think. James Morland was . . . possessed. But, as you said, that's, I suspect, simply being a parent."

"And Mrs. Morland?"

Amy breathed deeply, his eyes warm as if he'd been hoping for that very question. "Desolate. A shell. She wouldn't talk, couldn't even cry. Spent most of the month locked away in her room. I think, perhaps, she might have been in shock for most of it. After, she embraced her new faith, became a devoted Catholic. Francine Morland has always been a distant and frosty woman, but this was . . . another ten years before she worked her way back to that cold bitch you'll spend the week with."

Simon laughed.

"But, who are we to judge, yes? I sat beside her that final week while she shouldered the death of her only child, stoically planned a service for Mary Rose. Tragic. She'd gone so far as to order a bloody tombstone for the girl."

"Sounds like she and James weren't on the same page," Simon poked.

Amy shrugged, chuckled darkly. "Marriage."

Simon glanced at the man's ring finger for a clue, but both hands remained in his pockets. He thought maybe Anglican priests could marry.

"The church was enough for me," Amy grunted, answering the unasked question. "Did they show you the drawings she makes?"

"From when she was a girl? Yes."

Amy slanted him a glance. "Some are from college."

"Yes, I know." Simon felt unusually defensive. It'd become somehow beyond important to let this virtual stranger know that Simon Blake knew all about Mary Rose. "They told me," he added, for emphasis.

"Good, then they surely told you about the incidents with the professor. And the therapist?"

Simon braced angrily. "Sure," he lied. "But sounds an awful lot like gossip to me, Mr. Amy. You're not in the gossip business, are you?"

"Always." He winked. "But in this case, I'm only looking out for an old friend. And, his family. And you."

"I'll be fine, thank you. *We'll* be fine," he revised. "Obviously there's some kind of unresolved trauma. We'll find her help back home."

"They've tried 'help' before."

"Ah, and I suppose you think the answer is in the church?"

"Sometimes." To Simon's surprise, though, Amy grinned, shook his head. "I'm not sure yet about this. Francine seems to have found some rescue in her Catholic faith. Are you a religious man, Simon?"

He thought about the inquiry before answering, pictured Francine Morland touching that damn cross at the top of her chest. "No," Simon replied. "I mean—"

"Do you believe in good and evil?"

"Not sure I'm following you, Mr. Amy." As Simon answered, he scanned down the street for Mary Rose. Couldn't find her, then cursed himself for even looking. When they'd first started dating, he could go days without knowing where she was, what she was doing. Now, it seemed, he couldn't go five minutes. Was that all Amy had seen in his eyes, he wondered. Some emerging pathetic codependence?

"How is she?" Amy asked a second time.

Simon felt a flash of anger. "Feel free to ask her yourself. Know anything about that island? Some of the locals brought up witchcraft, occult ceremonies and the like." He expected Amy to laugh, to tell him the locals were merely playing with him.

"James was never afraid of the island," Amy said instead.

"And you?"

"I've never been and, so, couldn't say. Though I suspect there's good, *and evil*, to be found in every place."

"They also mentioned James. Not by name, but said it was believed by many the father was somehow involved. That must have been hard on him. Knowing that, I mean. What people were saying."

Amy shrugged. "The easiest suspect. The last to see her. The wealthy magistrate. It was natural to gossip, I suppose."

"And something about the uncle. You mentioned James's brother had been on hand for the search. What can you tell me about him?"

"David. Never met, but James still brings him up now and again. Bit of a drifter, apparently. His name, yes, also was dragged into this."

"Any particular reason why?"

"Unsavory past, some thought. Ran with a . . . a *creative* crowd as a younger man." Amy grinned thinly. "I suspect there's good, and evil, to be found in every place."

Simon watched him carefully. "Why are you afraid of Mary Rose?" he finally asked. He'd seen it on the man's face days before, and ten minutes ago, too. He'd only called it nervous then, but since Mr. Amy had called out some, apparent, new "fear" in Simon's eyes, the priest had given a new and better name to what Simon had perceived. And turnabout was fair play. "Well?" Simon pursued.

To Simon's surprise, Amy didn't deny it. "I don't know," he said instead. "I . . ."

"Yes?"

"Your father passed. Yes?"

Simon took a deep breath. Where was the man going with this? Why had James Morland brought it up with Amy? He'd assumed Amy must have been nosing about to find out what his father did for a living. "Yeah, when I was fifteen. Why?"

"When did you know—*really* know—that he was gone?"

Simon shuddered. Thought. "When we came home from the funeral, I guess," he said finally. "It wasn't the open casket or the graveyard or the lowering of the coffin . . ." His thoughts were half lost to memory, vivid images. "It was when we got home later that afternoon and he wasn't there."

Amy breathed deeply, huffing over Simon's answer. Then, without warning, he seemed to be done with the whole topic.

"Not sure how that," Simon observed, "in *any* way, answered my question."

"Perhaps not. Forgive an old man's wandering mind. I simply wanted to reach out to you, to both of you . . ." He stopped as if he was collecting his own thoughts. "The past should be left where it belongs, I suppose. We must let it go and take those actions necessary to leave it there."

"Fine," Simon agreed. "Simple enough. But the Morlands, and you now, are the ones who brought all of this up in the first place. If it's best to simply let it go, why the concern?"

Mr. Amy sighed again. He didn't deny the validity of the question. "Because all too often," he said, "the past can't let *you* go."

Simon weaved down the street, bypassing people more deftly, and rudely, with each step. Mr. Amy was five minutes gone, but the man's words of warning and support still remained, jumbled and confused in Simon's mind as he rushed a little quicker past each store. He still wasn't sure what he'd learned from Amy, or what to make of the priest's own strange emotions and energy. But the conversation had clearly affected him, had increased his own growing unease with the visit, the ancient history, and what it could mean for his and Mary Rose's future together.

Not a damn thing, he decided. Part of what Amy had said was right. The past wasn't anything to cling to. Hallways filled with old creepy portraits and creepier antique mirrors weren't any way to enjoy the present, build a future. He could see it easily with the Morlands, shambling from one room to the next with enough pleasantries and new purchases, two artifacts already in their own museum. Simon chuckled darkly; a mausoleum was more like it. He and Mary Rose would be nothing like that. They would—

A woman screamed.

Mary Rose.

He'd known it was her before the sound had even finished.

And it *hadn't* finished. She screamed again and again.

Simon sprinted the next block, following the turned heads and shocked expressions and pointing. He turned the corner and found a small cluster, two women and an older man, gathered and crouched around someone on the ground. A larger group had stropped on either side of the street to see what was happening. One teen boy even had his phone out, recording, no doubt. Mary Rose had stopped screaming.

Simon skidded into the circle, dropped to one knee. There, she sat on the ground, hands to her mouth, one leg caught awkwardly beneath her, the other out straight as if she'd slipped on ice. "Mary Rose . . ."

She stared ahead, eyes wide, fixed on the store behind him and he turned to see what she looked at, saw only the window and mannequins within, three faceless figures in ladies' clothes and fussy hats. He looked back, studying the terrible expression in her eyes.

"You hurt, love?" one of the two women asked, breaking his own trance.

"I think she might have tripped," another man explained.

"Mary Rose?" Simon tried again, put a hand on her leg.

She finally looked at him. "Simon . . ."

He grinned down at her, pouring warmth, reassurance into his expression. "You okay, babe?"

Mary Rose blinked back at him. "She . . . I saw her and then—"

"Saw who?" He looked up at the three above them uneasily, their help no longer needed. "You know what . . . How about we get you up? You okay to stand?"

She made to push herself off the ground. Simon and one of the two women helped lift her.

"Thank you," Simon said. "Very much. All of you."

Seeing Mary Rose was calm again and back on her feet, the three who'd come to help had faded back into the crowd. Others continued to stare, another older woman even approaching to pat Mary Rose on the back.

"What happened?" he asked quietly, when they were alone again. "Who did you see?"

She turned her back to the store window. "Let's go," she said. "I want to go home."

"Done." He took her hand. "Sure you're okay to walk?"

"Yes. I'm sorry. I—"

"Shhhh. No apologies. You're fine. *Everything's* fine."

"She's always been here," she said.

Simon stopped, glared down at her. "What?"

Mary Rose shook her head. "I shouldn't . . ."

"Mary Rose?"

She leaned, crumpled against him. "I don't want to be afraid anymore."

"Of what?" Simon hugged her close, putting on his best face. "What's there to be afraid of here?"

She gave no answer.

Simon couldn't breathe.

Every time he tried, the attempt was choked off. Blocked. His throat and lungs burning for air. The pressure in his chest mounting. The panic.

He'd been dreaming of his father and an empty coffin, and no matter where he looked—in various dream halls and dream rooms he didn't recognize—he still couldn't find it, the corpse. *Him.* Then he found another door at the end of some hallway and knew his father's body was behind that door, but first the handle wouldn't turn, and then the door had no handle *to* turn, and when the door opened, his father was standing at the end of a long hall, but it wasn't his father at all; it was a little girl in a blue nightgown, and she had bare feet, and the nightgown was tattered at the bottom, wet and sullied with sand, and her face was hidden at first in shadow, like pictures he'd seen, but closer he saw the stiches between her lips, pulled open enough so that she could speak, and her dark widening eyes became deep black sockets filled and squirming with life, and he wanted to wake but couldn't, because she wouldn't let him, not yet, and then he couldn't breathe and—

Simon lurched awake, gasped for air. Moaned in relief, and mitigated panic, in the dark room. He clenched a pillow in his hands, wondered if he'd somehow been holding it near his own face when he slept.

"Merz . . ." He gulped her nickname.

Someone was standing in the room.

Two pitch-black forms standing beside each other at the end of his bed. Silhouetted in the room's dim light. One shape barely above the bed, its tiny head tilted in the darkness. The second, an enormous figure, which took up the entire end of the bed, the contour of its shoulders and head almost bent beneath the ceiling, looming over him.

The smaller figure lifted its hands onto the bed.

Simon hurled the pillow, the only weapon at hand, and jumped from the bed with a long string of angry loud curses.

No one was there.

But a large shadow *had* moved across his opened doorway.

Simon pounced forward. He knew positively he'd closed his door hours before and pounded after the fleeing shadow into the hallway. His heart bursting in his chest, fist drawn to strike whatever he found, his—

He stopped. The dimly lit hallway was as empty and quiet as his bedroom. Only his panicked breath seemed to fill the whole house. He'd expected to see figures rushing down the steps or scurrying into the next room, but the stairway was empty, the doors to the next rooms all closed.

Simon couldn't help but think of the dream he'd been having, the same endless hallway and doors, and wondered some if he were *still* dreaming as he plodded down the hallway, toward Mary Rose's room.

At the very least, he'd just cursed a blue streak, and no one had woken up to see what had happened. *Seriously?* He couldn't believe it.

Her door was closed. No light or sound from the other side.

Farther down, a greater darkness caught his eye and he recognized the next room down.

The disturbing "cross room" at the end of the hall. The old playroom. Its door *was* open again.

This time, wide open.

So much so that the shadows within were splayed against the opposite wall in the hallway.

Simon gathered himself, his body trembling, knowing already he hadn't really seen anyone but equally knowing that if he *had*, then they'd be waiting, waiting for him, within that same doorway.

He marched to the door as before, stepped in, his hand slapping around for the switch. A waft of fetid ocean water suddenly filled the room.

Something stood in the room across from him. Crouching in the dark. The shape vividly crooked and inhuman.

The room's stench grew more putrid, like spoiled food.

The prayer kneeler again, no. Whatever this was stood *behind* the kneeler. It exhaled with the thinnest sound, and a puff of breath wafted out in a frosty cloud.

"Francine?" he asked, whispering. It was *her* room now, wasn't it?

No answer came.

"Answer me!" Simon shouted at the figure, no other words or ideas coming to mind. The cloud evaporated, though its chill had crossed the room and blanketed his whole body.

He found the switch and flipped on the light.

The room was empty. The nauseating odor faded.

Directly across the room, Simon's own reflection came unevenly off a dozen metallic crosses caught in odd angles like a fun house room of mirrors. He'd been screaming at himself. The wooden pieces hung and mixed within the reflective crosses cut his image, the impression, into many pieces.

He stepped farther into the empty space, Francine Morland's words about the room, its door, booming in his harried thoughts. And there was a new smell in the air. Yet familiar.

Sheets of paper had been draped over Francine Morland's kneeler. Painted sheets that lay, in this room particularly, like burial shrouds.

Simon crossed the room and lifted the first.

He could still smell the fresh paint. The painting was the two figures he recognized from Mary Rose's childhood art books: the giant dog man; the faceless little girl. A chill ran up Simon's back, one so strong as if the imagined girl herself had touched him with her tiny fingers. How he'd imagined these two at the end of his bed, he had no idea. He must have been thinking of them all this time.

The second painting was of the girl alone. The head, larger than his own, taking up the entire paper. A pear-shaped face and dark hair framing an empty circle where eyes and nose and mouth should be. Instead, lines of a dozen different colors, various shades of gray and green and yellow ran vertically, slashed in thick jagged strokes, down the face and into where the neck should be, each line bleeding off unevenly at the bottom of the page and running onto the top of the wooden kneeler.

Simon touched the paper, the paint still tacky beneath his fingers.

He stepped backward clumsily and saw himself in several of the crosses again, momentarily startled at the puzzled, weak man looking back.

Simon flipped the lights out again, pulled the door closed, though the handle turned in his hand easily enough if he wanted to reenter.

He looked down the hall to Mary Rose's room and stood for a while, hand on the doorknob, thinking. Simon crept down the silent hallway once more. He stopped at her door and opened it carefully, peering through the crack first before entering.

He could see only her blanketed legs. Lifeless. She was asleep, he decided, and—more important—had been this whole time. Simon looked up and down the hall again, and then crept fully into her room.

Mary Rose lay in the darkness, her head turned toward him. For a moment, he saw only an empty space where her face should be. Some trick of the moonlight spilling through the window. He approached the bed carefully, so as to not startle her. There'd already been enough of that for one night.

As he approached, he noticed—for the first time—on the bureau, a vase of long-dead flowers, wilted over, brittle and browned. Several purple petals lay curled together beside the vase. He shook his head; Francine Morland was proving more inattentive to her daughter every day. How simple to have replaced new flowers for their visit.

"Mary Rose . . . ," he whispered, sitting gently on the bed beside her.

She stirred, smiled thinly.

"My beautiful Simon." She spoke his name without opening her eyes, then turned herself to be closer to him.

Simon continued his crawl into the bed, pulling her closely against him. She lay a hand upon his bare chest, and he grasped it, trying not to flinch at the unexpected texture of the touch. He looked down at their entwined fingers in the night's darkness.

Hers were darker still.

Stained with fresh paint.

12

They'd been back in Philadelphia for more than a month, and any memory of the return visit to England had already become a condensed blur of images and remarks. Lunch in Kintbury. Arguing something about Mhoire's Point with her parents. Kissing Simon and pics on the London Eye. Mr. Amy floundering again over his decades-long desire for her—(sexual maybe, but something, she dreaded from experience, far deeper). Oh, and admiring some new art purchase of her father's. Getting to paint again in her old room. Seeing a mother fox and her trailing skulk of pups cross the backyard.

At least Simon seemed to have truly enjoyed himself, though he'd already thrown himself fully back into work. Slaving away late hours most nights, starting a big new case. She was glad, though. She missed him in the odd moments of the day that she herself came up for air, but she knew he needed work as much as she did. For different reasons, she suspected, and made a mental note for the two of them to discuss the differences someday. So many things they might discuss one day soon, when the world had stopped spinning so fast and time stood still, giving them a chance to truly see each other once more.

Or perhaps that wouldn't be such a good idea. Perhaps the rush and hustle was exactly what they both needed, why they'd always got on so well. Perhaps when everything stopped spinning, they would stare at each other, startled, unsure of what had drawn them together in the first place. Perhaps many things.

Regardless, she herself hadn't yet gotten back into the swing of work. Other than opening a few emails and making some excuses to clients, she'd not really done much. Some kind of vacation hangover, she decided. She already missed the smell of the ocean, the sound of the waves and the whistling sea wind.

The two candles she'd lit wavered as if caught in her imagined Scottish breeze. Mary Rose smiled at the thought, then continued scrubbing her hands and face at the bathroom sink. It was well past nine o'clock, Simon's text apologizing for working late several hours old.

She'd already turned off the lights, the bathtub still filling, scented with a new mixture of sea salt and calendula petals. She'd been adding sea salt to all her baths these days, and tonight she'd watched the swirl of it for several minutes before it disappeared into the foam of the soft bubbles. She imagined it against her skin as if she was truly back in the salt water of the North Sea, each granule scraping subtly, winnowing her away.

Mary Rose rinsed the sink's water onto her face and looked into the bathroom mirror. Tried picturing herself old.

Like *her*. Francine.

Mother.

Or perhaps more like the old crones who'd helped her on the street when she fell. The woman in the park, even. It was easy enough to imagine, once she began. The water ran down her cheeks and chin, creating unnatural ruts. The steam from the sink and bath filled in some hollows but created others, a streaky illusion of ugly wrinkles and blots and creases.

Many years before, Mary Rose had discovered that all she'd had to do was glare intently at her reflection, a staring contest that could go on for hours, and she could will herself to, well, look older. The skin around her eyes steadily retreating. Her face growing more gaunt and hollow like an old jack-o'-lantern. Her newly puckered cheeks holding up the deep sockets above. From seventeen or twenty-seven to seventy just like that. Her eyes sunken in, darkening.

Tonight she kept pushing the vision until only a haggard monster stared back. The skeletal eye sockets and gum-stripped grin. The reedy hair. A haggard monster who looked just like Nanny Dee, actually—her father's grandmother—the way she looked in her painting, anyway, the painting that alternately had horrified and fascinated Mary Rose since the very first time she'd seen it. The family resemblance was obvious enough, she thought, peering into the mirror tonight.

Just like that, and Mary Rose couldn't see Nanny Dee anymore, she saw herself. Herself old and frail. Alone and forgotten. Waiting, always waiting. Drooling apple juice from lips that couldn't keep the form of a smile anymore. Seventy more *years*, she thought, almost in a panic. She couldn't even imagine. Couldn't possibly bear it all so long.

She tried recalling the last time she felt truly alive. More than just getting by. As always, the same images sprang to her mind like a half-remembered promise: a sunny, green-bright day of blue skies and laughter. A little girl twirling and twirling until the sky became the grass and waves and the grass and waves the sky and how it all tumbled together, perfect in its hope and possibility. But tonight, that little girl seemed farther away than usual, her twirling, swirling body indistinct, blurred like the edges of the steam-streaked mirror. Tonight, she could hardly picture her at all. Not like she could picture Nanny Dee.

Mary Rose studied her imagined "old" self again, wondered once more if she could, should, push it a little further. She'd always been curious. That superstition about looking at your reflection in the dark and seeing your own death. If she could see herself *old* so easily, what would she look like *dead*? Maybe a flash of lying in her coffin, just before the lid was closed forever.

The lone painting of her hanging in the hallway back home, there were times . . . Many nights she'd looked at it over the years and seen only a dead thing. Rotted flesh and bone. And some sort of lavender-black fungus growing up the right side of her face like a deep, fuzzy bruise. The deep worm-filled sockets . . .

> *The worms crawl in, the worms crawl out,*
> *The worms play pinochle on your snout.*
> *They eat your eyes, they eat your nose,*
> *They eat the jelly between your toes.*

She hummed the childhood song, her gaze fixed on the now-familiar hag staring back at her, and blindly reached out to stub out the candles. The flames singed her fingertips and she savored the pain, embraced feeling something fleshy and alive for one last, perfect glorious moment.

The room went totally dark.

At first, she saw only that same darkness, but she kept her gaze focused on the now-unseen mirror. The reflection and future waiting for her eyes to adjust, to see what she was meant to see.

> *Your eyes fall in, your hair falls out*
> *they invite their friends and their friends, too*
> *they all come down to chew on you . . .*

Then something emerged slowly from the black. Like some creature crawling toward her from a great distance, getting ever closer, and Mary Rose felt her heart thudding strangely in her chest. It was coming—she could almost see it! This momentous reflection of her ultimate loss and liberation, her last feeble gasps, her horrible death—

But it was nothing.

She stared, wide-eyed, but only her regular face stared back. Shadowed and gray, yes. But young again. Definitely young. The imagined old face gone.

Mary Rose shifted and the face shifted with her, now even younger.

A little girl's face. Her face, she thought, no more than six years old.

A chill skated through the room as she stared, whispering through the stillness, and hoarfrost crisscrossed the lowest corners of the mirror beneath the steam. Her next breaths came out as small expanding clouds.

She stood like that for a long time.

13

He'd deleted the private investigator's email two weeks before.

It was a betrayal. Plain and simple.

Simon knew that. No matter what he told himself about "looking out" for Mary Rose or "protecting" Mary Rose or "doing his job"—as her husband, lover, friend—it didn't change the fact that this was a complete invasion of privacy. They'd been engaged for four months already. . . . Funny, he never *had* gotten around to asking her parents for her hand. How impressed they'd be with their future son-in-law—with such a fine "endowment" to mark their impending marriage: a detailed report of Mary Rose's past. Of the disappearance twenty years ago, the investigation. What Amy had said about some professor, her therapist. Her uncle. The house Simon had seen and found again too easily on Google Earth.

Before the report arrived, a dozen times, he'd thought to contact the British investigator—a retired claims adjuster named Tull, who a colleague had recommended—and call him off, to forget the whole thing. The violation was just too great. So the unopened email first lay, tucked aside in a personal folder, for three weeks, and the thought of it waiting there for him was almost as distasteful as the thought of actually opening the damned thing. And he'd finally deleted it.

But then, every time he'd almost dismissed it entirely, something would happen. Something strange. Sometimes, even something bad.

Mary Rose hadn't been the same since they'd come home. She'd been less talkative than usual, yet somehow also more restless. Needing more sleep and alone time than ever before. Of course she needed sleep, he thought. There'd been more nightmares than ever before. Several a week now. Startled awake by throttled screams with no explanation for what she'd just dreamed. Desperate gibbering in her sleep another night, the only line he'd caught clearly: "Why is *she* here?" Simon didn't know who "she" was, but he could tell from Mary Rose's voice this person completely horrified her, that "she" was powerful, and deadly. So much so that Mary Rose's nightmare—the way she'd whimpered in the dark beside him—had left *him* uneasy and chilled the rest of the night. Had *he* also dreamed of the rotted dirty thing dragging back beneath the bed, standing in their bedroom doorway?

In the mornings, she claimed not to remember the dreams or even waking. She was more fidgety, and her OCDish habit of scratching at herself, subtle unless you were looking for it, seemed unbroken now, all day long. She sometimes showered three, four times a day. And he'd found new pictures she'd drawn. Familiar pictures.

His hints that maybe she could seek professional help, someone to talk to about any anxiety she might have, any lingering depression, went ignored. His direct proposals equally rebuffed. She "was tired," was all, she claimed. Had the "winter blues." A euphemism too similar to the one her father had used. Too dismissive. No better than his own dumb and dismissive "October Country" quips. Simon had done some reading. Delusions, thought disorder, loose associations, ambivalence, emotional lability . . . these were the symptoms of genuine PTSD, a condition beyond only soldiers, and one far much more than "having a shitty day."

The only respite had come when he'd taken her down to the Outer Banks for a week over Christmas. Textbook rented the little house right on the beach and then checked off every requisite couple's cliché he knew: sat in the hot tub together at sunset, napped before the fire, exchanged gifts to the morning cries of gulls, walked the Hatteras shore in silence for hours beneath the gray sky, the sea foam tumbling like snow beside them. There, only then, she'd been Mary Rose at her best. Wide-eyed, alert. Bursting of life and bad puns and love. Standing before the whole Atlantic and, so, staring out over the whole of the world.

Simon checked the time. His call with the investigator was in less than an hour. He'd rescheduled that twice also. *Wasn't the report enough?* But he knew it never was. People always held back information, sometimes not even intentionally. He always liked to see faces when he could, ask old questions in new ways.

He thought a final time of *truly* deleting the email—as it had simply been moved to his trash folder—and canceling the call for good. Instead, he restored the email, glanced over the professional pleasantries, then continued to the report. He was rereading PDFs of old news articles when Tull's video call came through.

They'd spoken only by phone when he'd hired the man. In the tiny video-conference screen, Tull looked as Simon had first imagined: Michael Caine with a larger forehead, less hair, and enormous 1980s glasses.

"Good morning." Simon leaned into the screen, smiled broadly. This was just an ordinary call, he hoped somehow to convey.

"Good morning, sir." The man bowed slightly, his face revealing he knew it was anything but for Simon. "I hope you found the report satisfactory?"

"Very much so. Jennifer told me you were the best man for the job."

"Well." Tull leaned closer into the camera. "She's always been a bloody fine fibber."

Simon chuckled, as he was expected to. "Surprised how quickly the articles drop off. Appears that without Morland's family name, it wouldn't have made the press more than a couple times."

"Kids vanish every day, don't they." Tull leaned back again. "When this one came back, they ran a couple 'miracle' pieces, but then moved on to the other thousands who don't ever come back."

Simon nodded. "What's not in the report?" he asked.

Tull's face frowned in the small box, a thinking frown more than one reflecting insult. "Oh, perhaps the constable from Mhoire's Point. Fraser. Had more information to give, I think."

"You say as much in the report."

"Not as strongly as I could have, possibly." He grinned. "Usually, when one's told to fuck off so strongly . . ."

"I understand." Simon paged through the PDF. "Retired, still lives in Mhoire's Point."

"Yes, sir."

"What more can you tell me about Lockley? The history professor."

Tull smiled.

"What's so funny?" Simon asked.

"Jennifer told *me* you were a good lawyer. A twenty-page report and you got right to the most ominous bit."

More caveman-ish curiosity than any professed legal skills, Simon confessed to himself. Guy had wanted to bang his fiancé.

"He was in love with her?" he said.

"He was indeed." Tull nodded. "But, as I reported, the feelings were not, by all accounts, returned."

"Quite the scandal on campus." Simon paraphrased the report. "Sexual harassment accusations. Lost his job."

"And his marriage. His widow is still a French professor at the school. As he's been dead for seven years, getting people gossiping there was easy enough."

"Suicide?" Simon asked straightaway. This must be the "ominous" part Tull spoke of and had *not* been in the report. He could only assume, given the man's age: forty-two. Tull nodded again. Simon shook his head, disappointed the investigator had censored that important detail. "Why'd you leave that out?"

"The inquiry wasn't about Mr. Lockley. The suicide was four years after the incident at university, so . . ."

Simon frowned. "Well, it seems . . . fine. May I ask how he . . ."

"Ended his life?" Tull smiled again, but his eyes had narrowed. "Since you ask."

Now Simon leaned back, waiting.

"The coroner records logged only 'Suicide by hypoxia.' Asphyxiation."

"Why do they suspect suicide? Could it have been one of those, what is it, 'autoerotic asphyxiation' things?"

Tull smirked. "This wasn't some belt or plastic bag. Going from university rumor now, only, but . . . they say he'd wrapped his mouth and nose with duct tape. Not a piece of tape, apparently, but *wrapped* utterly around his face and the back of his head three, four, times."

Simon stared. "What the hell."

"That's what the wife had been told by the detectives. Suffocated in his apartment kitchen."

"And the psychologist, earlier." He shook off the image of the professor—slumped in his kitchen, or worse, flailing on the floor, ripping at the tape when he'd changed his mind—and checked his own scribbled notes. "Schaeffer. Lost his license also, it appears. Quite the pattern, don't you think?" Tull had clearly left such inferences to be made by Simon.

"The party was a minor at the time, so . . . Was relying primarily on more gossip. Not facts, and nothing verifiable."

Simon wasn't sure he liked Mary Rose being debased to "the party," especially since he was the one who'd put her in that role. "And the interview with Schaeffer," he moved on. "Surprised he'd speak with you."

"Him," Tull scoffed. "As the report says, he seemed more than happy to talk about Mary Rose. I implied merely that she was applying for some corporate job in London. He was glad to hear she was doing well, and blames others for the loss of his license, not her."

"She was thirteen, fourteen."

"Yes."

"And no chance of getting his notes, or . . ."

Tull shook his head. "No chance. Long since gone, he claimed. As I mentioned, he wouldn't give specifics about her case, only that she was a special girl, talented, creative, so on . . . that 'she shined.'"

She still did, Simon thought. "Okay, last bit to focus on. The uncle."

"Right, you've got the arrest sheet there. Couple rounds of disorderly conduct. Public indecency. Malicious mischief."

"Vandalism. Breach of the peace." Simon finished reading the offenses himself. "Doesn't look like he ever did any real time, though."

"The constable said it was just kids messing around in the woods. They arrested close to a dozen of 'em with the exact same crimes, hoping to end the pagan ritual bullshit."

"Morland was twenty-seven," Simon noted aloud. "That's no kid." Simon had been practicing law already. "Sure it was *all* bullshit?"

"Constable thought so. Said it was never a serious part of the investigation. Was the gossips and some of the less-reputable local papers done that. They found the arrest records at the courthouse as easily as I did. Didn't matter the uncle had come back to town and was helping to look for Mary Rose. If anything, that simply fueled suspicions. And rumors about a satanic cult, and what not, have apparently surrounded that island for decades."

"Or longer."

"Yes, I suppose so."

"You never went out to the island yourself," Simon said, almost as an accusation. He'd been disappointed it hadn't been part of the report.

"Didn't seem necessary." Tull lifted and drank from a coffee mug. "It's just another island."

Simon wondered.

"The uncle seems quite the character," he said.

"World's filled with them, mate."

Simon clasped his fingers in thought. "What else? What else *not* in the report?"

"Unsubstantiated rumor. 'Marriage troubles' with the Morlands, a brief separation, but nothing noteworthy. You'll see I've gathered and logged half a dozen boarding schools she attended but always made her way home again in a few months. One neighbor believed it was drug related, but that led nowhere. Another said something about a boyfriend who'd died. A teenager. Again, nothing substantial enough to put in the official report."

Simon had slumped in his chair, stared off, thinking. What would she find rooting around *his* earlier life? He'd started a short list when his gaze fell upon the copy of *Treasure Island* she'd bought him in Mhoire's Point. A first edition of a printing from 1891, to commemorate their first boat voyage together, his nautical gallantry. This version had included a strange short story added at the end called "Ola"-something about a soldier and this family, maybe, of vampires. He'd not given it—or Long John Silver, either—a genuine reading before bringing the book into work. Long-ago stories wakened to life again by Mary Rose's touch, then passed to his careless hand to beckon mutely from his shelf, forgotten almost as quickly as they'd been found. *Treasure Island.* He supposed there was something to that. A play on words, she was perhaps hinting at. The island had, in a way, been a treasure, of sorts. She'd been so happy there, and he, gratified to see her that way, not wrapped in a veil of worry or long-forgotten gloom.

"Anything else I can do for you, Mr. Blake?" the man on his laptop asked.

"No," he said, looking back at the screen. "I . . . no. We're, ah, getting married, you know. Mary Rose and I, I mean."

"Yes, I gathered as much. I hope you found the report satisfactory."

Mary Rose was already asleep in the next room.

Simon wandered her apartment alone, fixing the coffee for the next morning, collecting his work papers, shutting off lights.

It'd been several days since the discussion with Tull, the report and email saved onto a flash drive in his office. Never to be opened again. And over time, he decided, he'd convince himself it had never happened.

She'd shut all the doors again. The hall bathroom, her office, second bedroom. Every night, same routine. Making sure every door was pulled closed. Did the same thing at his apartment. Another one of the little quirks he'd gotten used to so easily. A few times, he'd even secretly reopened one to see what she would do. Sure enough, she'd find it and pull it closed without comment, shutting tight all the rooms before she turned in.

Tonight he'd decided to explore her office some. *In for a penny, in for a pound.* She'd been working all day, from before he'd been gone to work and had barely left the room for dinner and to say hello. He hoped it was work related, but what she'd been working on, he could only guess. So . . .

Simon opened the door, turning on the lights, admittedly expecting the worst.

On the drafting table was a colorful painting. At the sight of it, his whole chest clenched. He crossed the room, each step harder than the last, working through all the options. He wasn't going to freak out, he wasn't going to read too much into it, the image wet and gleaming on the stretched canvas. Mary Rose was tense, strung out. Painting was a release, a creative expression, a solace. He could allow her that solace without judgment. He could allow—

Simon came around the desk. Stopped as the painting revealed itself.

His breath leaked out in a soft, startled exhalation.

A face. But nothing ghastly. Empty. Or shrouded in any way.

It was simply Mary Rose. Her *face*.

A genuine self-portrait. All those denunciations, fears, about her never drawing a human face shot through his mind in quick succession. Yet here was not just *any* face, but her own, almost a photograph, as if rendered by a master. You could almost reach out and touch her. The slightest crinkles around her bright, flashing eyes. The sunlight shimmering in her windblown hair. The sprinkle of red leaves tucked into her ear; rowan-tree leaves. He stared at the portrait a long time, lost in Mary Rose's smile.

Mary Rose had told him once about the *Mona Lisa* and the debates over the painting's background landscape, some village and destroyed bridge in northern Italy looking enough like every village and broken-down bridge in Italy that arguments raged on for centuries over its setting.

Here, there was no debate. Behind *this* portrait was a place Simon knew well. Already too well. The last, and maybe first, place he'd ever been truly terrified. Its whitecaps, the cairn field, the mist. And the tree, the ancient, knotted sentinel, high and alone on the bluff, visible directly over Mary Rose's right shoulder.

Inspecting the painting more closely, he noticed she'd done something interesting—intentional, he assumed—with her shoulders and hair, the way they . . . the way, if you got right up on it and really looked, it was impossible to tell where the island ended and the girl began.

14

Two: Get your big coat.

Three: Put coat on.

Now, to four: Tell Simon you're getting some coffee.

"I'm getting some coffee," she called out from the front door.

Mary Rose moved through each step independently, a solution she'd developed many years before to manage stressful situations. To hammer out the next project, shatter the next deadline. It was almost impossible to get overwhelmed when dealing with only one thing.

"What?" Simon glanced up from the sofa. An NBA game lit up the muted television, papers spread on the table in front of him. "Did you say—"

Five: Lie.

"Want to get some fresh air." Six: Button coat—carefully. "Figured I'd pick up some coffee at Chic's while I was at it."

Simon put down the paper he'd been reading. "Let me grab my shoes. I'll—"

"Nope," she stopped him. "Do you want anything?"

Seven: Open the door.

Simon stood frozen, puzzlement on his face. "I'm good. You sure, you . . ."

"Be right back." She smiled and stepped into the hallway, pulling the door shut behind her.

Eight. The next "steps" got her down the stairs and out onto the street. It was late, but Chic's, down a couple of blocks on the corner, stayed open until two a.m. on weekends. Most of the other shops were already closed, the only light from streetlights and muted night lighting from inside the empty stores. Still, the streets remained busy, people out enjoying their well-deserved Friday nights. Bundled against the early spring chill.

Nine: Find a suitable public trash container. One half-empty so she could bury everything at the bottom. She carried her package tucked into her coat. The lump it made was part of the reason she'd left the apartment so quickly, fearful Simon would hug her goodbye. Then he'd feel the hidden bag, know what she had done.

Mary Rose passed several potential bins but felt the need to get still farther away from her apartment, away from Simon. What if he was watching from the window? What if someone they knew saw her? The package was surprisingly heavy against her chest and belly, shifting like something alive against her skin. Or worse, *inside* her skin. The pieces jostled with each step, tiny bones poking, cracking, and loosening. She scratched at her arm.

Safely a block away from her own building, Mary Rose pulled the bag free from under her coat and carried it like any other package. She walked past Chic's and continued another two blocks to where she could cross and get down closer to the river. She wanted to be near water tonight.

Ten: Cross the street. She sighed deeply.

It'd been a good week, except for what was in the package. There'd been no incidents. None that she knew of anyway, though she suspected Simon often hid them from her. As her parents and others had done years before. But still a good week. She'd felt energetic, well rested, had gotten some solid work done. Then the Rodin Museum, and it had all fallen apart.

Simon had surprised her, arranged a tour of their facilities for their wedding reception. She'd been speechless. He knew it was her second favorite place in the whole city; only at the park was she more at peace. And yet, despite all her excitement, her appreciation, her genuine gratitude to Simon for choosing such a perfect, special place for them to celebrate, she'd returned home agitated. Anxious. The museum hadn't offered its usual sanctuary from the real world but instead had brought all of it—the real world—crashing in. The next forty, ninety years. The nightmares. The marriage to Simon. Her dreams for her career. Children? Did it matter she'd never had a period, waiting, an "underdeveloped" uterus, waiting, that she might never be able to reproduce? She'd warned him having children might be a struggle, yet he remained convinced, in either case, it would all work out.

Ahead was the river and a public canister she'd passed a hundred times. Never realizing how some night it would help her to hide the truth.

Eleven: Walking straight up to the bin, she plunged the package deep inside it, her arm reaching down into the black hole of rubbish up to her elbow. Past the cans and tissues and knotted plastic bags and the . . . whatever. Making sure to get her contribution as close to the bottom of the bin as she could.

Fifty little bodies. Entombed together. Buried and hidden.

Twenty-five little wooden grooms and twenty-five matching brides.

She'd ordered them a month before from some bridal website; handcrafted party favors about six inches high each to decorate the tables, the tiny carved top hats and bouquets and painted smiles. And they'd been lovely, just lovely, and she'd imagined one couple each at the center of every table, surrounded by a whimsical scatter of silk flower petals and brightly colored confetti of hearts and stars.

They'd been in the apartment for weeks before she'd realized what she'd done. Whether the damage had happened the first day they'd arrived or only last night, she couldn't say. But she knew they hadn't shown up that way, was almost entirely sure they hadn't shown up that way. She would have remembered.

Every bride's face was missing. Gone.

Painted over with the single thick swipe of gray paint. Some faces had been deeply rutted in thick paint, in fact, the heavy acrylic trailing down onto identical white-painted dresses. The twenty-five little grooms were all fine. It had been only the brides.

Mary Rose knew she'd done it herself. Who else would have—could have? She'd returned to the bridal website to see if there was any possible way . . . But, of course there wasn't. She'd done this to all those little brides. An unfinished project, she'd told herself at first.

She'd probably planned to redo the faces herself, something about them, perhaps, she hadn't liked, but then got distracted somehow. Forgotten that she'd started and then . . .

But there was no explanation, she knew. As there was no explanation whenever she felt phantom bugs slinking across, or sometimes even *under*, her skin. Or when the invented smells of death filled her nose, seemed to seep from her own skin and hair, and she turned the faucet until it scolded her back red and stood hunched in the water until after the heater emptied and the spray turned ice-cold. And so she scratched and showered. Every day, every year. And then swept fifty little wooden bodies together into an old paper bag, and wrapped *that* bag into another. Hidden it in the top of her clothes' closet, knowing Simon would never look there. Hiding it like an alcoholic secreting away empty bottles. The shame, the fear of discovery, mounting each hour they stayed in her apartment. To have gone to sleep with them bound in her closet like that would have been unbearable. So, again like an alcoholic, a porn addict, a murderer with blood on her hands, she'd snuck out into the middle of the night to get rid of the evidence.

Evidence of what, she wasn't able to say. But she knew Simon couldn't see them. Not ever. Otherwise he would be just like the poor tiny grooms. Perfectly fine, yet still buried right next to all their ruined brides.

Mary Rose stepped away and exhaled deeply, no longer needing her numbers, no longer needing anything but to get closer to the river. To stand at the banks in the cold and watch unseen water flowing past in the night. When she closed her eyes, she could hear always the river streaming, its urgent sway, and then hear the blood inside her doing the same. It took her only a few minutes more to reach it, and suddenly—everything was better again. The chill wind whooshed off the water, lifting back her hair, stroking her face.

The wedding was less than two months away, a distant part of her remembered. She smiled into the darkness, hugging herself with a delight she could finally surrender to. Simon was so excited about the wedding—charmingly, flatteringly so. He truly wanted nothing more than for her to be happy. Happy and healthy and at his side, the two of them ready to begin their lives together in laughter and love, with nothing and no one to stand in their way. And why should there be?

Maybe it was time to try medication again. Therapy. Simon's caring hints had not gone unnoticed. But she'd been down that path before. On and off for twenty years. And it had, in the end, only ever added to the laundry list of neuroleptics or atypical antipsychotics they'd tried on her. Most of which had only made her hallucinations worse, and *all* of which had left her feeling more hollow and not fully part of this world. A feeling she'd fought her whole life and didn't need any extra help with.

And, the therapists . . . She sighed, smiled at her own failings. What had the last one's name been? Michael-something. Schaeffer. That had been difficult. The things he'd said to her in the end, *vowed* to her. He'd clearly proven as delusionary as she.

Mary Rose lifted her gaze higher, fixing on the water. It swirled with inky assuredness, familiar and true, an endless spill of life and hope and secrets and mysteries flowing along. As she watched it, her breath slowed, became more even. She could breathe, next to the water like this. She could think.

And her first thought was, she realized with a sigh, the most important one: She loved Simon. *Loved* him, more than anyone she'd ever loved in her life. She wanted to step into that life he so vividly had imagined for them, to do all of the things she'd been frightened to do on her own, to grab hold of her own future and live it—truly live it! To grow up.

No, pills weren't the answer, but she trusted there was one out there somewhere to be found. For Simon's sake, she hoped she'd find it soon. Even as she thought the words, however, the familiar panic gripped her. Growing up was something she'd never fully considered possible before, her existence caught like an unfinished painting, the still life of Mary Rose. And Simon—poor Simon!—did he deserve someone so unfinished, so broken as she was? Could she even *try* to be happy, or normal, or real?

Or should she simply let him go, let him go and never, *ever* grow up.

To tell Simon why she *really* needed away time, and to get away from groups of people. Not because she feared them, but feared what she'd do to them.

Mary Rose shuddered, a sudden, unexpected laugh bursting from her lips at this last thought. The laugh had been cruel and distant. It had been her mother's laugh.

Before the echo of it fully died, she turned away from the river. It was time to get the coffee she'd promised and return. If she was gone much longer, Simon might come looking for her. He'd been hovering around her all week, watching her. Asking odd questions, about her first boyfriends, even. And so she'd told him about Evan and most of what had happened. But there was no point in talking about such things.

Halfway to the trash bin, she realized several people were walking toward her, toward the river. Four young men, she saw. College kids.

"What do we got here?" she heard one of them ask, then snicker.

Mary Rose nosed her head down into her scarf and moved so as to get around them. One of the boys had stepped out from the others, however, blocking her path.

"Wow," the boy said, "you almost ran into me."

"Pardon me," she said, regretting the norm to speak, to apologize, and then turned sideways to get past. If anything, however, the wall before her had tightened. She'd literally have to push through them.

"'Pardon me,'" the boy mimicked. "Hey, that's some sexy accent. Where you from?"

"England!" One of his friends laughed. "You're so fucking dumb."

"You from England?" the first boy asked.

"Yes," she said, keeping her eyes down.

"Hey, you don't gotta be afraid or nothing," he said. "We're not gonna, you know . . . like 'rape' you or anything."

She nodded curtly. Made another step to get around them. One of the other boys had laughed at the rape "joke." A hand seized her arm, the hold tight and aggressive through the thick winter jacket.

"Please," she said. "I need to—"

"That accent is driving me crazy," the first boy said. "I could listen to you talk all night."

"Yo, guys . . . enough." It was one of the students who'd not yet spoken. He'd motioned as if to move on.

"Chill, we're just talking is all." The boy holding her leaned closer into Mary Rose. His breath was hot and rank with hours of booze. His fingers still dug into her arm. In the morning, she'd be bruised for sure. "We bothering you?"

"No," she lied. Because that's what you do.

"See?" He looked around triumphantly at his friends. Then he slid his gaze back to her. "You wanna party?"

"Brian . . ." The complaint of another friend came out as a drunken plea. "Come on, man."

"Shut the fuck up." He laughed again. "What about it, Hermione. You wanna party with us? Could be good, yeah? Bet you're some kind of wild European cougar or something. Got four young studs at your service, you know?"

"No, thank you," she said. Her voice had come out as a growl. Her eyes were down at his boots.

The fingers squeezed tighter. "How about it? I wanna listen to you talk some more."

Behind him, she could see the trash bin and the fifty tiny bodies buried within. Their faces turned in their bag, in the dark, to watch her.

Twenty-five of those faces blank, caked with dried paint. Watching.

"You," she said. Her voice flowed out of her with inky assuredness, familiar, true.

"What's that?"

"You want to talk," she said, and she'd lifted her free hand to his chest, still barely glancing at any of the boys' faces. "We'll talk." His hand had let go. She motioned her head back down to the river.

"You gonna throw me in the river, Hermione?"

"I'd so fucking help her," one of them said, and they all laughed.

"Only you," she said, and the boy flinched at her husky tone, but recovered quickly enough. With a ribald, crowing comment to his friends, he hastened after her, falling into step beside her, trying to take her hand. She let him, then her fingers closed around his, tightly. Quite tightly.

"All rightie then," he drawled, but his voice had shaken, ever so slightly.

The river seemed closer than it had the first time, and Mary Rose walked with growing certainty, feeling the strength in her hands, her feet, the sway of her hips. The whisper of the wind lifting her hair. *The river, this night*, she thought. Not the ocean, but enough. Connected. *Always* connected. The river and this night and her striding along its banks so real and so grown-up. So very grown-up . . .

She almost didn't notice the boy beside her when she stopped to draw in the cool, chill night air, to revel in the water's siren call. The stars now dripping blood. The ground yawning open by her resolve, its grim and stalwart shades scrabbling free to lay every kind of death in her employ. She, herself, making the ghosts. Roaming barefooted over their graves, hair unbound, passing through the infinite shades of night.

"Hey, look," the boy stammered. His hand moved in hers, tugging but not quite frantic, not quite a broken-winged bird scrabbling to get away. But close. "Look, I was just messing around. I didn't—"

Mary Rose looked up at him.

The boy's eyes had narrowed, then widened until his face looked like a skin-stripped skull. He groaned, more of a whimper, escaping like a death rattle from cracked quivering lips. "What's that . . . smell? Please . . ." He lifted both hand to cover his mouth.

Mary Rose came closer, stood on her tiptoes to better reach his face. Moved her face within inches of his exposed neck. Breathing in the warmth there, the familiar scent of salt water, cold and damp and so, so right.

He trembled against her, however unable to step away. "I . . . I . . . Please . . ." he whimpered again as bloody spittle dribbled down his chin. Must have bit the insides of his own mouth.

She stepped back again and stared at him, their eyes locked.

A minute passed, a month, or twenty years.

Until, eventually, she turned away.

She needed to get that coffee from Chic's. Simon would worry. He always worried, wanted nothing more than for her to be happy. For her to laugh. For the two of them to be together, joyful and filled with love, stepping into their fresh, new life together. Always together.

The boys were waiting near the rubbish bin where she'd left them, and they stared at her expectantly. Then one of them, then a second, started for the river bank, passing her with confused stares.

"What did you do to him?" someone shouted, the accusation only now shading into fear.

Mary Rose ignored the question, kept walking. She owed no explanation. And, to be fair, she still didn't know the answer.

One: Cross the street.

15

"That's a very big smile, husband."

Mary Rose beamed up at him, her eyes alight, her face so happy. And apparently mirroring whatever look *he* now carried.

In this moment, as they turned on the dance floor—Simon and Mary Rose *Blake*, his "wife," *Mrs.* Blake—he knew all of it was worth it: the rash decision to host the reception here (to hell with the price tag), the endless catering questions and last-minute rush to find musicians, the whittling down of the guest list to fit the space.

He'd have done it all over again to see her here, to see this one satisfied look. One, he realized all too well, he hadn't truly seen since they'd walked a Scottish shore.

Regardless, she clearly fit the Rodin Museum here and now, as if she'd been born to glide beside the garden's serene reflecting pond, to float and dance across this gray-and-white marble floor like sunlight playing in the clouds. And the museum's striking marble sculptures provided the perfect counterpart to the twirling guests that coursed around the newlyweds: guests chosen with meticulous care, secretly grateful that Mary Rose's family mostly sent back fond regrets and tastefully wrapped packages, rather than showing up with suitcases and slightly bemused expressions. For those, they'd made perfunctory hints of an "English reception" following a European honeymoon, though Simon suspected the Morlands weren't any more excited about such a gathering than he.

Tonight, her parents still seemed out of sorts despite everything he'd done to make them comfortable, two country mice in the big city no matter how much money they'd come from. They'd been enthralled by the reception venue, though, and that had felt good. Or, rather, James Morland had been enthralled; Old Franny, he was beginning to suspect, reacted to life with as much emotion as one of these statues. In any case, another box checked in a day and night of checked boxes.

How proud his father might have finally been to see him tonight. Guy had always been such a hard-ass, impossible to impress. Good grades, wrestling trophies, part-time jobs, always taking the high road with other people . . . never seemed to mean shit at the old Blake castle. But, he was a married man now. A card-carrying adult. Great career, money in the bank, a part of the city's political and social future.

A part of Mary Rose's future, too.

So much clearer and truer to him than her, or his own, past.

"Okay, you two, let's take a champagne break." Keith's bold voice, so near, it startled him, pulled Simon out of his reverie. With a smile that didn't need any practicing, Simon turned Mary Rose one last time, the gauzy embroidered fabric of her dress swishing against his legs like surf. The fragrance of vanilla and sandalwood filling his whole world.

He'd thought it was all bullshit, the things they'd told him. The friends and coworkers and even several of his lifting buddies at the gym. How he'd see everything differently on this day, feel differently, the world a bigger, brighter place. Filled with so many possibilities, his future suspended in front of him, glittering on a string. Damn it if "they" hadn't been right. He'd ignore those few pathetic guy friends seriously bemoaning his loss of access to other women. He couldn't imagine ever caring.

Keith and his news anchor—yes, still going strong—stood to the side waiting, each carrying two flutes of champagne so expensive that Simon was pretty sure it'd been bottled in Xanadu. "Time to toast the bride and groom," Keith said.

"Best man already covered that," Simon countered, taking the glass anyway.

"I'm giving it another shot." Keith, who'd clearly been "toasting" throughout the night, laughed. "To Mr. and Mrs. Simon Blake!" he whooped, and Mary Rose laughed, bright and full. Even the reporter on Keith's arm couldn't help smiling, and lifted her glass to complete the toast. The woman's elegant black-and-white suit was TV perfect, as if she might be expected to break away and report on this society wedding at a moment's notice. She might, Simon mused. Another two, three years, and he could be a big enough deal to merit such local coverage.

"Oh, major improvement." Simon laughed. "Appreciate the on-going dedication to your responsibilities."

Keith took a deep bow. "Anything for Snow White, here."

"We're so glad you're both with us," Mary Rose said, her voice rich with warmth, laced with that rolling English accent that'd partially earned Keith's nickname for her years before. Her beauty and gravitas, the rest. Simon didn't bother quelling another surge of pride. She was the perfect lawyer's wife, the perfect Philadelphia wife, the perfect wife.

"Killer party," Keith said wryly. "Invite of the season." He pulled the news anchor to him, nodded across the chattering, laughing crowd. "Good move inviting Wonderling and what's-his-name. They won't forget it."

"Lenfest." Simon grinned. The two Philly idols *had* seemed genuinely touched, he thought, more than Simon would have expected. "Well, you know. They're like family," he said with a wink.

"It was up there, wasn't it?"

The question came from Mary Rose, her gaze having gone up—and then up still further, fixing on the glittering glass ceiling far above.

"Or, rather, *down* here," she amended darkly, with a lifted brow.

Simon blinked, but the news anchor didn't miss a beat. "Oh, that's right," she said, with the mock dismay of a seasoned anchorwoman. "The suicide. I remember covering the story. Older guy—retired cop, right?—got all the way up there somehow and jumped. Fifty-plus feet." Her lips quirked, the perfect studied blend of horror and sympathy gilding her expression.

"Nasty." Simon shook his head, looking down on the floor between the four of them where the man might have landed. "Well, I can tell you his family's been offered close to a million-dollar settlement."

"So we drink to lawyers everywhere," Keith put in. He lifted his glass to the floor and chuckled, the moment that could have been bleak passing with effortless ease.

The music started up again. Keith and his date gave their early good-byes, moved off, then Mary Rose once more turning into Simon's arm as they strolled past the museum's prized replica of Rodin's *The Kiss*.

He watched her smile at the marble sculpture almost fondly, and another ripple of satisfaction moved through him. They'd posed here earlier for a series of pictures, and he and Mary Rose had quasi replicated —with much more clothing and the requisite amount of humiliation and arm pulling—the famous pose of Rodin's ill-fated lovers in a photo he suspected, regrettably, would prove the most memorable of the bunch.

"Mother's looking a little green, isn't she?" Mary Rose said now. He followed her gaze across the room. "I can't believe she's still here."

"On your wedding night? How could she miss it?"

"She didn't miss it." Mary Rose fluttered her fingers with exquisite grace toward the center of the room, where dancers swirled to Glen Miller and the rhythm of their own conversations. "She's seen it, all of it. Everything so refreshingly, reassuringly *happening*. Her daughter getting married, her son-in-law an acknowledged rising star." She returned her hand to Simon's arm, squeezed it. "What more could a mother ask for?"

"Apparently, a nightcap and a warm bed." Simon laughed as Morland caught his eye and waved. "You want to come walk them out?"

"Not at all," Mary Rose said definitively. "We've talked for *hours* today already, and if I saw them now, I'd exhaust all of us without meaning to. I want to stay here." She stepped up on the toes of her satin slippers and brushed her lips against his, then leaned back from him, eyes mirror bright. "I want to wrap up everything about this day and hold it close, never letting any of it go. It's all simply . . . magic."

"*You're* magic." He smiled back, and in that moment, he truly meant it. The knowledge of the secret he was going to share with her later swelled inside him, but it wasn't the moment for that yet. He could let it linger in his mind a little longer, turning it around, imagining Mary Rose's face when he told her. She would love it, he was certain. *Almost* certain.

"Well, then, husband, your magical wife is going to go get another magical glass of champagne while you go help her parents to their magical taxi." She squeezed his arm again, her expression going almost stern. "So long as you promise to come find me again the moment they're off."

"Deal."

He was still grinning when he reached the Morlands at the front of the room, stepping out with them to the cool evening. Tonight, the reflecting pool shimmered with dozens of floating lights, and more of the fairy lights were strung through the trees and bushes, another museum planner recommendation that was worth the price. Though by that point he'd long since grown numb to the figures and could focus only on the hoped-for outcome. Which had all come to pass exactly as advertised.

"Congratulations, Simon," James Morland said gruffly, and Simon took his proffered hand in a warm shake, though he'd already fielded this comment from the man twice today. Mr. Morland apparently didn't know what else to say. "Mary Rose is lucky to have you."

"I'm the lucky one," Simon replied, a variation on the same response he'd given earlier. They strolled along the pool to the front of the museum, and he exchanged a still-awkward but what he suspected was a very British hug with Francine. His new mother-in-law did look a little green, he decided, but she smiled with genuine relief at him.

"Thank you," she said, and she held both his hands too tightly, releasing them only when Morland stepped in beside her. Simon waved a taxi forward, confirmed a brunch date the next day, then stood patiently by as the couple folded themselves into the car and sailed off. With their departure, a layer of tension unspooled he hadn't realized he'd been carrying, and he turned on his heel.

It only took a few minutes for the *third* Morland to sidle up to him, as he'd suspected he eventually would.

He'd seen the man at the wedding, of course. Handsome, athletic, for a guy in his fifties. An old-school Alpha, for sure. Stepping into the final pew at the back moments after Mary Rose's parents had been seated. Even from that distance, he'd seemed strangely familiar, a bright, far more vibrant version of the staid and stolid James.

The miscreant uncle, Simon realized. Had to be.

The guy was dressed in a well-cut suit with a collar that didn't quite hide the tribal tattoo stretching up his neck. His hair was dark brown dusted with silver, swept back from a sharply angled, sun-bronzed face that accentuated the dark intensity of his eyes. David Morland was weathered but not old, his manner relaxed and alert at once. Simon had also watched him leave the wedding hall the moment the ceremony had come to a close, slipping out as quickly and stealthily as he'd arrived.

Mary Rose's uncle. She'd laughed when sending the invitation, seeming wholly charmed of the possibility. "The black sheep of the family," she'd said with affectionate curiosity. "Nothing like weddings and wakes to draw them out." And now that black sheep fell into step with Simon, nodding as Simon turned to acknowledge him.

"I'd hoped you'd say hello." Simon smiled to ease any inference of rebuke. Guy was even more good-looking up close, wavy hair curling at his shoulders, like an eighties rock star who'd somehow kept the weight of. He shook the man's hand. "Good of you to come."

"Good of you to invite me." David Morland's grip was noticeably stout, and his voice held the echo of the Morland brogue as well, but faint, almost lost. "A bit of a shock, too."

"Your brother gave us the address." An address in Colorado, to Simon's surprise, not exactly the first place in the world he'd expected the outcast English uncle to have landed, but seeing him now, it made a certain kind of sense. Nothing could have gotten farther away from the buttoned-down civility of the Morland estate than the rugged American West, he supposed. Though David Morland would never pass as a cowboy.

"Did he now," Mary Rose's uncle said, his voice dry with layered meaning, but he offered no other comment. This close, David could more clearly see the family resemblance. He could have been Mary Rose's brother. "Sorry I didn't RSVP. I wasn't—"

"No worries," Simon stopped him. "We're glad you're here. Weddings are for family."

"Well, thank you." David Morland looked around, approvingly. "Cool place for the reception. Your choice or hers?"

"She's always loved it here."

"She would." Morland nodded, though how he'd have any idea about the tastes of a woman he'd last seen when she was a little girl, Simon didn't know. David Morland had been in Germany when Mary Rose went missing that fateful summer, estranged from the family even then. But he'd come back to help with the search within two days of learning of her disappearance, and hadn't left Scotland until she'd been recovered. Perhaps that was why Mary Rose still remembered him fondly.

"I'd hoped to speak with her, if that's all right," David said, his voice suddenly hesitant. "I—wanted to make sure it was okay with you first, of course. Or, rather—" He laughed nervously. "I suppose to broker 'her' okay. It's been a while, and I wouldn't want to blemish her special day. I won't take much of her time, just wanted—"

"No brokering needed," Simon said firmly, even warmly. He patted him on the shoulder, charmed by Morland's sudden reticence, as if Simon was going to bar him from speaking to his own niece at an event they'd invited him to. "You in town long?" Unsure if he'd asked to be courteous or because he wanted to ask this precise man a hundred questions.

"Just tonight."

"There's a small breakfast planned. Maybe . . ."

David Morland smiled warmly, shook his head. "Maybe someday," he lied for both of them.

When would he get this chance again? So many questions. *Not tonight*, Simon admonished himself. *Let it go tonight.*

"I know she'll be thrilled to see you," he said aloud. "You've only made our day more special." He nodded to where Mary Rose held court with three young women he recognized from several art gallery shows she'd dragged him to. The heavier one was cute; the other two worked too hard at being serious—and he could never remember their names. "You'll be rescuing her, trust me."

David Morland flashed him a grateful smile, then moved off.

Simon drifted to one of the dozen buffet tables set up around the space, but he didn't stay idle for long. There were always more hands he could shake, more shoulders to clap. More smiles and nods and acknowledgements of how lucky he was. He kept his position steady, though, never letting Mary Rose and David Morland leave his field of vision completely.

The initial moments of the meeting seemed to go well. Mary Rose greeted the family black sheep with a squeal of delight he would have heard across the room even if he hadn't been staring at her, her welcome clear and full. She threw her arms around the man for a brief hug, then stood back, her head tilted in that way she had while scrutinizing a person's exact cranial structure, as if she planned to draw it later. There was even a strange flash of jealousy, he admitted. This attractive man who'd, even though absent for decades, been part of Mary Rose's life longer than himself. Not sexual, of course, but an intimacy he had to swallow as David spoke and she listened with rapt attention, but she didn't seem to say much back to him, instead offering up a throwaway smile when it came her turn to speak.

Simon grimaced. If Morland hoped to get any real information out of Mary Rose—about her life, her parents, her new husband—Simon suspected he was having a poor time of it. Mary Rose wasn't one to give up her secrets. Of course, she was his wife now, he mused as he plucked another glass of champagne from a passing server. She might give them up to him, at long last. Or, even better, wouldn't have to. They'd simply fade away on the tide for good, once he finally got her back to where she'd been content. At peace.

He kept tabs on Mary Rose and her uncle through three more congratulatory chats and goodbyes. Throughout each, he checked his watch surreptitiously. Approaching ten thirty. The final dance would occur at eleven, and the place would be cleared out by eleven thirty, he'd been assured. Even the more stalwart of partiers were finally showing some wear after almost four hours, and he applauded himself for holding firm about the cash bar. The wine, beer, and later champagne was more than enough, and the champagne sparkled and caught the light in the tall flutes, a testament to the celebration of the night, but also a nod to decorum, good manners, and discernment. Hard to believe champagne qualified another checked box, but there you had it.

A knot of dancing couples spilled off the dance floor briefly, blocking his view. When it cleared, he stopped midway through lifting the flute to his mouth again—

Mary Rose and her uncle were gone. They'd disappeared.

Simon stiffened without meaning to, then turned sharply, his gaze darting around the crowded but well-lit space as unexpected panic clawed up his throat. Not by the table, not on the dance floor, not near the doors, not by the—

He determined it wouldn't bother him. She was with her uncle, for God's sake. The guy wasn't some kind of serial killer. He hadn't stolen her twenty years ago and returned to do it again. And they hadn't gotten in his UFO on the roof with the ghost of a dead cop and taken off to Mars.

Simon backed away from the party slowly, decided to inspect some of the sculptures closer. He honestly hadn't given any of them, or the paintings on the walls, a second thought. He suspected Mary Rose would ask him about them hours after—a little game they played every time they visited any museum, *which* piece in each room he'd want for their house someday—maybe it was a good idea to file away a couple of answers. Pillow talk for after nine-or-so degrees of consummation.

Fittingly, several in the front hallway, away from the noise, drew his attention, and the center display depicted two featureless naked bodies entwined in each other and the supporting marble beneath. He thought the one had a small tail, some kind of ravaging satyr.

"Getting any ideas?"

Mary Rose appeared by his side as if she'd been spirited there, tucking her arm into his with a rustle of swishing fabric. Her smile was wide, and her eyes fairly danced with animation.

"Most definitely. Several."

"Good." She grinned. She'd listed her head to study the sculpture. "He added the tail and changed the sculpture's name to the Greek poem after a bit of a scandal. Originally it was simply two women embraced."

"Hmmm." Simon restudied the carving. "Ah, yes, I see now. Two more breasts."

"Getting more ideas, I assume."

"It's a gift."

"One worth sharing, I hope."

"Well . . ." He checked his watch. "Our limo awaits out front, Mrs. Blake."

"You sent Uncle David over to me, didn't you?" She grabbed his hand. "He even asked your permission. How very lord and master of you."

"You all right?" Simon's heart still raced, his mouth dry despite the champagne he drained. "Did he take off?"

"He did, and I'm perfect," she said, sighing with what seemed to be true contentment. "He was delightful. He hasn't changed so much since I last saw him, isn't that funny? Stopped to visit me at various boarding schools a few times over the years. But it's been more than ten years now. Like one day he walked out of our life and another, he walks back in! And nothing so much is different no matter how many years have gone by."

"No?" Simon was back to scanning the hall, but there was no tall, slender man with dark hair shot with silver, ink reaching up his neck above his sharply cut suit collar. No man with intense eyes and a mysterious, knowing smile. "What'd you two talk about?"

"Oh, everything," Mary Rose with the vagueness Simon expected. "He's a real estate broker in Colorado, isn't that odd? So—prosaic. I'd imagined him as much more *alive*, you know? Not selling condos and time-shares or whatever it is he does."

Simon didn't bother responding to that. He suspected David Morland wasn't a real estate agent, no matter what he'd told Mary Rose. "You enjoyed catching up with him."

"Not nearly as much as I'm enjoying being with you."

He let her lead him past the table and into the side gallery. The location suited him as well, and when she pulled him into a quick, passionate embrace, he was struck with the utter rightness of everything. This was it, he thought. This was happening. It would all be all right.

"I have another surprise for you," he murmured, and Mary Rose's eyes flashed up at him again, consumed once more with an interest so bright, it almost bordered on avarice.

"What!" she cried. "Tell me now. What have you done?"

"It's not what I've done—it's what we'll do." He watched her carefully. She was turned toward the light spilling out from the main display rooms. It seemed to skate along her features, adding to her luminescence.

Her brows lifted as he extended the moment, and she gave his hands a hard shake. "Well, what is it?" she demanded.

"Our honeymoon," he said, without further preamble.

"*Italia*. I can't wait."

"After Italy," he said.

"Simon . . ." She scowled seductively.

"I've rented a house for ten days in June."

Mary Rose markedly shivered.

"On Mhoire's Point."

"Mhoire's . . ." Her eyes flared wide as comprehension dawned, and for one sickening moment, Simon thought he'd gravely miscalculated. Mary Rose stood, her mouth opened in surprise, brow lifted, her skin gone icy pale. Then she exhaled in a sudden rush and repressed an almost childish squeal of pure and unadulterated happiness.

"Mhoire's Point," she breathed, the word a mixture of relief, excitement, and curiosity. "Yes. Oh, Simon, yes. Thank you. It couldn't be . . . more perfect. Back at the start of it all. And an end, too, I suppose."

"A new beginning," he added, because it somehow seemed necessary to say, important. "The beginning of *our* life together."

"Together," she echoed. "Mary Rose and Simon. The beginning."

His new wife had said it in a way he believed her.

And, in a terrible way, she was right.

Ghosts only appear to those who are looking for them.

—Scottish proverb

16

The run-down house on the Scottish bluff was easy enough to find.

Simon stepped out of his rented car unhurriedly, squinting into the late-afternoon sun. The driveway was dirt, the path deeply rutted and weed filled. He studied the house again, once more deciding it was surely empty and had been for many years. The screen door was blown back and hanging unevenly off one bottom hinge against the entrance. Most of the windows had been busted out by sea storms or, more likely, kids tossing rocks at the neighborhood "haunted house." And it looked like part of the roof was rotted out, evidence of a long-passed fire and/or water damage blackening the corner. He also saw where someone had nailed something to the front door; on closer inspection, the barely recognizable rotted remains of a squirrel or some such creature pinned by its scraggy tail. Decidedly more mischievous than throwing rocks. Simon frowned.

Approaching the steps to the porch, he heard, maybe, the distinct sound of a growling dog. He stopped, waiting to see if the noise had come from inside the house or beneath the porch. Nothing. An imagined sound in the wind, then.

He rapped the door frame to make absolute certain no one lived here. No point getting attacked by some local squatter or Scottish meth heads. He could see the headline: NOSY GROOM KILLED ON HONEYMOON; BRIDE-WIDOW TO MARRY LOCAL CLAM SHUCKER. Still, he knocked at the doorway a second time. Firmer. Paint flakes drifted down off the cobwebbed porch cover onto his shoulders.

Simon chuckled, tried the doorknob. It turned, but apparently the door was locked or otherwise bolted.

It's never locked. It's held.

He stepped to the closest window and cupped his hands to peer inside. The interior looked as forlorn as the outside, a single rotted couch overturned in the middle of the one room he could see. The rooms beyond, the hallway, all lost to imagination and cast in long shadows. One of the window's panes was already smashed, the glass shards and culprit rock still lying on the wood floor within. Simon looked around for something to knock out the rest, climb through the window.

Thinking better of it, he left the porch to walk the perimeter of the house, looking for a more civilized way in. Wind off the ocean—getting more familiar to him but, even in June, demanding full attention—slammed against him as he came around the corner. He pulled his jacket collar up and kept going.

The windows on the side of the house were boarded over, the slats nailed from the inside. Out back, he located a basement door covered by weeds, rust and old spray-can graffiti that also ran piecemeal along the entire back of the house. Most of the graffiti was crude or old-style name tags, no different from what he saw in Philly every day. The rest had the look of, he assumed, traditional Gaelic words and symbols and then the little figures: stick girls, cartoon faces, each one enough like the pictures Mary Rose drew to send a shiver up his back, but was he trying to make a connection when—

When he looked again, they were gone. Replaced with only the swirling graffiti Os and lettering he'd seen before.

He sidestepped back, trying to recapture what he'd seen, but the illusion was gone. He laughed at himself, hoping to chase away the last of the creeping chill.

A cellar door, despite several kicks, held even harder than the front door had. Again, locked from the inside. Two smashed windows in the back gave view to a small deserted kitchen and then a bedroom, the discolored mattress and rusted springs leaned up against the far wall, the rot of several Scottish winters draped in dark stains down every wall.

Simon turned to look out over the roiling ocean. A good hundred feet below and continuing for another thousand miles in three directions. He covered his eyes from the sun and squinted out to where he and Mary Rose had been when she'd fixed on this specific house. Tried going farther to see "The Island," but it was lost, lying low in wait deep within the black waves. He wondered again if this had even been what Mary Rose had been looking at. With her wandering mind, she could have been thinking about something else altogether and merely been staring at whatever was ahead of her, or, perhaps even, looking at some passing cloud or bird above the house that day.

He checked his watch again. Mary Rose planned to spend the morning shop hopping and then painting a little, maybe, down on the beach outside their rented cottage. They'd had their week dashing across Italy: Venice, Florence, Rome. Now for a week of quiet and leisure, one he hoped would bring Mary Rose the serenity she so craved. He'd promised to meet back up by four for "a nap" and then a late dinner. It wasn't even noon yet.

Simon decided to try the front door again, a good shoulder would pop it open probably. What harm could come from looking inside?

Coming back around the house, he recoiled.

An older man stood in the driveway, eyeing Simon's car. The man turned: "This yours?"

"Yeah, sorry. Hi. This your house?"

The man shook his head.

"You know the guy who lives here?" Simon asked.

"No one."

"How long's it been empty?"

"More than ten years now. What you doing back there?"

Simon strode closer. "Someone in town said it was for sale. I'm maybe in the market, and was checking the place out." The lie, he thought, had been delivered casually enough.

The old man's crinkled eyes narrowed into slits, a thin smile forming within his white beard. (So, maybe not casually enough, Simon realized.) "No one lives there," the man said.

"Yeah, understood." At this point, Simon knew there was nothing to lose. "Any idea why?"

The man shrugged.

"Well, you think anyone would mind if I took a look inside?"

The man sucked something from his top gum, thinking, said: "I would."

"It's not your house." Simon grinned, challenging, surprised at the man's response.

"Not yours, either, young man."

Simon laughed pleasantly, held out both hands in surrender. "Fair enough. You got any idea where I'd find the owner? Gillis," he expounded from memory. "Benjamin Gillis."

"No."

"What about Jean? *Jean* Gillis?" It had been the other name on the online property records. "That a wife?"

"One of his daughters."

"They still around?"

The man shrugged again.

"Okay then." Simon clapped his hands, rubbing them together against the cold blowing from behind. "It was great talking with you."

The man saluted with two fingers as Simon crawled back into his car and backed slowly down the driveway away from the house, the Scot's receding shape no more than another dark skeletal weed in the rearview mirror by the time Simon had made a quick K-turn to pull onto the main road.

The local constable in town was proving almost as helpful.

When Simon had directly asked about the disappearance of Mary Rose Morland, a case from twenty years before, they'd looked at him like he'd asked for their Loch Ness Monster file. "Any such records are long gone," they claimed. "Stored in Glasgow, if at all." The current constable was not much older than Simon and hadn't lived in Mhoire's Point when it had happened anyway. The office receptionist, an older woman, remembered the monthlong disappearance vaguely, but could only recall the "father was somehow involved," a version of the story Simon had heard before. No matter how hard he tried pursuing the notion, he couldn't picture it. He supposed that was naive, that anything was possible, but it just didn't fit the guy he'd met. James Morland was more of a lazy explanation than anything.

"Why so interested in this old case, Mr. Blake?" the constable asked.

Because my wife has terrible nightmares. Because sometimes she scratches at her arms until the skin breaks. Because something happened to her in this shit hole twenty years ago. Something terrible. And a part of her was, is, broken. *And now here I am, the motherfucker who's gonna try and somehow fix it.*

"Took a tour of the island," Simon responded. "Thought it was a remarkable story."

The guy seemed unimpressed with the answer and done with the discussion, so Simon gave him something he could talk about with authority. "Also heard you guys still have an issue with kids out there," he prompted. "Drinking, that kind of thing."

"Sure, sometimes. Mostly fines for broken fire restrictions, underage drinking, misdemeanor drug offenses."

"Don't forget the bull," the receptionist called over the counter.

Simon pulled up a good laugh from somewhere. "Sounds like another good story!"

The constable smiled thinly. "Three, four years ago, caught a boatload of guys bringing a bull out there. Damn near sunk the boat. Said it was a prank."

"It was for *sacrifice*," the receptionist countered, her eyes wide with playful secret knowledge.

"Woo." Simon made an exacerbated grimace. "You sure it's just 'fire restrictions' and 'underage drinking' going on out there?"

The sheriff shook his head at the receptionist. "'Sacrifices' . . . You're talking mince, woman." He made a dismissive whistling sound, though he kept his gaze on Simon. "You got any supposed haunted places in Philadelphia, Mr. Blake?"

"Sure, I guess so."

"Well, bet they bring all the idiots out also." It'd come out as "*eejits*," and the implication was that Simon had joined their ranks. "Anything else now, Mr. Blake?"

"Unrelated. Any idea where I could find a Benjamin Gillis? Was hoping to discuss buying his property out at the bluff overlooking the bay."

"Don't know him," the constable said.

"Moved away years ago," the receptionist added. "Don't recall where. His daughter might know."

"Jean?" Simon asked, turning.

"Right," the woman said, thinking. "Jean *Osterby*. Kept her married name." She pointed out the front window. "Lives right down the street."

Jean Osterby stood in the crack of her doorway, filling up the narrow space she'd allowed open. She wore an oversize Iron Maiden T-shirt. Simon suspected, with a twinge of guilt for even thinking it, that she was ten years younger than she looked. Hard lines around her mouth from smoking, eyes dark and hollow from the exhaustion of life. A look he knew well from his work for Philadelphia's underprivileged. Still, even if beaten down some by life, there was no mistaking a nice-looking woman.

"Don't know where he is," she said.

Simon laughed. "Didn't even tell you why I was here."

"Isobel Grierson, from the police station, called. Said you were coming out here."

"Word travels fast."

"In Mhoire's Point?" She laughed, and the sound was guttural, filled with decades of whiskey and nicotine. "'No man can live longer in peace than his neighbor pleases.'"

"Got it. Well, do you know if there're plans to sell the house or—"

"Nah," she said. "He won't sell."

"Why's that?"

She winked. "It's haunted."

"You're kidding."

"Never about money, love. Anyway, that's why he won't sell. Why he won't live there. But when he dies, I'll sell it to *you* right away. How's that?"

"Any chance I could talk to your father directly? Is he still around? Maybe he and I could—"

"We're not interested, thanks." She'd started to close the door.

"Mrs. Osterby . . ."

"Ms," she corrected him, held the door. "And I don't know anything about any missing girls, neither."

Simon lurched back.

"Yeah, she told me about that, too," Jean Osterby said. "Got nothing to do with us."

"No, I didn't mean . . . Unrelated stuff."

"Okay. Still, don't know anything about it."

"Got it." Simon retreated from the door. He'd been clumsy mingling the two stories, not thinking the locals would talk. If someone showed up at his door asking about a missing girl, what would he do? "Sorry for the intrusion. I appreciate your time." He turned and was halfway down her walkway when she spoke again. The woman's words lost to his own jumbled thoughts.

"What's that?" He'd stopped and turned back.

"I said, 'You could maybe have a talk with Brodie Rothes.'"

"Yeah?" He checked his watch. It was almost three, already. "And who is he?"

"The local druid chief."

The local—huh? "What's that? Like 'magic' stuff?"

"Something like." She grinned darkly.

"Why would I talk with him?"

She looked past him, down the street, out to where the sea was, hidden by four blocks of development. "To learn all about your cursed island, love. Ain't that what you come here for?"

Simon half expected a guy in a hooded cloak, something out of Middle-earth with black contacts and maybe a pentagram branded into his forehead. *This* "druid chief" looked more like the local geometry teacher and sported only a bushy beard and a fancy water bottle. "What's in the bottle?" Simon finally asked.

"Cinnamon sticks and black currants." Brodie Rothes offered it for Simon to try a sip and Simon held up his hand to say no, thanks. They sat together at one of the half dozen picnic tables on the front patio of a local restaurant. Jean Osterby—who'd come along for introductions and, more likely, a free meal—sat with them. "May I ask how an American tourist got so interested in our little island?"

"Stopped there on a boat tour a couple months ago for a few hours. I don't . . . I guess there's something about the place."

The two locals exchanged looks.

"Guess you think so, also?" Simon leaned back, inviting them to drive the conversation as they saw best. For now, anyway.

"'The Little Island That Likes to Be Visited' has been part of local lore for a thousand years," Brodie said. *"Thaeilean-beag'toighleisa'bhith a'gabhail luchd-tadhail."* The last came out slowly, in the notes almost of a song. Brodie allowed the tune to linger over the table for a moment before speaking again. "It's a sacred place, for sure. Charged with the lifeblood of the world."

"And what's that mean, exactly?"

"Some places are natural conduits to the earth's life force. And to those worlds beyond and between our own. Gaelic tradition believes in the Otherworld, a place before and after life, before and after death."

Simon leaned forward, genuinely intrigued. "Like heaven? Hell."

"Like." Brodie Rothes nodded. "There *are* portals out there. Some quite dangerous. Most not."

"Dangerous, how?"

"Not all thresholds are meant to be crossed, yes?"

"You mean actual entryways to other worlds? *The* 'Otherworld'?" Simon shook off the idea. It was absurd. Next thing, the guy would be showing off his collection of twenty-sided dice. "Seems too fantastic to believe."

"The belief is considered more metaphoric than literal, as most enduring beliefs tend to be. You can research the true origins of Halloween, winter solstice, and Easter yourself. As to 'literal' possibilities of an Otherworld, there's a growing theory called the 'many interacting worlds' hypothesis, which submits not only that parallel worlds exist, but that they conjoin with our world on a quantum level and, so, are quite detectable. It's a spin-off of the many-worlds interpretation in quantum mechanics focused on some universal force of repulsion between 'nearby' worlds. Various measureable quantum effects could be explained by factoring in this very force, and could prove that bridges, or portals, or whatever you want to call them, *do* exist between these parallel realities. Traversing what folk are calling 'branes,' quantum boundaries. Think of a 3-D raindrop running down a 2-D windowpane, believing that's the whole world—when it's not, and the raindrop somewhere at its core always carries the smallest prickle that it's not. Spatial dimensions or spiritual planes, the net result is the same."

"Interesting." Simon admitted this guy was possibly more than hugging trees and twenty-sided dice. "I take it you go out there. You and, what, like . . ."

"His 'coven'?" Jean Osterby laughed. "Fly in on their broomsticks, they do." She playfully scrunched her ten fingers into claws and made a wild face.

Brodie shook his head. "Doesn't quite work that way, and she knows it. But, yes, I joyfully confess many of us still go out to the island at special times of the year. As folk have for centuries. But if you're expecting wild orgies and blood sacrifices, I'm afraid you'd be quite disappointed. There's some hand-holding and just-bearable original poetry. Music, meditation. We're, like our ancestors, worshipping nature. The natural cycles of birth, growth, and death. Not the devil."

"Understood. I didn't mean to . . ."

Brodie smiled, showing no true offense was taken.

"Are you . . .?" He turned to Jean Osterby. "Do *you* go out there, too? I mean, does everyone here, or . . ."

She laughed from somewhere deep in her throat. "Not me, love. I've got enough on my plate without worrying about offending tree gods. Brodie and me are just old chums. But you, you want to know if Mary Rose Morland stepped into one of his magic portals, yes?"

Simon frowned in confusion. He'd never given Mary Rose's name to either of them.

"Don't look so surprised," Brodie explained. "The 'little English girl' is still a bit of a legend around here, and probably will be for generations. She's one of dozens of people to vanish over the years. There's a list. But"—he paused—"one of only two we know who came back."

"Two?" Simon sat up straighter. This was quite promising.

"Paul McAllister passed over more than ten years ago. He'd vanished in 1942, in his twenties." Brodie breathed deeply. "For exactly thirty-three days."

Simon blinked, a chill skating through him. "Thirty-three . . ."

"Yes, same as the Morland girl."

"Some kind of copycat, then? Or, could McAllister have been a suspect and—"

"Thirty-three is a very important number to the original worshippers of these parts. There were thirty-three Celtic immortals and thirty-three Fomorii leaders, sort of like the more-monstrous Greek Titans. Cúchulainn, a major hero, kills thirty-three opponents in the Otherworld. The Desi have to wander thirty-three years after their expulsion from Meath. Chief druids are said to have first studied for thirty-three years. The Picts had thirty-three pagan kings, and thirty-three Christian kings. The great cities of the Celtic world are listed as thirty-three. Several major mythic and historical kings are each attributed with siring thirty-three children. You get the point."

"I do. So, is this—and, again, no offense meant—a fan of druidism making a statement, a sacred symbol of some kind. By keeping her away for thirty-three days?"

"The alternative is that thirty-three is an important number for a *reason*." The man leaned forward to let the notion sink in. "Perhaps she really was somewhere else for that specific amount of time. Portals that open and close on a schedule of some kind. McAllister returned with no memory of what had happened or where he'd been. Everyone assumed he'd been drunk somewhere the whole time. Anyway, a few years later he landed on Juno Beach with the 51st Highland Division. Swore he was protected all through the war and beyond, protected by unearthly forces. In his eighties, he spoke more of strange lights and hallways and the 'angel people' he'd once visited for thirty-three days and hoped to see again soon. I take it you know the Morland girl personally?"

Simon sat back. "Why would you say that?"

"Because, for the first time today, you look terrified." Now the middle-aged man *did* look like a sagacious wizard. "You know this girl."

Simon grimaced, gathering his thoughts. His next questions.

"Should I be?" he asked. "Terrified?"

"Not if you're to accept McAllister's testimony. There, it appears he found the 'right' portals." The alternative was left hanging unspoken between them.

"What should I do?" Simon asked. "What would *you* do?"

"Doesn't that depend what you're trying to do?" Jean Osterby asked, pointing a half-eaten sausage roll at him. Brodie rose his brows to indicate she'd made a good point and sat back, waiting for Simon answer.

"I don't know," Simon admitted. "Still gathering information, I guess. Trying to learn as much about this island, about Mhoire's Point, as I can. Even the, well . . . *this* kind of stuff."

Brodie smiled. "Does she ever talk about it?" he asked. "'*This* kind of stuff'? Anything like about 'strange lights,' 'hallways,' 'angel people'?"

She'd said nothing, of course. Perhaps never would. Maybe she would when she was eighty. Simon, instead, evoked things she'd said in her sleep, though only for himself, determined not to betray so this guy could gossip over campfires for the rest of his life. No, thanks.

"No," said Simon. "I can tell you I've seen her there, on the island, and she seems happy. But, I suppose . . . It seems that place has a certain . . ."

"'Hold' on her?" Brodie offered.

Simon looked between them. "Yes."

"Like old Paul McAllister," Jean Osterby noted.

"I guess. And I'm not sure it's very healthy for her. Whether that's 'supernatural' in origin or more earthly is . . ." He could say no more, the less insane criminal possibilities were obviously his best course. This woo-woo stuff was only getting in the way of a *real* abduction, real trauma. "I suppose, I'm exploring her disappearance. Trying to make sense of what happened."

"For her," Brodie added.

"Right."

The Scotsman studied Simon carefully before answering. "It's the 'Little Island That Likes to Be Visited,'" he said. "I'd start there."

Jean Osterby winked, then gazed at Simon thoughtfully.

"Anything else?" he asked.

"Yeah," the druid said. "Maybe plan to end there."

17

Mary Rose examined the stars through the open bedroom window, listening to the reassuring cadence of Simon's breathing joined with the always more tender whoosh of waves at night. He'd fallen deeply asleep hours ago, the furrowed line of her husband's brow easing at last, his tense mouth softening until it seemed he was smiling as he slept, wrapped in the comfort, she hoped, of good dreams. He was always handsome, as stark and sharp as sunlight refracting through glass, but she never loved him more than when he slept.

Still, she couldn't seem to follow him into slumber, no matter how she tried. She'd been at it for hours, yet all she'd been able to manage was an endless count of the stars in the deep indigo sky, a fruitless endeavor dogged by an increasingly nagging concern: What had caused those anxious, secretive looks from Simon when he'd finally returned from town, that cautious tone?

She'd done nothing. *Have I?*

Ten days in Italy and then whisking up here, everything exactly as they'd, he'd, planned. The joy of being Mrs. Simon Blake in full flower finally, as real and certain as the ring on her finger. She'd fairly burst with that joy throughout their trip so far, she knew she had. And yet . . .

She tried to remember what had first roused her. An elusive memory. A dim nightmare of some kind that had frightened her awake.

Moving slowly, barely making any sound, Mary Rose slipped from her husband's bed.

The stars were too far away, she thought. That was the problem. She'd maybe step outside and see them more clearly for a moment—not relying on the view through the window. Outside, they'd be close enough to hold in her palm, to touch their light. Fresh air was what she needed, nothing more.

The patio doors moved unresisting at her touch, gliding open into the night. The flagstones glistened with the damp that never fully went away this close to the water, their smooth surfaces echoing back the starlight. It wasn't too cold, she thought. Warmer than she expected, certainly, the breeze light and comforting against her flushed skin.

She frowned. Why was she so anxious? There was no reason. She was doing everything right—she was Mrs. Simon Blake, a married woman, prepared to step out into her new life. Simon, too, was everything he'd promised he would be: Doting. Engaged. Passionate. Concerned over her every reaction. *Too* concerned?

Shaking her head, Mary Rose lifted her hands up into the sky as her feet picked their way down the well-worn path to the water's edge. The stars *were* closer here, and she stretched out long white fingers, pale and elegant in the moonlight, almost touching them.

When had she noticed the tension in Simon—had it started today? If so, it hadn't lasted long. When they'd first driven into Mhoire's Point, maybe, but then they'd reached their quaint little cottage down by the sea, and she'd turned to him with a smile, and they'd reached for each other with that simple, instinctual knowing. They'd fallen into bed that afternoon the same way they had when they first met, their hunger for each other a tangible thing, leaving them gasping, laughing, tangled in sheets.

Happy. Yes, they were happy. *She* was. There'd been no incidents since they'd left Philadelphia—none that she remembered, anyway. And she would have remembered . . . or Simon would have told her, she was certain. He would have. Was that the tension? Had something happened?

Was it time to see a professional again? Dare she? The last time had gone so poorly, and anyway, surely, she'd improved a great deal since. So much so that the medications she'd tried seemed a silly, melodramatic solution, unnecessary. She wasn't crazy. That wasn't what was wrong. At least, she didn't think so. Besides, things simply weren't that bad. She was so close. So close to her future that she could cup it in her hands, a thousand and one stars waiting for her.

Mary Rose smiled as she came to the last tussock of grass before the land gave way to the thick, granulose sand that trailed down to the water. Such a perfect location, this cottage, with its view and its position on the bay. And Simon had chosen it himself—for her. To bring her here, so close to her lovely island.

They'd see it tomorrow, she knew. Simon had promised, and he always did what he said. They'd rent a boat and go crashing across the bay and then walk along those pristine beaches again, climb the gentle hills, revel in the sunshine and warm breezes and memories. So many happy memories—her father, always remarkably robust and carefree, fishing for hours as she drew and wandered and daydreamed. Her own drawings, coming to life beneath her fingers, first hinting that maybe, one day, she could be a real artist, a real painter—or a princess or astronaut or rodeo star.

Anything was possible on her magical island.

She smiled, staring out over the darkened waters, a tumble of inky waves rumbling somewhere in the middle distance. If she tilted her head, she could almost see shapes out there, floating, bobbing, dancing in the waves. Her island. She wanted to go back there so badly, too—this one final taste. One last walk along its shores, re-membering, remembering . . .

Then she would go back home to Philadelphia with a happy, full heart. She'd start her new life as Mrs. Mary Rose Blake, American artist, and embrace wide-eyed all that life held for her. She'd throw herself wholeheartedly now into Simon's career also, and it would be both their stars that she would cup in her hands, stars that would shine so brightly, it would keep her awake at night, content and watchful as he breathed beside her in the darkness.

All of that awaited her, and she was ready for it—more than ready. Eager. Excited. She just wanted to visit her island one more—one *last* time. To get a final fix of happiness to carry her another twenty years and more.

Mary Rose marched closer to the rolling surf, the tide reaching out to her like a petitioner, beckoning her in. She steeled herself for the icy cold touch of North Atlantic water as it washed over her bare feet—but it wasn't cold, she realized, despite the delicious chill that ran up her legs at the sudden shock of its touch.

Impossible.

It was *warm*. Like stepping into a bath.

Her delighted laughter rang into the night, caught by the breeze, and then lifted high and away.

18

The guy who'd first taken them to the island saw Simon coming down the dock and grimaced, stacking long tubs along the side of the boat. "We're not hiring," he grumbled.

"Hello again." Simon examined the boat, the sea lapping against the row of pilings between them. The morning sun had lifted over the closest buildings. Closer, he saw the tubs were filled with huge fish and crushed ice. "Are these cod?"

"Haddock." The man thumbed containers still on his ship. "And *those* are lobsters."

"Very nice." Simon took a moment to officially admire the haul. "Was hoping to reserve your services a second time."

The man shook his head. "Mr. Blake was it?"

Simon nodded, still fighting to remember the fisherman's name. Somewhat concerned the man had somehow remembered *him* after nine months.

"Cameron," the man said, as if reading his thoughts—more likely, reading Simon's face—and then lugged up another ice-filled tub. "Where's the girlfriend?"

"Wife," Simon corrected, reaching out in an offer to help lift it onto the dock. Seabirds squawked overhead.

"I see." The boat captain lifted it over himself. "Well, congratulations, mate. This the happy honeymoon?"

"Part of. Just flew in from Italy." He regretted the clarification, knew he was bragging to knock the guy down a peg. Playing the

Ugly American far too well, it seemed. "But staying here for the week, and was aiming for this afternoon or anytime tomorrow. If that works for you."

The captain shook his head, indicated the tubs. "Booked all week."

Simon smiled. "Got it. Could you recommend anyone who'd take the job?"

Cameron looked up and down the docks. "No one comes to mind," he said. "Sorry, mate."

"Okay, 'mate.'" Simon's grin hardened. Actually, hiring the man had been the least of his goals this morning. "You knew it was her right away, didn't you?"

The boat captain wrapped his hands around the ship's railing and leaned forward to stretch to indicate he wasn't all that interested in Simon Blake and his new wife. "Not right away," he said finally. "But thereabouts."

"She been out here before?" Simon knew what answer he wanted to hear. The notion that Mary Rose had snuck out here by herself any time after her disappearance was unnerving.

"First time in twenty years, for all I know. But I helped look for her that first night and seen her picture a hundred times. Hasn't changed hardly at all."

"Why didn't you say something?"

"Didn't I?" The man looked up, eyes cutting. "Took it she wasn't too keen in following that particular course, so I dropped it. Not really any of my business, anyway."

"She doesn't remember what happened to her," Simon admitted. Hoping this man might. "None of it."

Cameron squinted, considering this news. "Probably for the best."

"Why's that?"

"Don't know. But, like I said, not my business."

"Yeah." Simon stepped forward. "You keep saying that, but it's been clear since that first day you got something on your mind. Why I'm here now. So, even if it's a final 'Fuck off,' I'd like to hear it."

"Right." Cameron nodded. "Fuck off."

Simon laughed. "Are you scared of it? The island."

The pilot shook his head. "Give the missus a kiss for us."

"Trying to keep her safe is all," Simon said. "Can't blame a guy for trying." He didn't know why he did it. Something—something about the men in her file, in her whole life. It was the word "safe" that did it, Simon could see immediately, with his lawyer's intuition pinging sharply. The man's head came up, and his eyes were mirror bright. "You know more than I do. Thought you could help."

"Safe," the Scotsman said bitterly. "Right. Taking her out there again . . . For fuck's sake, keep her off that bloody island."

Simon tried to keep his voice even. "Why? You helped look for her that night. Did something happen?"

Cameron shook his head. "Haven't stepped foot on its shores since the night young Mrs. Blake first vanished."

"So what happened? To you, I mean. It seems—"

"Nothing. Something. I don't know." Cameron sighed. "I was thirteen. Got lost looking for a dead girl and spooked myself is all. At least, that's what I tell myself when the lights are on."

"And in the dark?"

His face collapsed, in exhaustion. Or relief. "I saw a glimpse of something," he grumbled quietly. Simon could barely make out the words with the accent. "Or maybe some*where*—that night. Lights and power not of this world. The Otherworld, maybe. I couldn't say. And I heard things, too. A certain name breathed in the wind. Mary Rose, Mary Rose, Mary Rose . . ." He imitated the memory, barely making a sound.

Simon tried not to listen.

"Which is why I wouldn't bring her back out there. Why would . . . I went back myself. Maybe fifteen years ago. Twenty-two years old. Hadn't been back since that night I was thirteen and looking for a little English girl. I'd just gotten out of four years with the Royal Navy, Surface Fleet. Seen the world. Bought a beer for me da once. Lived with a woman and her son in town. Felt I was too old for ghost stories. For being afraid. Ready to go back, understand?"

Simon nodded.

"I wasn't. Still never set foot on it. When I brought the boat up close to do so, the waves rolled onto the shore, and when the surf pulled back, the sand and rock was covered in blood. Dark, red blood like a winding ribbon around the island as far as I could see. Every time the tide ebbed, the blood only grew darker and covered more."

"A trick of the light," Simon offered. "It was sunset."

"Aye, I told myself the same. It was algae. It was iron-rich water coming up from some underground lake. It was a trick of the sun. But then looked out to the cairn fields. You know what—"

"I know it," Simon stopped him.

"All the rocks were gone, and they were replaced with things. Shambling things. *Dead* things. Staggering out to the water, toward me, in various stages of rot. Wasted. Tattered suits and dresses hanging, dripping wet. Sodden bone glistening in the sun. Two dozen gaping sockets staring back my way. And standing with them was a shape I knew, clothes I knew. It was my own father. Alive and watching the telly back in Mhoire's Point. But out there, somehow decomposed, the flesh hanging from his bones. Calling me to him."

"Bullshit."

The pilot turned again to look over the water, not meeting Simon's eyes. "I never went back again. Not until Mary Rose Morland and her American husband-to-be showed up at my boat. It doesn't want me out there. Never did. Probably doesn't want you 'visiting,' either, Mr. Blake, but is playing nice enough . . ."

"To get to her," Simon finished the warning.

"There's something out there. The place is . . . unnatural. 'Good' or 'evil,' I couldn't say. But you shouldn't . . ." He stopped, pointed into the sky. "You notice there weren't any birds on the island, Mr. Blake?"

Blake glanced up to see a dozen soaring every which way, several cawing. All of the man's jokes about gull shit notwithstanding, Simon hadn't actually thought about it. He couldn't remember seeing any now. The docks and trip down, there'd been birds everywhere.

"They won't go near the place. Nothing will. *Nothing*"—he let the word sink in—"lives on that island. There's a presence, but that's not the same thing, is it? Not at all. Whatever it is, it's not of this world. It's older. The whole island, it's, well, aware, and . . . and hungry."

"'Hungry'? An island? For what?"

"I don't know. Attention, maybe. Love. Blood? Control."

Simon groaned in protest, despite his best efforts. Damned super-stitious Scots. "What would an island want with any of that?"

"I imagine the same as any of us," Cameron said. He'd reached for another tub of dead fish. "Ain't that right?"

The small sport boat cut an easy line down the Scottish coast. Midday sun flashing off its bow, water splashing off the sides as pearls and streaks along the edges of the front window. The engine, an inboard 300 hp V8, purred beneath them no louder than the Jeep Simon had driven through his twenties. This trip out, they were both warm and comfortable. Simon feeling quite capable behind the wheel of a boat for the first time in his life. They'd rented it for the afternoon from the lodge they were staying. If this Cameron guy wouldn't take them out again, there were other options.

Mary Rose sat one seat over, shrouded in a black scarf and hidden behind her giant sunglasses, considering the water ahead. Twice, he'd glanced her way and imagined the sunglasses as the dark enormous sockets of an old skull, tilted to watch him. He cursed himself for even thinking such a macabre, and stupid, thing. She looked like Jackie Onassis or one of the Kardashians, not some horrid death's head. But it was the damn island. The druid guy's business about portals and spirits and whatnot, Cameron's insane story and palpable fear. These people had managed to creep him out in less than a week. He could hardly imagine what spending your entire life with these horseshit stories would do.

But he'd gone looking for that, hadn't he? He already had the boat rented, didn't need Cameron the Highlander to get them out there. He'd really been working on instinct, knew nine months before the guy had more to say. *Needed* to.

The island drifted low in the distance, cradled within the lightly rolling waves. Too often, it vanished completely, disappeared behind some cresting swell to remain inexplicably hidden long after the wave had passed again. A trick of the sea, Simon supposed; or of the sun overhead or the ever-changing water. How easy, he thought, for those ashore to imagine the island wasn't there anymore. How simple for a local fairy tale to begin.

Finally the island elevated completely, and continually, from the water. It seemed smaller than the first time he'd seen it. And its colors more vibrant. Vivid greens spread across its center and shocking Caribbean blues edged its coast, so very different from the inky black of the rest of the sea. A special oasis, the same Mary Rose's father had found so many years before, or a genuine mirage beguiling passersby.

He couldn't help but think of Cameron's claims that the island sometimes changed sizes and locations depending on *its* mood.

They motored along, Simon acutely aware of the squat gray house watching their journey from above like some devoted sentinel. Whether or not Mary Rose had any real connection with the place beyond looking at it strangely once, he couldn't yet say. He, however, now found the property creepy as shit.

It's haunted.

Now Jean Osterby's words echoed in his memory as they passed beneath. He'd gathered half of Scotland claimed to be haunted by something, but there was no denying he'd allowed this particular place to get under his skin. As for Mary Rose . . .

"What do you think of that house up there?" he asked. He hadn't come back to Scotland for subtle.

Mary Rose looked up and down the coast. There were a dozen to choose from. So, maybe not as formative as he'd first imagined.

"The little gray one." He pointed.

She nodded to show she found it, but her eyes betrayed no further interest or reaction than anything else they'd passed. "Poor house," she replied.

"Why would you say that?"

"It's very lonely, I think." She looked back to the sea and island ahead. "There's no life inside at all." She'd closed her eyes to the sun, smiled. "You're almost there."

Simon turned ahead to the approaching island, Mary Rose clearly content to let the gray-house discussion end, showing none of the angst he'd read—imagined?—the first time. Fine, maybe its only purpose had been to help him find Osterby and her druid pal. Maybe there *were* "magical forces" at work out here. Benevolent ones.

Simon laughed at the thought, and Mary Rose turned, curious.

"Nothing," he said, wiggling his eyebrows playfully, echoing her own habitual response whenever she did the same.

She shook her head, reached out to touch his arm.

"My brave Captain," she said.

"Ha, yeah, speaking of . . ." He shielded his eyes from the sun. "We better start focusing, cocaptain. Going to try and bring it in exactly where we did the first time. Don't want to give any locals the joy of us running into some damned rock and sinking to the bottom of the sea."

"I wouldn't worry about that." She smiled, gripping the top of the boat window. "The island wouldn't do that to you."

"Yeah? What makes you say that?"

"Because it likes to be visited." She laughed.

"Ahhh, yes. Of course."

"And"—she turned—"you're with me."

In the distance, below the hill, lay Cameron's "field of zombies"— the cairn field—they'd passed through earlier, "finding" among dozens the one stack they'd built together and, then again, the one Mary Rose claimed to have erected as a child. He couldn't tell one from the other but admitted they *were* familiar. As if they truly had sat waiting through the winter storms and most of a year, enchanted beacons for their eventual return. *Jesus.* If only such things were true, he thought. Still, it was impossible to pass through the field of rocks without imagining the rotted phantoms. Lying here on their blanket, gazing over the paperback page he'd read three times to no avail, he could almost himself see the bloodstained sands, the moldering dead walking.

Mary Rose sketched above him, once more on her old stump. Over her, above them both, the rowan tree drifted in full bloom. Rounded and lush with what looked like streamers of red flowers enfolded in the green.

Today's visit was, for Mary Rose, already proving far more relaxed than their first. His bride wasn't bouncing from one memory/location to the next. She was moving across the island without schedule—loose, sated—as if she had all the time in the world. As if she'd never left, would never leave. Simon hoped it was simply because there wasn't someone waiting offshore for them, giving a two-hour deadline, that they *were* on their own timetable. But there was something else: she radiated a genuine joy and serenity he'd only fancied at the Rodin museum.

Which, truth be told, was fucking annoying. *Was this pile of rocks two thousand miles from home really the only place that made this woman happy?* He found the notion ludicrous and himself growing bolder each minute they stayed.

Simon lowered his book.

"Do you have only *good* memories here?" he asked.

She tilted her head. "What do you mean?"

He breathed deeply. Unsure how dangerous his next questions could prove, yet also unable to spend the *next* twenty years completely ignoring what had happened to her here, living like her parents, pretending it had never occurred. "There are people in town who are afraid of this place."

"That's ridiculous." She shook her head, smiled.

"Yes. I thought so, too. But . . . So, you never got scared here? I mean, when your dad was fishing, or whatever, and you were here. Alone? Drawing? Exploring the island? A little kid. You never saw anything that scared you?"

"Here?" She laughed at the idea. "Hardly, never once."

He forced his own smile. "The warrior princess."

She winked back. "Fierce."

"Did . . ." He paused, yes, but had to keep going. Pushing her. "Did you ever get lost here?" Running out of subtle now, the next question would have to openly address the thirty-three days, her disappearance.

She thought. "Not that I recall."

The lifelong dilemma in one reply. He steeled himself against the next ten minutes. But he hadn't come all this way to let some ancient event haunt the rest of their lives. "Come here," he said, and waved her to join him on the blanket.

Mary Rose closed her sketchbook and lay it beside the old stump, then climbed down to his side. "What?"

"I love you," he said, taking one hand.

With the other, she reached up to flatten the tuft of hair on his head. "My beautiful man . . ." She gazed into his eyes.

"I think we should talk about something," he said. "I'd like to, anyway."

She frowned, puzzled. "And so serious."

He forced a chuckle, hoping to seem more at ease. "You know I'll never do anything to hurt you, right?"

"Not *my* husband." She squeezed his hand.

"I think we should talk about the last time you came to the island. When you were a little girl, I mean. Twenty years ago."

She sat back on her legs, her face cheerful in the sunlight. "Okay," she agreed.

"What *do* you remember? About the last day you came here with your father."

She thought, staring out past him. "Do you hear that?"

He heard only wind, surf. Rarely sidetracked in court, no such attempts would fly here. "Nope," he closed that diversion. "What *do* you remember?"

"I'm sure it was like any other day."

Simon shifted so that she'd look only at him.

"What?" she asked, a hint of irritation in her voice.

"I don't think it was," he said. "Mary Rose, it wasn't like any other day here. Something happened. Something happened to you."

She shook her head. "I don't . . ."

"Mary Rose?"

"We should go for a walk," she said, standing. "In the woods."

"Not today." He remained on the blanket. "We need to get out of here long before sunset. And we need to finish this talk."

"Talk in the woods. I've never shown them to you. I think . . ." She stared off again, pursuing some thought. "I remember . . . Something about the woods." She looked directly at him. "Come on." She'd already started down the hill.

"Mary Rose, wait. . . ." He dragged himself up. She was already twenty yards away. "We need to . . . it's too late today. What about our stuff?" So much for avoiding diversions.

He followed after her and caught her halfway down the hill.

"Right down here," she explained, pointing.

"I see it." A thick grove of birch and rowan waited ahead. Maybe an acre of dense woodland. He checked his watch. Another two hours until sunset. They had some time. "You'd come here as a little girl."

She nodded, then turned, grinning. "See? There it is again."

"The call of the island?" he asked, but there was no humor in the question.

She closed her eyes for several steps and then led him down and across the short field to the edge of the wood.

Mary Rose took his hand. "Trust us," she said.

He thought he'd misheard.

It was another few minutes before Simon also heard the music. Barely, at first. Only a soft indefinable sound carried somewhere deep within the enduring rustle of cool summer wind in the surrounding trees. Fading in and out. Obviously imagined. A trick of sound. Then, more distinct. Deliberate. More melodious.

"That *is* music," he agreed, still doubting enough. The island was deserted. There'd been no other boats. "Right? I thought you were kidding."

Mary Rose continued without remark.

They followed a slender and loose trail, overgrown with scrub, the trees stretching overhead in a heavy canopy that allowed the sun to split through only in well-defined fixed beams, and the sunlight somehow made the copse seem darker, casting blacker shadows than what should be. The musical drone had grown stronger, more real, with each step.

Twice, he'd turned. Convinced they were being followed. They weren't alone anymore. That someone had stepped onto the path no more than twenty yards behind them, and then jumped back again into the shadows each time he'd turned. The unique prickle of being watched coupled every step they took. "You know where we're going?" he asked, striding through a wide shard of light.

"I want to show you something," Mary Rose said. Her voice startled him and he took a deep breath to bring his racing imagination back to real life.

"Something you saw as a girl?"

She only nodded.

"Did you ever—"

Movement at the corner of his eye passed between several trees at their far right. Shadows, maybe, in the shifting sunlight. Or someone running. He'd automatically reached out a hand to stay Mary Rose.

"What's wrong?" she asked, turning.

He held up his other hand for quiet. "Wait . . ." he whispered, listening, and also squinting ahead. The music had become unmistakable words. Chanting, even. And not in English, for sure. Several voices intoning as one relentless drone of those concealed within the innumerable trunks and the thick boughs overhead. It was a sound that somehow evoked the pounding of animal-skin drums and dark primordial shapes swaying in the moonlight before open fire—he could even smell it—and antlered demigods, or maybe just Brodie, "The Druid," painting bull blood on some virgin's bare ass.

What a load of shit.

But there was definite movement between those trees. Not another swaying birch, but *someone*. If it was such a "load of shit," why was he holding his breath? Why did it feel as if his whole body were trembling?

"We should go," he decided. He had even searched the ground for a fallen limb as some pathetic sort of weapon.

Mary Rose looked at him oddly, puzzled.

He tugged her backward. "Come on. We can't—"

A terrible scream filled the woods.

A woman, or some animal, maybe, the shriek of something having its throat slit over an ancient stone altar. The horrific echo drifted away between the trees slowly and deliberately.

Simon was frozen, mostly wanting to pull Mary Rose to safety, but knowing someone was—

Mary Rose had made the decision for them both, jerking her hand free and sprinting ahead.

His mind exploded with panic, and anger. "*Mary*," his voice hissed in warning, but it was a voice for dogs broken free from their leash or unruly children in public places safe from spankings: a voice with no real control. She'd gone straight at the sound, and he dashed after her.

Between the trees ahead, straight beyond Mary Rose, he glimpsed tall distorted figures coming directly toward her. And then the unmistakable shine of bare flesh—sinewy, powerful, bronzed and glistening in sweat, a flash of plump pale breasts—the skin and surrounding trees spattered in vibrant dripping blood.

He could hear two voices, their words clear now.

Their dark incantation.

". . . a snare without escape, set for evil, a net whence none can issue forth . . ."

He leaned forward to grab a random stick from the ground.

"Evil spirit, or evil fiend, hag-demon, ghoul, phantom, or night-wraith . . . or evil plague or unclean disease . . . That which may do harm . . ."

Snapped and turned it in his hand, finding the sharpest point. He'd braced himself to stab and stab and stab . . .

"Which hath broken the Barrier, let not the Barrier of the Gods . . ."

Mary Rose had stopped, turned, hands to her mouth. But hiding a smile? It made no sense. Her eyes were wide with joy.

"Its Throat May They Cut. Its Face May They Smite. Its—"

"Holy shit!" a deep voice yelled, followed by laughter and more cursing.

Simon had caught Mary Rose and finally overlooked the same clearing. Five people—teens, at most twenty—stood frozen in various poses before them. Both guys were bare chested, one of the girls still pulling up her beach towel around her own topless form. Simon got another flash of bikini bottoms and a long thin thigh. The other two were also girls, eyes wide in panic. The sweet pong of marijuana hovered over the whole clearing, the "fire" he'd smelled. Simon spotted beer cans, a couple of book bags, beach towels, and iPhones. There was no blood, no daggers, no primordial demigods. He'd seen only clusters of rowan flowers and five kids getting high.

"Who screamed?" he demanded, using a voice his father would have once used. He laid a comforting hand against Mary Rose's back.

All the teens turned to one girl, whose wide eyes grew despondent. "I was . . . I'm sorry." Already welling with tears. "I was . . . just joking."

Simon shook his head. "Everyone's okay?"

The kids all nodded. "Hey, man," one of the boys said. "Sorry to freak you guys out. We were . . ." His voice trailed off, then started up again to match his abashed grin. "You know."

"Yeah," Simon said. "I know."

"You guys American, yeah?"

Simon ignored the question and studied their stuff again. "How'd you all get here? I didn't see your boat."

The other boy pointed away from where Simon and Mary Rose had entered the woods. "The cove over by the lake," he explained. Simon had seen the lake only from afar—*they dragged the lake for her*—but didn't know the cove the kid spoke of. Obviously an easy place to store a boat, grab a little girl, and vanish again.

"You were calling them," Mary Rose said.

The teens exchanged quick looks.

Simon whispered to her: "Calling who?"

One of the girls held up a sheet of paper. "My aunt gave me these."

"It's almost solstice," one of the boys said, as if that explained everything. "You know . . ."

"What?" Simon snipped. "Like magic stuff."

The boy shrugged. "Yeah. You say the words the hour before sunset? Light a fire. Yeah, all that stuff."

"Do any of you truly believe?" Mary Rose asked.

Again, the group exchanged looks in the telepathic speak of all teenagers. "Aye," one girl said, and the others nodded in agreement.

"And you're afraid," Mary Rose said.

The girl lowered her head.

"Don't be," Mary Rose said.

"Do you know how to do it?" another girl asked.

Mary Rose only smiled.

"Can you show us?"

Simon held out a hand. "It's late. We'd better get going. Sorry to scare you guys."

"No, man, that's totally on us. *We're* sorry."

The girl held out the sheet of paper for Mary Rose to take.

"Inviting me in to help?" Mary Rose had crossed her arms.

"Yeah, sure," the first boy answered. "We don't know what we're doing."

Mary Rose stepped into the clearing, and Simon followed, tossing aside the stick he'd been holding. For the first time, he noticed that several oblong upright boulders encircled the entire opening. "This is what I wanted to show you, anyway," Mary Rose said, looking back to him. She took the sheet of paper and studied the words.

"Are you, like . . . a Wiccan?" The one girl asked.

Mary Rose shook her head. "Not at all. I'm not sure . . ." She thought. "I used to come here."

One of the boys cautiously offered Simon the half-burnt joint he'd been cupping in his hand. Simon shook his head, and the kid licked his fingers to stub it out. "Sorry, man," he apologized again.

"Not a problem." And there wasn't. Simon had certainly spent enough of his teens doing shots and partaking in the occasional hit to not worry about these kids having a good time on summer break. "You guys okay out here?"

The guy smiled. "Yeah, sure." He leaned closer. "You mean all that weird stuff. Ghosts and stuff?" He laughed. "We were just 'concentrating the magic circle.'"

"*Consecrating*," his friend corrected, and they both snickered again. "Look, the girls sprinkled salt between the rocks."

Simon pretended to look but turned more to watch Mary Rose and the girls. They were, all four, laughing and whispering quietly. Even, especially, the freckled one who'd first looked afraid. Mary Rose was lifting her hands in the air, making her twirls while the others giggled.

"That your wife?" the kid asked, clearly impressed.

"That's what they tell me." Simon couldn't believe how easily she'd fallen in with the girls, already almost one of them. Like long-lost sisters. He grinned. No wonder men got so nervous whenever women gathered together alone.

"We really should go," he declared loudly, checking his watch. Damn, they'd now be leaving at dusk at best. He'd be coming back into Mhoire's Point in the near dark. He'd completely lost track of the time. "You guys, too. It'll be dark in less than an hour."

"We're staying all night," the second boy said.

"On the island?" For some reason, Simon found the idea loathsome. Maybe because he suspected Mary Rose would stay with them if they offered. "It'll get cold tonight. You guys should—"

"Got blankets and the fire." The first teen smirked. "And the girls."

"Plus, we're used to it." The kid with the sideburns tried a wink.

Simon smiled politely, started backing from the clearing. "Mary Rose . . ."

She waved, whispered something else to the three girls, and then jogged across the clearing to join him. "Be good, guys!" Simon called out to all five of them. "Keep safe."

The five teens waved and nodded back.

"They okay?" he asked Mary Rose.

She smiled. "Should be."

"What, exactly, did you tell them?"

"Oh, I don't know. Just to have fun. Not to be so serious. To dance and sing and love."

"Great." Simon chuckled. "The guys will appreciate that."

She shrugged.

"Who are they 'calling' now?"

"Spirits of the island. The Fae. That kind of thing."

"Do you believe in that stuff?"

"What did you think of the standing stones?"

"The circle of rocks? And how do you know that?"

She looked off. "I don't know. I must have heard it somewhere before."

"It's fucking absurd your father used to let you wander alone back here. I'm thirty-four and, honestly, half-scared to death." He stole a look. "What if you'd run into somebody?"

"Those five were harmless."

"Yeah, *they* were. You ever run into someone who wasn't?"

He expected a flash of fear, sadness, or even anxiety to cross her features, but Mary Rose simply threw up her hands. "Simon!" she said, exasperated. "Will you stop with the cross-examination! I don't recall anything that happened here—I know something did. I do. I'm not an idiot. But my mind has lost it—*I* have lost it. I'd appreciate it, if you love me, if you'd lose it, too." She reached out for him, and he let her take his hands in hers, drawing him close. "Isn't it enough that you are here, and I am here, and we're happy? Isn't that all that matters, husband?"

Her face, in that moment, was so transcendent with happiness that Simon went perfectly still. Her eyes were enormous, and their gaze so piercing, so intent that she'd never felt more real to him. The lawyer in him gave way to the man, and the man *was* in love with this woman. She was his wife; she was happy. Something terrible had happened to her but—she was not where he'd find his answers. She was only someone he could protect.

"Deal," he said, and her smile lit up her entire face, reaching even to those beautiful, fathomless eyes, and in that moment, he felt that it all would be all right, eventually. Every last part.

"Thank you," she whispered, stepping up on her toes to brush his lips lightly. Simon's heart was racing now, only he couldn't say why.

She turned and led him onward.

They made it out of the woods, more quickly than they'd entered. So much so that Simon would have sworn they'd taken a shortcut of some kind. With the whole sun resting on the farthest horizon, they jogged up to the top of the hill and collected their things. Mary Rose was laughing, having fun, enjoying the new challenge of making it back to the boat in time. Simon, now that the woods were behind him, not as much. The idea of returning to Mhoire's Point in the dark wasn't a pleasant one, especially in an unfamiliar boat on unfamiliar waters.

They waded back to the boat, the tide higher than the first time they'd come out. While Mary Rose toweled off and sorted through their tumbled provisions, Simon got the boat going and turned out of the shallow inlet as quickly as possible. The sun was behind the island, only its glow in the sky providing light.

Minutes later, the island was a retreating silhouette in the background, looking hardly bigger than a sporting boat itself. Simon turned back to watch it plunge into the darkening ocean. He was convinced he'd spotted a single spark on the island, a small fire finally blazing to life somewhere deep in the woods.

The kids.

He smiled, finally feeling better. If they were willing to chance it overnight on the island, how bad could it be?

"Simon!" Mary Rose's laughing call drew his attention away, and he fixed his gaze on her as she leaned over the edge of her boat, catching the spray in her outstretched hand. As the setting sun edged her figure she once again looked almost incandescent against the murky water, the blue fairy come to life.

When he looked back to the island again, there were now *several* small lights glowing in the shadows, scattered across the whole island, and even as he watched, another flared to life on the island's farthest edge.

A trick of the sunset and shifting water, he decided.

Like all the things Cameron had once seen.

There was no other explanation.

19

The light was terrible for drawing.

A low fog crept up from the bay the way it sometimes did on damp Scottish mornings, casting a strange glow over everything, most of it caught in a muddy haze, with some items inexplicably highlighted in sharp relief: the shovel by the corner of the cottage, the thatch of rhododendrons by the walk down to the shore. From her vantage point, on a clear day Mary Rose could almost see all the way to the island.

This morning, she could barely glimpse the water's edge, its dull gray surf creeping up and receding again with a restless petulance. Still, *nothing* could cast a pall over her day.

For the first time in longer than she could remember, she'd fallen asleep even before Simon, the two of them wrapped in each other's arms like an infinity loop, no clear demarcation of where one ended and the other began. They woke up with equal laziness, murmuring and shifting beneath the covers, lost in a world unto themselves. It was like everything around them was limned in magic, somehow more special because they were the ones seeing, touching, tasting it.

They'd breakfasted like newlyweds in love—they *were* newlyweds in love—laughing and talking about nothing, staring into each other's eyes as they held hands over plates of ignored scones and fruit, coffee growing cold. Every moment seemed more perfect than the last, and when Simon had gone into town for a pint and to explore alone, she'd almost defiantly brought her easel and pastel pencils to the wide patio behind the cottage.

The day simply had to be wonderful, she decided. She was far too happy for anything less.

She lifted one pencil, then another, examining the points. Then she picked up her sharpener, allowing herself to become mesmerized by the tiny spiraling flakes of wood as they curled off the blade, each fragile shard falling toward the worn gray and blue and cinnamon-pink flagstones before skating off in an errant puff of wind. A bird cried far out to sea, and she shifted her gaze up, as if she could pierce that looming bank of fog, see all the way to the island.

Those charming, laughing girls on the island. So soft and young, alive. And so dreadfully pliant. So frightened, too, beneath all their brash excitement. Mary Rose frowned, a thread of unease skating through her despite her resolution for nothing but happiness to color her thoughts. This nagging thought: The teens they'd met on the island. If they'd decided to stay there the whole night. If they'd listened to her advice. If they'd attracted the right . . .

"Energy."

She'd said the word aloud. Others came as easily to mind, but they weren't words she ever wanted to use. Not in all these years. "Energy" was a term others would nod at in total agreement and understanding. "Energy" sounded sane. Believable. Safe.

She looked over the sea, veiled almost entirely now in fog, down toward where they might be even now. For not the first time, she pondered if she should—*wished* she could—have stayed with them. To keep them safe, maybe. But mostly out of jealousy, for all they might see and hear and feel. Silly thought.

She wondered if Simon would take her out again. Later today, even. When the fog burned off in the midday sun. Or tomorrow. Tomorrow, they had no specific plans. Dare she ask? Would he take her again? Would he continue to do everything he could to make her happy? For, if so—

The fog had expanded to shroud most of the shoreline and something was moving within it. A familiar shape. Strolling a good fifty yards away down along the water's edge.

Mary Rose found she'd stood and backed her way to the cottage door. Her hand fumbled sluggishly for the door's handle. The figure had stopped, appearing to stare across the ghosted shoreline between them. In the mist, its posture appeared loose, slouched.

Who . . . ?

A breath later, Mary Rose had reentered the house. Turning back, she could see the small figure was closer now, farther from the water. Behind it, deeper in the mist, loomed another hulking form.

Mary Rose found enough strength to shut the door. Two, lock it. Three, her hands pressed against it, trembling. Cold. To her panicked eyes her fingers were strained, ashen, rutted with marbled veins like the withered fingers of a rotten corpse. Beneath those fingers, the door trembled.

> *The worms crawl in, the worms crawl out,*
> *They invite their friends and their friends, too*

She retreated to the far wall opposite the door and crouched on the floor as the whole room filled with the imagined—what else could it be if not imagined—rumble of the surf breaking against the walls of their cottage. She covered her ears and stared wide-eyed at the front windows, half expecting to find sea water splashing against the glass.

There was no water, but the mist had continued its spread from the shore, enveloping the front porch and anything that might still exist beyond.

Within the fog, she could see the smaller shadow had continued to drift toward her, had walked all the way up to the cottage, in fact. Pressed its small face and hands against the glass.

Why here? Not here. She shouldn't be here . . .

Mary Rose dropped her head, closed her eyes.

> *They all come down to chew on you*
> *and this is what it is to die*
> *and this is what it is to die*
> *and this is what it is to die . . .*

In the welcoming blackness, a surging wind rattled both front windowpanes. Or was that the sound of tiny fingers slapping at the glass, its patter dancing along her skin like a frigid memory.

A memory of what she sometimes called "energy."

20

"Who are you, now?"

"Simon Blake." He gave his warmest grin, the one a moment ago employed on the guy's wife. "I was hoping to—"

"Not interested, Yank." The retired constable shook his head, reached up to shut his front door.

"Please." Simon lay a hand against the door. "If you could just give me ten minutes. I . . ."

Fraser first glanced up at Simon's hand, then met his eyes.

Simon withdrew his hand slowly. "Sorry." He chuckled, embarrassed. "It's obviously really important I talk with you."

"About the Morland case? Got nothing to say."

Simon rocked back. He'd said nothing specific to the wife.

"The PI from London," the man explained, then paused to think. "Ah, 'Tull.' He's the last to ask me about an old case, only one in years, as a matter of fact. Said it was for some American fellow. You show up here eight months later." He lowered his head to look at Simon through thick gray eyebrows. "I'm retired, lad. Not stupid."

Simon smiled again. "Understood, sir."

"You writing a book or something?"

"I'm the girl's husband." Simon held up the back of his newly ringed hand.

"Ahhh. Well, may you both be blessed with long life and peace." He started shutting the door again. "Girl came home, case closed. Nothing else to talk about."

"*Five* minutes," Simon hounded, cutting his asking time in half. "I'm sorry to seem so anxious, but to track you down, travel all the way out here, it must be pretty important, right?"

The man's return look implied: *Only to you.*

"Look, Mr. Fraser . . ." Simon's voice had taken on an unexpected, and new, pleading sound. "She seems to have no idea what happened to her. She's internalized the trauma, whatever it was, for twenty years. Fights depression, has nightmares." He held out his hands in surrender. "I'm just trying to figure out what the hell it is we're dealing with here, so we can . . ."

"Fix it."

"Yeah, I guess something like that."

"Ah, to be a young fool again."

"Well . . ." Simon shrugged. "Guilty as charged."

Fraser scratched his chin, stared awhile longer, the weathered lines of his face seeming to deepen into ruts. "You want coffee?" he asked gruffly.

"Yes, sir." Simon didn't in the slightest, but the man could have offered cat piss. He'd gotten his minutes. "Thank you."

Fraser waved Simon into his house and started down the hallway, calling out to his wife. Simon followed mildly. "Living room on the left," Fraser's retreating back called out. "Be there in a minute." In the kitchen behind, Simon caught Mrs. Fraser trying to sneak another curious look.

Simon entered the dim room, every square inch seemingly covered in framed photos, knickknacks, hand-knit afghans, newspapers, and stacks of paperback romance novels. Not hoarders by any stretch; the house was tidy and inviting, but cluttered. A lifetime of keepsakes. He stood, waiting, glancing at the photos. Tried imagining what his living room would look like in another thirty or forty years, the lifetime he and Mary Rose would/could have on display.

Would their walls include pictures of children? Grandchildren? Vacation homes on the Scottish coast? Or would they be filled with photos of him and Mary Rose at gala openings, on the steps of the justice building. Recognition awards for his community service. Shaking the hands of presidents. No children, but plenty of scuba shots and suntanned faces. So many different directions they could go, if they only got the chance.

Simon frowned. Where had that thought come from?

Fraser came in and tossed on another light. "Sit," he said, and indicated a specific chair. He then dropped a thin folder, bound with string, onto the table between them. "Be right back with that coffee."

Simon sat as asked and stared across at the folder like Fraser had brought something alive into the room. Something alive *and* dangerous. Wondering what, if anything, waited inside. He reached a hand out to touch the string holding it all shut. So much more real than any email report.

Fraser returned with coffee. "Here you go."

"Thank you, sir."

"So." Fraser took a seat on the couch on the other side of the table. "You flew three thousand miles to talk with me for ten minutes?"

"Honeymoon."

Fraser sipped his coffee. "Here in Mhoire's Point?"

"Right."

"Interesting. Not *that* concerned about 'depression' and 'nightmares,' then?"

"She has nightmares back home also. In fact, the only place she—"

Fraser lifted his head, interested.

"Only place she seems to be at peace is on that damned island."

"'The Little Island That Likes to Be Visited.'"

Simon had shuddered as he said it. "Yes, sir."

"You've been out there?"

"A couple times now, yes."

Fraser shook his head. "What'd you think?"

"I don't know, it was an island. I suppose there's something a little, what, 'creepy,' about the place, but you hear enough stories . . ."

"My nana swore 'Auld Hornie' himself sometimes lived out there."

"The devil? You believe that?"

"Swore she'd known certain girls in town to bring their newborns out there. Fisherman from Beckfoot killed his entire crew in 1933. Claimed they were all possessed by evil spirits. Half a dozen suicides over the last fifty years I know of out there. Pair of kids hanged themselves together in the 1950s, and we cut the whole damn tree down. There've been drownings. Couple drug overdoses, too. If that ain't the devil, I don't know what is."

"What do you think happened when—"

Fraser held up a hand to cut him off. "I want you to think about what you're really doing here. Digging around in business that happened twenty years before she knew you were alive."

"We've been together almost three years now."

"Oh, aye." Fraser widened his eyes. "The one in there . . ." He pointed out toward the kitchen. "We've been together almost *fifty*. Still madly in love, we are. Wanna know the secret to our marital bliss?"

"Sure."

"We've never once had a serious conversation."

Simon grinned as he was expected to, shook his head.

"And"—he held up a lecturing finger—"we never felt the need to go rooting in each other's baggage. Couples collect an awful lot in seventy years, son, believe me. From before you met and long, long after. Your Mary Rose *ask* you to do this for her?" He waited. "Didn't think so. So, it's prying, plain and simple." He shook his head. "There was something about my lass's high school math teacher, I recall. Quite the town scandal in 1952." He wiped his hands dramatically.

Irritation flared through Simon, sharp and full. "Excuse me, Mr. Fraser, but when's the last time your wife woke up screaming? Last time she woke up choking? From a dream. A memory."

Another shrug. "Get a shrink. Maybe best to leave the past where it belongs, don't you think?"

Simon watched him closely. "That's what her parents seem to think."

"Sure." Fraser looked away, affecting disinterest. *Affecting* it—and not well. He knew something. Something he wanted to share.

"Okay, that's what I thought. So, how 'bout we cut all the 'you don't really want to do this' stuff, and you can get on with telling me whatever it is you brought me in here for." Simon leaned back, waiting. "I'm 'young,' Mr. Fraser. Not stupid."

Fraser watched back at first, then firmly pushed the folder over to Simon.

"I assume," Simon began, unwrapping, "you don't believe it was 'Auld Hornie' or pixies."

Fraser snorted. "Investigation focused almost entirely on local suspects. Lots of transient fishing labor in town that summer, and we worked a short list of known pedophiles, along with anyone with a history of sexual assault or solicitation."

"But you wanted to look elsewhere. The British?"

"They've come up every summer since long before I was a boy. Mostly keep to themselves."

"'Mostly?'"

"The younger crowd has always gotten together. Drugs, sex. Magic business."

"What do you think about that? The magic stuff?"

"Horseshit, mostly. I got no stitch with druidism and the like, but some of it's darker, to be sure. Different problem altogether."

"You think any of that had something to do with Mary Rose? Her disappearance, I mean."

"Well, she hadn't drowned. There was no evidence of sexual assault, dehydration, hypothermia. She was *somewhere* safe for thirty-three days. I always had the feeling someone, or several someones, had tucked her aside for a ceremony, maybe."

"But then, what, they lost their nerve and brought her back."

"Or"—the old constable sighed deeply—"completed it and returned her."

Simon started down that terrible path, but he clamped down on it as quickly. He nudged the file. "I see David Morland's name in here a lot. The brother. What's the story there? I met him once. Seemed a nice enough fellow."

"David Morland was always trouble." Fraser shook his head. "I knew all of 'em from when they was snot-nosed kids. David was the chief cock around here for three or four summers—there's always one—and I can't say I was sorry to see this one go."

"Why's that?"

"Pulled in a bigger circle than usual. Tourists *and* local kids. He was very charismatic. Clever, rich, moody, and looked like that fella in the Doors. Morrison something. Poor lasses never stood a chance.

Must have been a dozen or more of them every damned night getting into one kind of mischief or another. Sometimes the mischief was criminal. Sometimes dangerous. Lot of fines those summers, but those types never seem to care about that."

"They go out to the island?"

"All the damn time. Got to the point, we stopped chasing them off. Wasn't worth the trouble. Of course, if any of them had gotten hurt out there, there'd have been hell to pay."

Simon flipped to the next arrest sheet. Read the name at top.

Francine Hughes

Someone had written the note "mother" in pencil beside the name. He looked up from the sheet, incredulous.

"Mrs. *Morland*?"

"Yes." Fraser nodded. "She was seventeen. The records were sealed. Opened only on account of the incident with Mary Rose."

Simon read the charges, trying not to gape. "'Indecency'? 'Disorderly conduct.' 'Malicious mischief.' The same charges David Morland was arrested for."

"Well, whattya know."

"Were those two, like, an item?"

"David Morland would've flanged a snake if it'd lay still long enough." Fraser drank his coffee. "And don't let her pearls and dour expression fool you. Francine Hughes spent her summers here for twenty years before she got respectably married, and ran around with all the rest of them."

"And you believe they had something . . . something to do with Mary Rose's disappearance?" Simon frowned. "Francine must have been at least thirty by then. And I was told she didn't even come up here anymore."

"David Morland was still here then, on and off. And there were always new ones coming. Tourists and local kids to introduce to salt circles and totems and written spells and the like."

Simon thought of the five kids he'd met on the island the night before. Hadn't they done something with salt? Reading words written by an older aunt. How many more decades, centuries would these same traditions trickle down, he wondered. Realizing the island would likely still be welcoming its "visitors" a thousand years after his own death sent a strange chill up Simon's back.

"Did you ever bring David Morland in for questioning?"

"He was living in Munich then. Had a rock-solid alibi for the day of her disappearance. Came and helped with all the other locals, doing everything he could. Reputation was the only thing he was guilty of. There was, officially, nothing to ask him. And after she was brought back, didn't matter. She was back. Case was closed for good a couple days after her return. There were a hundred other troubles to get to."

"I see you interviewed James?"

"Naturally. The father became a suspect easily enough. That said, *I'd* never suspected him. The man was heartbroken. And as baffled as the rest of us. Genuinely so, I believed."

"And Francine?"

A careful pause. "Never interviewed her myself. The Yard done that. She stayed in Alderley Edge throughout. Was mostly unresponsive. Medicated, was the insinuation. In shock, perhaps. If I'd been in charge of the investigation . . ."

"Yes?"

"I don't know." Fraser grimaced, as if to reject the words as soon as they were spoken. "Thought it odd she never came up during the search is all."

"My understanding is James asked her not to. Thought it best to keep her out of the chaos."

"Yeah, well . . . that 'chaos' was her little girl."

Simon riffled through the paperwork. "I don't see . . ." A picture fell free of its clip, the photo transfixing him. Mary Rose. Couldn't have been more than six years old, eyes bright, smile wide and open, so pretty, so *alive*. She had no idea what was to befall her. He cleared his throat. "There are . . . no notes for any interviews with Mary Rose." The photograph gazed back up at him, innocent and unaware, and Simon gently closed the folder. "Did anyone question her?"

"Of course. Several times, and I conducted the initial interview as a matter of fact. No more than an hour after she turned up again. She seemed completely unharmed."

"Why no notes?"

"As you said, she claims not to remember a thing. Did then, too. Didn't seem to realize she'd been gone at all."

"Did you believe her?"

Fraser nodded.

Simon considered that. "Do you recall her demeanor? Behavior?"

"She seemed . . . joyful. Peaceful. Content, I guess you'd say. Like a little girl watching a passing parade or the circus, a bag of candy in one hand. The kind of child you want to pick up and hug, you know. Because of how good they are, how blissful. Despite, or maybe because of, what the world's done to 'em." Fraser did look away at that, giving himself over to the memory.

Simon couldn't blame him. It was the same essence that had always drawn him to Mary Rose also. He picked up the folder and stood. "I'll get copies made in town and get this right back to—"

Fraser held out both hands, the same gesture he'd used to dismiss some love affair his wife may have had as a teenager more than fifty years before. "Keep it," he said.

Simon grunted, puzzled.

"She's yours now," Fraser told him. "You take care of her. I'm done."

A hundred questions raced through Simon's mind. *"Done"?* This guy hadn't "done" a damn thing for Mary Rose in twenty years. Certainly hadn't even solved the case when it *was* his responsibility. What right did he have to claim he'd *ever* taken care of her?

As if reading his thoughts, Fraser spoke again. "This whole matter has unnerved me for twenty years. I did everything I could to help find that little girl, to protect her from this world. And even after she'd come back, I continued to feel that need. Almost like an itch. A punishment, I suppose, guilt maybe, for not being able to solve the case. Not being able to protect Mary Rose."

It was the same "itch" that had first drawn Simon to Mary Rose. More than her beauty and talent, he recognized. It had been that need to take care of her, to—what had Fraser said?—to "protect her from this world."

"I think you came to my door at the right time, son," Fraser continued. "I needed this. Badly, I realize only now. But now it's your turn to solve this. Or let it go. But, don't get stuck, like I did, somewhere in the middle. That's never a good place to be."

"How did you 'need' this? I don't understand."

Fraser's smile was thin, the lines of his face seeming etched more deeply. Too deep, really, for a long-retired constable of a sleepy little backwater town. He asked quietly, "You think your new wife's the only one to have nightmares, Mr. Blake?"

The drive back to Mhoire's Point went quickly, Simon turning everything he'd learned from Fraser over in his mind—and all the questions he still had as well. What he knew: the constable hadn't done shit when Mary Rose had gone missing, barely managing the basics of his job. He'd done less after she was returned. No in-depth interviews, no follow-up. Yet the man felt like he was some kind of hero in all this— what was that about? That he'd somehow had a hand in saving Mary Rose. He also had a chip on his shoulder about the English who came up from the south. Typical territorial bullshit, but was it enough for the constable to turn a blind eye to a suspect right under his nose? Probably.

Also, the information about Francine was a surprise. Arrest records from her teen years, rumors of her being some kind of party girl connected more to David one summer than the little brother and future husband—yet now was all creepy crosses, strands of pearls, and tight lips. Hell of a jump. He shook his head, tapping the steering wheel absently. Probably not the first woman to turn over a new leaf when she got married. And James Morland would've sucked the life out of anyone.

On to what he didn't know: the why of any of this. *Why* hadn't they done more to pin down who'd taken Mary Rose? *Why* had they let the investigation die so quickly—a kidnapping had occurred, for Chrissake. Whoever'd done it had remained at large, could easily have struck again. Then there was the strange nightmare comment, the constable's strange demeanor. Why'd the old man feel so attached to Mary Rose—hell, why had any of the men she'd encountered? Simon grimaced. *Why do I?*

He pulled up to the cottage, his attention immediately caught by a large sheet of cream-colored paper stuck in one of the flowering bushes to the right of the front door. Had to be one of Mary Rose's wayward sketch pad sheets, lifted away by an earlier sea breeze.

Simon frowned as he exited the vehicle. The house had a peculiar abandoned look to it, and rather than entering immediately, he angled around the cottage, scanning the beach and backyard. There, the bushes fluttered in the steady breeze coming up from the ocean, the sky clear and the sun bright and full, beating down on the wreckage strewn across the cobblestoned patio.

"Mary Rose," Simon called out, starting forward.

Her easel lay collapsed on the cold stone, pages flung everywhere, her pencils scattered in a wide arc. Before his brain could fully process what he was seeing, he'd already dashed up to the back door, turning the doorknob, and—it was locked.

"Merz!" he shouted, and then rattled the knob once, twice, before fumbling with the keys still clutched in his hand. It was the smallest key on the ring, he remembered, the smallest!

A moment later he burst in through the back door.

The parlor was nearly empty.

Nearly, except for the form of his wife.

His beautiful wife . . .

Crumpled against the interior wall, rocking slightly.

Her eyes wide and glassy, arms wrapped round her knees.

Shit.

"Mary Rose?" His voice no longer urgent or panicked. Some sixth sense commandeered his emotions, cautioning him to go slow, go quietly, easing up to her with his hands out, his voice peaceful. "Baby, are you okay? Are you hurt?"

She stilled against the wall at his voice, her head turning toward him before her gaze followed. "Simon?" she whispered, the lone word plaintive, and his heart seized in his chest.

"That's right, honey." He dropped to one knee, and to his intense relief, she moved, too, holding her arms out to allow him to gather her close. "You okay?"

"Simon. Oh, Simon," she half whimpered, her face pressed against his shoulder.

"Shhh . . . ," he soothed, though his eyes were wide and staring, focused on the wall as his mind churned through all the possibilities. "Are you hurt, baby? Did something scare you?" No response, and he tried again, tightening his grasp on her the barest amount. "What happened?"

"Nothing happened," Mary Rose said quickly, too quickly, her voice shaking. Tension gripped her whole body. "Nothing. Everything is all right. Everything . . ."

Anger seethed through Simon. "Well, *something* clearly happened." Said more harshly than he'd intended. When Mary Rose didn't speak, he pulled away, trying to catch her eye.

She shook her head, staring beyond him toward the back door, the open water far beyond. "Maybe . . . maybe it's time to go home."

"Yes, and finally *talk* to someone." Simon nodded, trying to keep the anger, the fear, at bay. This was something, at least. Progress. "I know people who can recommend the best in Philly, someone who can finally help. We'll go together, if you want." He could sense her stiffening again, and he resisted the urge to shake her. "We have to talk to someone, honey," he said. "We can't keep doing this."

"No." Mary Rose shook her head. "My home here. In England." She straightened a little, her pale face streaked with tears, but she wasn't crying anymore, and her words were stronger. More determined. "You're right. We should . . . There's something I need to do. It's time."

Simon stared at her hard, his hands tightening on her shoulders while he coerced himself to smile reassuringly. Her gaze darted back to him, jumpy as a bird's, the relief in her face profound as he nodded to her.

A talk with Francine and James Morland sounded like a good idea.

"Okay," he said simply. "Let's finish this."

21

James Morland opened the door, clearly baffled to see them.

"Simon!" he said, his face still puzzled but finding a welcoming smile. "Thought you two were still on the continent. This is quite a surprise. We were just having lunch. Franny will be so delighted."

"As we're delighted to see you both," Simon replied with enough brusqueness that Morland caught it, and the Brit's gaze measured Mary Rose, as if making some determination about the state of her mental health.

Irritation cracked through Simon, even though he'd been doing the same thing himself the whole drive. She'd calmed considerably during the trip, but was too quiet, her manner more detached as they'd crossed back into England. As if whatever strange spirits that drove her along the shores of Mhoire's Point had lost their strength upon exiting Scotland.

And if that were the case, then this—all of it—was completely on him. Whatever had happened earlier today. Whatever had terrified her. It had been *his* idea to honeymoon in Scotland. To force Mhoire's Point and the damned island on her again. Because, *he* thought, it's what she'd most wanted. Because, *he* thought it would help. Had he driven five hours to give her parents a hard time when *he*, and he alone, was the one who fucked up everything?

"Come in! Come in," Morland said, turning back to him as Simon took Mary's hand.

Her fingers were slender, cold, and her touch grounded him, as always. He'd parked close to the door, vowing to himself they'd leave as quickly as they came if this went south. If he was honest, though, he looked forward to the altercation with the parents. To get everything out in the open, finally, deal with it straight on. It was obviously far past time.

Inside, the house was as before: hulking, stultified. Entombed. They followed Morland down the hall of portraits into the dining room. It was as if Simon were seeing the whole house for the first time, under the spreading lens of dysfunction and mendacity.

"Look who's here!" Morland sang out to his wife, who'd risen from her lunch to stand awkwardly at the end of the table, in her usual day dress and single strand of pearls. Her face scowled in disturbance. Her hair was curled tight to her head, her makeup subdued—everything about her subdued, Simon thought uncharitably. "You have to tell us everything," Morland continued. "Where are you in from?"

"Mhoire's Point," replied Simon evenly.

"Mhoire's Point?" Francine Morland winced. "Why, in the name of God, would you go back there?"

"Because it's our honeymoon, Mother," Mary Rose answered for them both, with a lightness Simon envied. He was about to boil over at Francine Morland's indignant irritation, but Mary Rose seemed wholly unconcerned. "It was Simon's gift to me."

"Really, Simon, I should have thought—" Francine pursed her lips and leaned against a wing-backed chair as if drawing strength from it. "Well, this is quite the betrayal."

"Now, now," Morland waded in. "Good time to visit Scotland. My family went every summer, you know . . ."

"Yes, I know," Simon said. He watched Morland, waiting for the flinch. "And Mary Rose has good memories there. Memories with you."

Morland chuckled, his gaze turning to Mary Rose but not really seeing her, Simon thought. Seeing someone else, instead. A young girl, drawing and laughing as he whiled away the days fishing in the surf. "They were, at that." Morland sighed.

Mary Rose, for her part, paid him no attention. Letting Simon's hand drop, she drifted to the window, touched the lace curtain, as if she needed to check on their car.

"Wonderful memories," Morland echoed himself.

"Wonderful? Are you even *listening* to yourself?" Francine's voice rose, thin and strained. Mary Rose, Simon noticed, didn't turn from the window. "How are we even *talking* about that terrible place? We had an understanding. An agreement."

That was the opening Simon needed, and he turned directly to Francine, his adrenaline spiking. "Because I only agreed to so much. We spoke less than a year ago, Francine, and I'm already tired of hiding her, what happened to her, in the shadows. I'm not going to spend another twenty years pretending nothing happened and tiptoeing around because it's uncomfortable for us to talk about. Mary Rose deserves more from us."

"This is absurd." Francine threw her hands up. "Now is not the time to—"

"I talked to the constable who worked the case. Fraser. Still lives in Mhoire's Point."

"Him," she sniffed, disgusted. "Never did a thing but get in the way of the real investigators. What's he know?"

"Well . . ." Simon fought to keep from striking a familiar pose he used in court, but Francine was making it hard. Everything out of her mouth seemed to damn her further. "He seemed to know an awful lot about James and David, and *you*, coming up every summer with your families to raise hell with the locals."

"Well, I'm not sure how much hell-raising we did," Morland said, but his chuckle had grown a touch more threadbare. "Simon. Franny, too. I believe you're right in saying now is not the time to discuss this."

"When *is* the time?" Simon countered. "Don't worry, James. At this point, it's got little yet to do with Mary Rose. I'm more interested in your lives *before* Mary Rose." Simon's question was low, direct, all the more impactful for the hysteria he didn't employ. "The people you associated with, all that occult shit in the woods. Your brother."

"What would David have to do with this?"

"This is unacceptable." Francine Morland visibly shook, her fingers nervously touching the tiny crucifix hung at her throat.

"It's time." Mary Rose's voice breathed out a startled gasp, and

Morland shot a glance at her, then back to Simon.

"That's what this constable told you?" Morland shook his head. "That has you all riled up? That was always all nonsense. Silly games, nothing more."

His words carried an indisputable ring of authenticity, but this was a man with a black mirror in his hallway, so Simon pressed his point. "What about the arrest records, then? David's, but also those of specific minors arrested with him. The constable has them all collected in a nice little folder." He turned to Francine, who froze, her hand now clasped around the cross. "Actually, as a matter of fact, I have them now."

"Who do you think you are?"

The accusation came so quickly, so stridently, that Simon was caught off guard. Francine strode forward, her eyes blazing, her hand no longer wrapped around the cross of Jesus but stretched before her, pointing at him in righteous fury.

"What right . . . what right do *you* have, rooting around in our private history, our past. Like we're the ones on trial? Don't think I don't know what you're doing, with all your fancy degrees and your fancy friends back in Philadelphia. Well, we're not in Philadelphia. We're in England and here, we are *grateful* for what the good Lord gave us—not condescending—and he gave us Mary Rose *back*. That terrible day she left us all those years ago isn't nearly as important as the day that she came back to us. It's a miracle that God saw fit to return her and it is not our place nor our privilege to question that miracle. It isn't! She is blessed and we are blessed to have her. Our lives before Mary Rose, or even now, are none of your damned business, Simon. How dare you come to our home casting horrible accusations and demanding anything."

Simon turned to Mary Rose—but she was gone. Vanished from the room in the midst of her mother's tirade. Simon grimaced. Smart girl. He would've escaped, too, if he could.

"Be satisfied she was able to put such terrible trials behind her. That's the most you deserve from us."

"Behind her?" He turned back at Francine again, pinning her with his glare. "Are you kidding me? She's racked up twenty *years* of problems, and they're only getting worse. Problems you have to know about." At their blank looks he advanced, forcing them to focus on him. "The professor—the man killed himself. Wrapped tape around his face until he suffocated."

"I don't have to listen to this," Francine Morland sneered, making to leave the room.

"But first, the boyfriend, yes? Evan something. Shot himself but lived. Institutionalized, disfigured."

"That was an accident," James Morland protested. "Not . . ."

"Then how about the shrink who lost his practice over her."

"That odious man." Francine stopped, blew out a breath of frustration, and it was all Simon could do not to strangle the woman.

"Hell, your own priest won't even look at her straight, and don't tell me that he's 'odious,' too. There's something not right here. Twenty years of issues, and how much of it is connected to the fact that you guys won't talk about what happened that day? There's gotta be someone you can bring in, someone to mediate this, because you all sure as hell haven't done a good job on your own."

Francine drew up stiffly. "Don't dare take that tone, Simon. This is a family matter."

"You're right," Simon shot back. "It is a family matter, and guess what, families talk. They talk, and they get everything out on the table, and they don't let it fester and rot in the dark where no one can see it, no one can acknowledge it, until the wound has grown so great there's nothing anyone can do to heal it. I don't care if you've decided that's how best to treat this issue, but Mary Rose is my *wife*. Mine. And I'm not about to let her suffer through this terrible silence of not knowing what happened to her or why. Do you understand? So this is how this is all going to work out. You're going to—"

"Look, here." Morland roused himself, turning on Simon. "Your concern for Mary Rose is all well and good, but it's certainly nothing we need to talk about tonight. We should—"

A hideous cracking noise sounded from the front hall, ripping across their argument. Simon was halfway to the hall before Morland turned and reached to grab at his arm. "Don't—"

"What *is* that?" Simon huffed.

"Careful!" Morland stepped into the hallway first, his attention drawn directly past the flowing staircase stretching up to the second floor and on to the imposing mirror at the head of the corridor. The source of the cracking sound was obvious now.

The enormous mirror's flat, black surface had been riven from the top to its center with an angry gash, a long fracture spidering out to fill the upper half of the glass. Only—there was nothing that had seemed to strike the mirror. The space before the antique was empty, save for a few shards of glass that lay on the rug, spit out like broken teeth, ragged and glistening in the dim light from the hall sconces.

Morland was beside him now, babbling, still pulling at Simon's arm. "They said, they said that could happen—any time, to expect it almost, that any time—nothing to worry about, nothing to—"

"What in the hell . . ." Simon's gaze lifted to the wall above the mirror. "Mary Rose."

With that he was off and up the stairs like a shot, taking them two at a time. He crested the stairs, and all the doors of the long guest wing stood open to him, welcoming, but there was really nowhere else Mary Rose would be, he knew. Nowhere else but the room directly above where the mirror hung, flat and dark and lifeless all these years.

All these years until now, when it cracked down its center, speaking for the first time.

But speaking of what?

Morland and Francine were on the stairs behind him, and Simon surged forward, bursting past the doorway of Mary Rose's former playroom.

He staggered back, wobbled. "Jesus!"

The room was almost exactly the way it had been when he'd seen it last. The eruption of crosses lining the walls, the kneeler at the far end of the room. Tonight, a childhood easel had been set up in one corner, papers stacked neatly beside it, drawing pencils carefully arranged.

But there was something else new on display in the room, new and terrible.

Mary Rose lay on her back, stretched out on the hardwood floor.

At her head, propped up against the wall, was a tombstone.

Simon recovered and moved into the room, rushing toward her.

He knew she was alive, knew this was some dark, macabre playacting, but when he dropped to his knees beside her and she drew in a startled breath, he still nearly burst into tears. Her face placid, eyes closed, hands folded over her chest. Humming a song of some kind.

"Oh my God—oh my God!" Francine's voice wailed from behind him, filling the whole room. Simon noticed where dark spatter from Mary Rose's late-night paintings months before still speckled Francine's kneeler like dried blood. "What is the meaning of this? What have you done!"

"Mary Rose," he managed as her eyelids fluttered open. "What in the world are you—" His head spinning, but at the center of the maelstrom, the extreme center, Mary Rose remained, so beautiful, so real. So alive.

Her humming, the words barely a murmur: "They invite their friends and their friends, too, they all come down to chew on you, and this is what it is to die, and this is what it is to die, and this is what—she's still there. She's still there. She's still in the house."

"Who?" Simon asked, barely a whisper. "What house?"

"Very lonely, I think. She's still in the house . . ."

"Mary!"

She stopped, finally looked directly at him, her hand coming up to his cheek. "Hello, Simon. I didn't mean to startle you." She lifted from her sepulchral pose and twisted back toward the tombstone. "Eerie, isn't it?" she asked, but in a strange, distracted voice, as if she wasn't really seeing it.

MARY ROSE MORLAND
BORN OF LOVE, FOREVER BELOVED

"Where in God's name did you find . . . *that?*"

Simon pulled his attention from the tombstone to Morland, who'd just spoken.

It was Mary Rose who answered, even as she sidled closer to him, still sitting on the floor. "It was in the closet, Daddy." She pointed. "I thought you knew."

Simon's gaze shot to the closet, its door cracked, bedecked with several crosses. Mary Rose must have dragged the stone out to the center of the room, must have known it, and her old playthings, had been stored together within. Something she'd discovered only months ago or years, he couldn't say. But she'd known. Known that terrible thing—testament of her death—was in her house. It was unimaginable.

"Uh-huh." Mary Rose grinned. "With all my toys and paints."

Morland turned on Francine. "Why do you even still have that abominable thing? You told me you destroyed it."

"I tried." Francine's bleating voice took on the trailing edge of a whine, her attempt at anguish as thin and pale as her faded dress. "I meant to get rid of it, I truly did, but at the end I—I simply couldn't. It held too much meaning—all those prayers answered, all those hopes, those dreams—"

"It's a bloody tombstone! You don't think it's something we might not keep in the goddamned closet of our child's playroom?"

"James! Do not blaspheme in front of me."

"You've been carrying around that chunk of stone for twenty years, and you're going to lecture me on my language? What's wrong with you?"

"You don't understand." Francine bowed her head. "That thing . . . that stone was the symbol of Mary Rose—our glorious Mary Rose—who left and came back to us, when there was nothing left *but* hope. Don't you see?" she asked him, looking up with eyes welling up. "Don't you see? I couldn't destroy it. Toss it away. No more than I could destroy, destroy . . ."

With a wracking sob, Francine turned and stumbled from the room, her low histrionic moans trailing behind.

Simon ran his fingers across the etched lettering of the headstone, feeling his wife's name.

MARY ROSE

He looked up at Morland.

"Tell me again," Simon taunted, "how we don't have anything to talk about?"

22

The long miles and hours back to Mhoire's Point had vanished before Simon as if driving in a dream, passing in only a few fragmented moments: scowling at the dim road ahead, replaying what he might have said, could/should have said, to the Morlands, *l'esprit de l'escalier*, possessing his whole mind and soul; Mary Rose slumped in the passenger seat against the window, holding back tears, broken and lost, a single reflection of her face flashing against the rain-pebbled window as a truck passed, then lost to shadow again; long dark empty fields with darker shapes looming far in the distance behind them, monstrous rises lost to the night; the moss-stained stone bridge; a lone house beside the road, a single lamp in one of the windows and the dark figure peering back out at the night, watching them pass.

The plan was to get home as soon as possible. Spend the night, get some sleep, then head to the airport together in the morning. There'd be half a dozen flights back to somewhere on the East Coast, and anywhere was fine. Hell, he'd rent a car in Dayton, Ohio, if that's what it took. He was done with this fucking rain and fucking Scotland and Europe and dark beer and William Wallace and Heathcliff on the moors and Gaelic witches gathering bones from still-warm tombs to dance for the fucking devil.

It was time to get Mary Rose home, away from merciless memories and a first-rate dysfunctional family, get her some real help, a professional to better get her through this. Whatever *this* was.

Plans . . .

Simon found he'd turned off the main road through town, instead cutting up the seaboard again, *away* from their cottage and away from their most simple escape. If Mary Rose knew where he was headed, or had even noticed he'd changed course, she gave no indication. Her eyes were lost to the night outside her window, her broken thoughts her own.

The downpour intensified, pelting the car, cutting what little visibility he'd had on the dark narrow road down to almost nothing, as if the very rain was telling him to turn back. The road revealed itself ten feet at a time, and any memory he'd carried of traveling it earlier in the week was replaced with the strange notion he'd made a wrong turn somewhere and this was another road altogether, one he'd never been on before in his life.

Turn back, he thought again as Mary Rose absently dragged her finger down the glass of her window, mirroring a long vermicular streak of rain on the other side. Any landmarks he might have recognized were lost to the dark and rain, the car's headlights providing the only light, somehow making the drive even darker than it truly was.

She's still there. She's still in the house.

Very lonely, I think. There's no life inside at all.

She's still in the house . . .

She'd definitely said these things. He hadn't imagined it. Her words particular, resonant, and had to have significance. Had to . . .

The ocean churned and roared somewhere to his right, a hundred feet or more below. One slip and they'd career over the unguarded overhang. He thought a final time of stopping, turning back, but a second pair of headlights appeared in his rearview mirror, and he feared some sort of accident. So he kept driving.

"Where are we going?" Mary Rose asked finally, speaking for the first time in an hour. She'd wrapped her arms around herself, visibly shivered. "We shouldn't . . ."

"You okay?" Simon asked.

She shook her head. "I can't . . . Simon, what are you doing?"

"I need to show you something."

Mary Rose's confusion turned to sharp, quick anger. "No. We should go back to the cottage. Don't—"

"We will." He scowled back at her. "After."

Finally, a structure he recognized. An old barn painted tawny orange. He'd been on the right road all along, of course he had. It'd been a trick of the rain, the night, his rattled nerves. "We'll be home by this time tomorrow," he promised. "*Home* home."

In response, Mary Rose simply looked out her window again toward the sea, any argument now within herself. He tried not to make too much of it. Another quarter mile, around the next bend, and they'd be there.

Finally, Simon turned the car down a familiar driveway. The worn gray house emerged through the rain beyond in the flush of the headlights.

"Why are we here?" She asked, sitting up. "It's not necessary. It doesn't help. Not really. I didn't want to . . ."

"This house is owned by a man named Benjamin Gillis." He looked over at his wife for some sign of reaction. "Do you know who that is?"

She shook her head again. "I'd like to leave, Simon. Please . . ."

He stopped the car. "What's the matter?"

"I don't feel well. I want to go back to the cottage."

He wasn't sure why he was doing this, why it was so important. He'd never before done anything to force Mary Rose into any decision. Not what to have for dinner or where to go for vacation or what to watch on TV. But here, now, he had no choice but to force her. Here, now, it was time she faced these demons that kept gnawing at her from the shadows. If she didn't, she would never be fully rid of them, he knew.

He *knew*.

"Come on." Simon opened the car door and got out into the rain.

"Simon!" He heard her shout over the closing door.

Mary Rose stayed within the car and he crossed to her side, rapped at the window with the knuckle of his ring finger.

The door opened, and she crawled out. "I don't want to be here," she griped into the rain.

"Why?" He brought his face to hers, imploring.

"I don't know. I just . . . I don't."

"Well"—Simon looked back at the house through the downpour

—"there might be a reason for that. Let's check it out."

"Simon, please . . . If this has something to do . . ."

"C'mon, let's get out of the rain." He took her arm and pulled her up toward the porch. He'd left the headlights on for some light, and their shadows spread over the front of the house, monstrous in size and shape.

Safely on the porch, he looked down at her, Mary Rose's hair wet and fallen into her eyes.

". . . something," she murmured, as if she hadn't heard him, as if she was still focused on what she needed to say. ". . . something to do with what you and my parents were talking about. . ."

"I think it might," he said. Simon could do nothing but push ahead. "When we first visited the island. We were on our way back that day, remember?"

She covered her face with both hands, murmured something. The pose almost identical to the one which had gotten them here.

"Coming back from the island, we passed this house. You looked up at *this* house. You . . . well, you looked terrified."

"I don't remember that," she barely whispered, and dropped her hands. "*Doing* that. I . . . I've never seen this house before in my life."

"Well, then let's know that for sure. Because I think it's maybe part of . . . part of what happened to you twenty years ago."

She frowned at him, once more resolute. "Nothing happened to me."

"That's not true." He took her hands. Ice-cold. "You vanished for a month, Mary Rose. A *month*. And no one knows where you were during that whole time."

"I don't . . ." She looked at him with gloom. "I don't believe that. I have no memory of that."

"Well, I think you remember more than you know." He waited. "And feel you've been trying to tell your parents, and me, for years. And . . . I also think you might have been here."

"Because maybe I looked at a house oddly? That's not . . . I don't feel . . ." She exhaled unevenly, beginning to tremble. "I think I'm going to be sick."

"Do you remember this house? Is that why you feel sick?"

"No," she said again. "Please . . ."

Simon braced himself and then slammed his shoulder, and full weight, into the door.

It burst open, rotted wood splintering off its frame.

"Simon!" She stared in horror. "What are you doing?"

He reached to take her hand again. Wind whooshed through the opened entryway into the empty house, swinging unseen doors and debris within. "We're going inside."

"We can't. I can't."

"No one lives here," he explained. "Not for fifteen years, apparently." The headlights flushed the front room and hallway and roaches, he thought, or little pieces of trash, scurried away from the light. Again, their shadows appeared dimly on the opposite wall. "There's no one here tonight but us."

"You shouldn't be here. I . . ."

"Damn it, Mary Rose." He turned on her, glaring. "You were lying in front of a fucking tombstone. In some kind of trance. Totally out of it. I doubt you had any idea what you were even doing until we burst in on you and you turned it all into some kind of joke. A joke! It was your own goddamned tombstone!" She'd looked away, clearly mortified. He crouched to make her turn back, look her eye to eye. "'She's still there,' you said. 'She's still in the house.' Who's 'she,' Mary Rose? Another girl who was once here with you? Or, is it you?"

"I don't . . ."

"Come on, baby. We need to put this behind us. Once and for all."

"Fine, you're right," she said, her voice as dead as granite and every bit as cold and hard. "It's time."

Simon tugged gently but still felt as if he were the one being led into the forsaken house.

The air was damp, fetid with moldering walls and damaged furniture. A single piece of old newspaper caught in the wind drifted across the room between the deeply shadowed corners. An empty closet gaped open, its door hanging awkwardly from one hinge at the top. In the other corner of the room, someone had once started a small fire.

Behind him, Mary Rose laughed.

Simon turned, the light from the headlights blinding, casting his wife in outline only.

"Sorry," she said, her expression hidden as she turned away from him.

He stood frozen, staring. The sound of her breathing seemed to fill the whole house. Then he turned and started back to where he understood the kitchen to be, first entering a short narrow hallway and coming upon a closed door. A decaying smell, the same from the Morland house months before wafted from underneath the closed door.

He grabbed the doorknob, expecting it to be locked, turned, and then threw the door open.

"Fuck!" Simon staggered back, put up a hand to hold Mary Rose back.

"Blood . . ." Her tiny voice wavered behind him.

Glistening, wet, and spilling down the wall. Several twisting lines that emerged from the ceiling and then pooled together along the floor. The wall behind spattered in wide black splashes of gore.

The stench of decay suddenly seemed to fill the whole house. Rotted roadkill, bad meat. Simon yanked his cell phone free, fumbled, finally found the damned flashlight icon. Its dim light penetrated the dark room.

"Jesus . . ." Simon slumped in the doorway.

It was nothing more than rainwater. Leaks in the ceiling. The trickle, no more than, glistening in his light. And the spatters of blood only decade-old patches of mold rotting away the drywall. The odor, only rot.

Why was he acting like a scared little kid? Jumping at shadows. He'd been crazy to think—

But, she'd seen it, too. Mary Rose had been the one to say the word aloud. Had she said it first? Put the idea in his head? Or had he only imagined she'd said anything. Or was it simply a trick of the light, a ridiculous possibility, they'd somehow both jumped to.

"Stay there," he told her, and entered alone, clearing his throat of the stink. A dresser lay tipped sideways against the closest wall. One drawer was missing, no doubt once used as firewood by kids in the other room. Using the light of his phone, he inspected the other two drawers, tugging each free one at a time. Nothing and, otherwise, the room was empty.

"We should go," Mary Rose said from the doorway.

"Come on." He turned off the cell's light and passed her to continue down the hall.

The small kitchen was as he remembered when he'd peered in from the splintered window outside. Within, he could better see how months of dust brushed the whole room, from the bottle-stuffed sink to the floor. One doorway led to the first bedroom he'd seen, the one with the mattress and bedspring propped up against the wall. Another was an empty pantry, nothing but smashed shelving and shards of dozens of various beer bottles.

He turned to Mary Rose, still waiting for a reaction. Some kind of recognition. She stood, looking smaller and more forlorn than ever in the center of the dim kitchen. In the moonlight from the back window, her expression was empty, lost. She turned to the back door. Outside was only more darkness and the rain and, somewhere, too far below, the ocean. He could almost hear the waves breaking beneath the rainfall.

"I peeked," she said.

Simon shivered. "Mary Rose?" Had he heard right?

But she'd shaken off whatever next comment, or thought, she might have had. Simon closed the space between them, took her in his arms. "What did you say?"

She trembled against him.

Simon whispered against the top of her head. "C'mon, baby. I need your help here."

He felt her shift. Moving her arm. She was pointing at something. Simon turned slowly to look.

There was a door.

Set in the bedroom, or more accurately *between* the bedroom and kitchen, it was little more than a panel of wood slightly offset from the wall around it, positioned in such a way that he hadn't been able to see it from outside the house, or even when standing directly in the kitchen. But now that she was pointing at it, it was so obvious, he could hardly believe it'd been there when they'd first come in.

A full-on shudder passed through Simon's whole body as he stared at the rectangle of wood. Ice-cold and jagged. A sensation he hadn't had since the afternoon he'd lost Mary Rose on that damned island for an hour. It was exactly like that. Even though she was wrapped in his arms. Even though he knew she was safe.

He released her to reach for the door. The handle was a short vertical bar screwed in on both sides, not a doorknob to turn. The smashed remains of two dead bolts, or rather, *padlocks*, hung from the door frame.

"Simon . . ." Her voice seemed far away from him. Too far away.

He looked back at his bride, then pulled the door open.

A single concrete step led to the darkness below. A crawl space or basement of some kind. He turned on his phone's light again, cast it down into the opening. There were at least five more steps. Graffiti covered the walls. Names and initials and more visual tags, no doubt, of those local kids who'd braved this far.

It's haunted. Isn't that what Jean Osterby, the daughter, had said?

Simon blew out deeply, gathering his nerves. He looked back toward the kitchen for some kind of weapon. But why? There was nothing down below but a flooded basement, unless he missed his guess. He descended the first stairs.

The darkness intensified until it was infinite. Absolute.

The dim light of the phone barely cut to the bottom step.

"I peeked," Mary Rose said again, behind him.

Simon stopped, caught halfway down the steps.

He saw she hadn't followed him but, instead, stood silhouetted in the doorway. Looking smaller somehow. Looking, he realized, like a little girl who'd vanished twenty years before.

"When we were in the boat . . ." She looked down at him, but he couldn't see her, unwilling to shine his light in her face. Unwilling to take the light away from the darkness waiting behind him.

"What boat?" His voice trembled. He *heard* it tremble. And anger had been the emotion that shook it, not fear. Someone had put his Mary Rose on a boat and . . . someone had . . .

"There was a space between my nose and my cheeks," she said.

"Where I could still see." She sounded almost happy. Proud. She sounded like a little girl. "And when I looked up, I could see."

"Jesus . . ." Simon started back up the steps to her when the reek of decay filled his nose again. So strong this time, he gagged. Stopped climbing.

"She's still down there," she said.

Simon found he'd put a hand against the graffitied wall to steady himself. "Mary . . ."

"They both are," she replied.

He peered back into the darkness below, covering his mouth.

But as quickly as the odor had come, it was gone again.

Simon stared into the dank basement as genuine fear finally *did* wash through him, supplanting the growing anger, hollowing him out. But this would never be over if he crept back up those stairs. There would always be this basement to conquer.

And he was here, now. The two of them together.

He straightened, held out a hand to lure her down.

For the memories were here, too. Down in the dark where such memories should be. The trauma, the past she'd buried so long. But not deeply enough. Instead they kept clawing away the dirt, dragging themselves free. Tonight would be different. He would see to it. Tonight, they were coming up one last time and then being put to rest.

"What else?" he prodded, stepping back up to take her hand. She reached out and allowed him to pull her forward. "What else do you remember?"

One. Simon led her down the steps. Two. Three. He felt an insane compulsion to count each step, another small victory, out loud, but stifled it. At the sixth step Mary Rose pulled her hand back, then lifted her fingers to scratch nervously at her neck. The downpour above had grown muffled, cavernous. Simon glanced from her face to the room uncovering below.

A crawl space no more than six feet high, one that ran beneath the moldering room they'd found upstairs. The walls were heavily splintered concrete, and there was more graffiti. Different graffiti, though.

Someone had spray-painted a pentagram. Several inverted crosses.

Enormous eyes. The faceless drawing of an antlered spirit covered one whole wall, with tiny stick figures drawn below and around the enormous head, in its mouth. Strange animals that didn't exist. Letters that weren't English, like those he'd seen on the walls outside the house.

Some of it was in paint, some scratched in with rocks or a knife. Some, it looked, had been made in blood.

He looked for them—the faceless little girl and a dog man—but saw nothing that matched, that made sense. He supposed many of the figures had no faces, but as he crouched down to enter the room—

Simon's phone light dimmed.

He thought to take some quick pictures, checked his battery life first. Twenty percent already. It'd been *ninety*, he thought, when they'd entered the house. How many flashes before the phone quit? Had to get a few, though. Then they'd come back in the morning. He and the Mhoire's Point police would come back in the morning.

There was a fallen chair in one corner of the room. In another, he saw a wooden tray. He leaned forward, watching his head, and when he toed the tray over, he saw that someone had crafted a homemade Ouija board on the other side. He crouched to retrieve the board.

"Don't," Mary Rose said, and her voice was dead. Shriveled.

Simon stared up at her, horror snaking through him even more. He'd never imagined she could sound like that.

"Don't touch it." That quickly, her voice sounded normal again. She looked past him at the walls.

Taking a shallow, shuddering breath, Simon let the board lie where it was and continued his slow bent-over search of the room. On the next wall was a snake that crossed and ate its own tail like an infinity symbol. Tiny beings with wings. Crescent moons. Figures with stars for heads.

"The walls were empty," she murmured.

Simon turned.

Mary Rose had righted and set the rusted chair in the center of the room and was sitting in it. Her legs were close together, her slender hands folded neatly in her lap. "She was here."

Simon crossed to her and kneeled, putting his hands on her legs.

"Who?" he asked. Had there been another girl in the room with her during the ordeal? Or was Mary Rose merely imagining herself?

He could feel her whole body trembling. Or maybe only his own.

"Sat right like this. Here, waiting. And . . ." She stared off. "And the doggie man would bring dinner." She smiled thinly. "And, sometimes, light."

Simon's eyes welled with rage, shame. This revealed explanation of the "doggie man" pictures she'd drawn for years was trivial against the rest. *Blindfolded.* They needed to leave right away, get the police. *Bound to a chair alone in the dark.* Her parents. *Rough hands grabbing her arms, legs.* And when he—*Stroking her face*—found Benjamin Gillis—*Standing over her in this same dark room, undressing her*—and he would soon—*making promises, telling her to . . . Inside her . . .*

He would kill him. Simon glared around the room, soaking in all the hate and darkness he could. Yes, decisions best made in such places.

He again studied Mary Rose. She stared at a particular spot on the floor, as if something was there. Simon glanced at it also, but there was nothing. He looked back at her, and Mary Rose's eyes had grown wide with terror. Her mouth frozen into the smallest of Os.

"She has no face," she gasped.

"What?" Simon slumped in uncertainty.

Mary Rose scrambled away from the chair, toward the stairs, and he fell back. "My God . . . Why don't I have a *face*?"

The room went black.

He heard the chair clatter to the ground, skid across the floor.

Simon cursed, fumbled with his phone in the dark to see what he'd done. It showed a 0 percent charge and then even that faint light shut off completely. He'd somehow burned through a quarter charge in less than five minutes.

"Mary Rose . . ." He glared around the room blindly, the dimmest of light in one corner showing where the steps must be.

"Mary Rose?"

He needed to find her, to take care of her, protect. Couldn't fathom what she must be feeling now. The memories. The horror.

The room had grown colder. And he could suddenly feel all the pentagrams and snakes and stick people on the walls, skirting closer in the darkness. "Mary Rose . . ." He called out again, and his voice had sounded chillingly fragile.

"It's okay," her stronger voice floated back. "I'm right beside you."

Simon froze, his eyes staring wide but seeing nothing—nothing at all. Or, rather, something enormous now squatted in the farthest corner of the room. Impossible. He saw nothing. It was a darkness so complete, it was like he was the one blindfolded, he was the one captured, hidden away in the ground.

Something touched his hand, and he flinched.

Mary Rose.

Her fingers wrapped around his wrist. Cold and skeletal in the dark. He grimaced in the void, ashamed at what had been the best word to describe the feeling.

"Don't be afraid," she said. "I know where we are now."

23

I know where we are now.

Simon couldn't say the same. Not even close. Not anymore. They might as well still be in the basement with the lights off. They were, he was, somewhere too extraordinary, too unfamiliar now. Beyond family secrets or cursed islands or things that went bump in the night.

The love of his life was in full breakdown mode, recalling a horrible crime from her childhood, and the evil fuck who'd done it to her, who'd surely stolen and ruined her innocence, was likely somewhere only a few miles away.

What *wasn't* only a few miles in this shit hole, of course, was a damned hospital. The nearest almost an hour away. He'd hoped to maybe get Mary Rose a shot of something, take the edge off. Or, rather, to bring her back to normal. Whichever. She was withdrawn more than ever. Hadn't said two words since they'd escaped the basement together. Her whole posture rigid, resolute. It was like he'd moved only the hardened shell of Mary Rose back through the rain into the car.

The final frustration was the cops. Even after he'd gotten the phone charged again, he knew it was pointless to call. They wouldn't arrest Benjamin Gillis tonight. Or tomorrow, either. There'd be interviews with Mary Rose first—and what, if anything, might she say to them, what would she remember, in the morning. As far as he knew, she again wouldn't remember a thing. Was what she'd said admissible? Was it evidence they'd act on? They'd need to build evidence, find a judge for warrants. "Yes, Your Honor. She stared at a house funny." "Yes, that's right, and then she said she 'had no face.'" It was lunacy. There wasn't enough evidence to arrest Gillis. That would take weeks, at best. DNA lasted fifty years, a million. They could prove Mary Rose had been in that basement, but it would—again—take time. These rubes wouldn't have the means. This was Mhoire's Point, Scotland, not downtown Philly. The Scottish FBI would have to get involved: more time.

He'd already decided to find Gillis himself. To get enough information somehow to arrest him tonight. The notion of "killing him" subsided to some form of citizen's arrest. His only fear was that that notion would somehow subside also. That he'd be left standing there, impotent and pathetic, unable to close. The man who'd abducted, and surely molested, his bride grinning at the memory somewhere in perfect comfort.

Would Gillis run when confronted? Become violent?

Simon hoped so. Monsters on the run, those not hiding in their little caves, were far easier to find. The authorities would know his guilt then, might even kill him in the process of arrest. And if Gillis became violent, Simon was ready for that, too. It would be the catalyst needed to follow through with his original plan.

But first, he had to deal with this.

James and Francine Morland.

Here, in Scotland. Standing together on the porch of the cottage.

And to keep things interesting: playing new roles tonight. Morland's face surprisingly hardened now, showing an emotion Simon didn't think the man was capable of: rage. Controlled rage. Francine's going with exasperated. Overwhelmed. The drama queen he'd only gotten a taste of just hours before.

"What are you doing here?" Simon asked, getting out of the car.

"We came right away." James Morland striding forward, bristling with fury. "You had no damn right to—"

Simon held up his hand to stop him. From talking, from moving. "Now's not a good time, James," he warned, and hurried to fetch Mary Rose. She was *his* responsibility now, not this guy's. Not anymore.

James Morland could fuck off. He'd had his chance for twenty years and not done a damn thing. "She needs rest. Peace." Simon fought to keep his voice calm. "We didn't ask you to come here."

He got her out of the car and hurried up the steps through the drizzle. If she recognized that her parents were there, she gave no notice. Simon could feel his legs shaking. This was not the confrontation he'd expected tonight.

James Morland assessed the situation immediately. He approached slowly, touched his daughter's back. "Mary . . ."

She stared ahead, eyes glazed.

Francine, Simon noticed, had turned away. Waiting for someone to notice *her* pain, no doubt.

"What happened?" James asked.

"We went to a house," Simon replied. "Owned by a man named Benjamin Gillis."

Francine Morland groaned, gripped the banister.

"'Benjo' Gillis?" James Morland winced. "Why in God's name would you do that?"

"You know him, then."

"Know him, no. Haven't heard that name in more than thirty years. He was one of the locals. The town drunk, from what I understand."

Simon had gotten Mary Rose into the cottage and was leading her to the bedroom. He turned, "He's more than that."

"Meaning *what*, exactly?"

Morland's curt words hung in the air as Simon worked Mary Rose's wet jacket and shoes off and got her into bed. He pulled a blanket from the end of the bed, tucked it around her gently, so gently. Behind him, James Morland hovered in the doorway.

Mary Rose gazed into Simon's eyes, her expression a harrowing mix of sorrow and fear and loss. *She knew*, he thought. Maybe she'd known all along. Trembling in the darkness, hiding from shadows that never slipped away. "Oh, Simon . . ."

"Shhhh . . ." he whispered. "Just sleep. I'll be right outside if you need anything." He held her until her eyelids drifted shut, her breathing steadied. Stepping away quietly, he closed the bedroom door.

It took him three steps to return to the front parlor. And by then he was boiling over again. "What do you know about ol' 'Benjo'?" he asked James, who now stood between him and Francine.

"I told you, he's a local. Drove delivery trucks, I recall. Some odd jobs around town. Older guy who hung around with the teen crowd, some. Bought kids booze. Sold pot. That kind of thing."

"Mary Rose remembers being in his house."

"This is absurd," Francine Morland hissed.

Simon snapped his glance to her. "Why's that?"

"All of this!" She waved her arms to include, perhaps, the whole world. "You bringing her here . . . This . . . Dear Christ, what have you done?"

"Simon . . ." James interrupted Francine's tirade.

"Yeah?" Simon turned, keeping half an eye on Francine as she fumbled through her purse, yanking out a rosary that she gripped in her hands, still moaning.

"Why Gillis?" Morland asked.

"She recognized his house. The first time we came out here. She saw an old house of his from the sea. Stared at it, in horror I think. She knew it. So, tonight, I took her there. Not soon enough, maybe."

"I can't believe we're listening to this." Francine, apparently tired of God not listening to her either, rounded on both of them. "She needs to get to a hospital. Needs to talk with someone about what happened on that island."

"It wasn't *on* the island," Simon countered. "Gillis is long gone, but we went into his house. She remembers that, too. Said she 'peeked' under some type of covering he'd put around her eyes. Remembered the basement. Being in his basement for days. Being fed dinners. Waiting for him to open the door so she could see *light* again."

Morland started at that, as if Simon's diatribe had finally cracked his carefully polished surface, like the shattered black mirror in the belly of his house. His face lost all color as he stared at Simon, his eyes haggard. Terror welled in them from somewhere deep within, a terror that Simon realized had never fully gone away. "She had no light?" he asked, the question almost a groan.

"She said something about not having a face."

"It's madness!" Francine spluttered. "She needs help. *Real* help. You've put all this into her head. You're the one whose—"

"They'll find her DNA in the basement," Simon said. "I believe her. I know she was there."

"Oh, Jesus . . ." Francine Morland collapsed onto the couch, the rosary still clutched in her hand. "Gillis is *gone* from there, long gone. God only knows who's been there since. You said the house was *empty*. What good can come from this?"

"Do you?" James Morland asked. "Believe her, I mean."

Simon nodded once, holding Morland's gaze. "With all my heart."

James Morland dropped his head, sighed deeply, then looked up at Simon again. "What should we do?"

Simon drew in a sharp, steadying breath. "Stay here," he decided. "With Mary Rose."

Almost without thinking, he found himself putting a hand on James Morland's shoulder. In the face of Morland's obvious horror at what Simon had found, his genuine despair at what that discovery meant, Simon's respect for the man had returned as quickly as any anger. Morland loved Mary Rose, too. Had protected her— or had tried to, as best he could—for more than twenty years. One of many who'd tried, tried and failed. "I'm glad you came. Will you do that?"

Morland nodded brusquely. "Of course. What are—"

"I'll be right back." Simon turned away, his mind already on the trip ahead.

"I suppose you're going to *find* him now?" Francine whined from the couch. "Gillis."

Simon scowled down at her, looked back at James and held up his newly charged phone. "Call me if Mary Rose needs anything. Wants me back or—"

"Go," James Morland said. "She's safe now."

Simon wasn't too sure about that but believed she was tonight somehow closer than in many, many years. He burst through the front door and down the porch steps to the car. Adrenaline rocketed through him, stronger than any time he stepped foot in the courtroom, no matter how big or how connected his opponent. This feeling surging through him knocked any court case in the dust. He was on the side of the righteous here, and he had twenty years of payback to deliver. First with one shocking blow, and then the right way, the proper way, bringing in the authorities and making sure every last shadow was stamped out in every last corner.

It was time to go monster hunting.

First he needed to find the monster's daughter.

Simon's fist slammed against the porch door.

"Jeanne!" he shouted. "It's Simon Blake. Open up!"

He heard cursing from inside the house.

The door opened. Jeanne Gillis looked, at best, half-awake. The stench of pot hung on her like a cloud. Like your old man, Simon thought, glaring heatedly. "What do you want?" she grumbled, but smiled when she said it. "You see a unicorn or something?"

"The house up on Route Thirty-Eight."

"What about it. Told you, it's not for sale."

"Did you live there as a child?"

She sneered. "Not since I was ten. My mum left him, my parents divorced. I moved with her over to Paisley. What's this about?"

"I need to speak with your father."

She wiped one eye awake. "Yeah, well . . . Why you *here*, then?"

"So you can tell me where he's living now. Where he's staying."

"Don't know." She looked past Simon, staring blearily into the darkness behind him. An erratic drizzle had replaced the earlier rainfall. "I don't know where he is."

"Bullshit."

Her gaze sharpened again on him, not quite so wasted that she didn't know danger when she heard it. "Look, you fud, how about you get the fuck off me property?" She went to shut the door, and Simon slammed his hand against it.

"Where *is* he?"

"I'm calling the police." It had come out "*polis*."

"Call 'em," Simon said calmly. "Go ahead. I was about to myself, so you can save me the trouble."

She stiffened. "What's this about?"

"It's between me and your father." Simon leaned in closer. "And my *wife*, Mary Rose."

She tried to hold her expression, couldn't. And Simon saw it then. Saw the whisper of fear that snaked over her face, quick and dark. "The 'wife.' What's she got to do with it?"

Anger ratcheted up, burning through his patience. "Where *is he*? All the bullshit about druids and other worlds and that fucking island. It was all only ever a distraction from reality. But I suspect you knew that. That it was part of your intention from the first day we met."

"Look"—turning away, unable to stand before his accusation—"I can't—"

Simon slammed his fist on the door. "Jeanne!"

She cringed back, and her fear suddenly changed—not the fear of being caught, of having the truth come out, but a different fear. That of a woman afraid of being smacked around by a bigger, stronger man. A fear she'd clearly experienced before tonight.

A wave of cold self-rebuke sluiced through Simon. *What was he doing?* He stepped back immediately, held up his hands. Drew in a shaky breath. "Hey, I'm sorry. I just . . ."

To his surprise, Jeanne still stood at the door. Clung to it, in fact, as if she was drawing strength from it. "Does this have something to do with . . . with when she disappeared?"

"Yes."

Jeanne closed her eyes briefly, then opened them. Those eyes had seen things, Simon thought suddenly. Maybe some bad things. Maybe some things she couldn't fully admit to herself. "What did he do?" she asked.

Simon breathed deeply. Didn't know how to answer her.

Jeanne Gillis peered up at him more intently. "*What* did he do?"

"I don't know exactly. But . . . probably something bad."

She winced as if he'd struck her after all, her lips going flat, pressed together. She didn't close her eyes, though. Simon got the feeling that when things got bad enough, Jeanne Gillis Osterby had learned not to shut her eyes. Better to know the blow that was coming at you than let it catch you unawares.

His stomach twisted at the flash of misery in her face. The misery and the weary, hard knowing the bad news wasn't over yet. "Jeanne, I . . ." He didn't know what else to say.

"Come in," she said. "Let me get some damn shoes on." She'd stepped back into the house.

"The address is all I—"

She turned her back on him.

Simon followed slowly, carefully. The notion that she might shoot him or hit him with a candlestick or some shit and toss him into the Atlantic had finally crossed his mind. In any case, he'd had no intention of bringing her along to her father's but didn't know how he'd stop her.

The house proved cluttered, and stunk of weed. A small pipe lay on the coffee table. The one wall covered in dozens on framed photos. The TV showed some English sitcom he didn't recognize.

"He lives over in Branmak now," she said, slumping back into the room. Sans candlestick, he noticed immediately. Instead she carried a pair of boots. "Two towns away. Thirty-minute drive."

"Sounds good," Simon replied, not sure what else to say. The woman looked overcome, drained of the salt-of-the-earth brazenness he knew her by. He had to say something. "Hey, Jeanne, I—"

"Forget it," she stopped him, then plopped down to pull on her boots. She looked up at Simon with a weary finality to her expression, suddenly decades older than her years. "I know who raised me. I know . . ." She sighed. "Someone was going to come knocking on my door someday."

"He told you the house was haunted."

"Yeah." She smiled woefully. "I guess he did. I thought . . ." She held her next thoughts, stood and grabbed a jacket from a hook on the wall.

"We can take my car," he offered.

"No. I'll follow you," she said. "Let me grab my keys."

She plodded back to some bedroom. Simon couldn't imagine what thoughts were in her mind. What, if anything, she knew. If she'd lied about her father's address, would she call and warn him from her car.

But he didn't think so. Something in her broken gaze.

He'd wandered over to the wall of photos, looking for his first image of Benjamin Gillis. To see what a real monster looked like. To see into the eyes of the kind of man who'd abduct a child. Keep her locked in a basement. Or worse. The man's mugshot, how could a man like Gillis not have one of those, hadn't even made it into the folder Constable Fraser had given him. On the wall, there were many pictures of men, but nothing from when Jeanne was a girl. These were old boyfriends, husbands, male friends. There was even a picture of Brodie, the druid. Funny to see a familiar face already when he'd only been in the village a total of a week. He could hardly fathom how many faces he'd know, how many lives and secrets he would share, had he spent every summer with these people, or even lived here.

His own reflection mirrored in one of the larger frames. His hair ruffled, he needed a shave, eyes shockingly dark and fatigued. He looked like his damned father.

He scanned the wall of photos once more, hoping to see if he'd missed one. Funny, no older men, either. Clearly, whatever relationship the two had had was strained enough that he hadn't made it to her wall. There was a certain—

Simon stopped at one of the photos.

His throat clenched like he was being choked. He couldn't move. Couldn't breathe.

The older photo featured three grinning girls standing together in their Halloween outfits: a pink Power Ranger striking a karate pose, a classic pointed-hatted witch giving the rock-on sign, and a dog with its arms crossed.

A dog with a brown shirt and fluffy tail and, the keystone of the whole costume, a cartoonish mask with big black button nose and two loping Snoopy-like ears hanging from each side.

"Who . . ." Simon managed, his voice like gravel. His shaking finger touched the frame.

"What's wrong?" Jeanne Gillis asked.

He half turned to see her frozen at the mouth of the hallway. "Who is this?" he asked, amazed he could keep his tone steady.

She approached to see. "Me and my friends, why?"

"Who's *this*?" His finger stabbed at the dog.

Her face scrunched into an exasperated scowl. "Me . . . Why?"

"Do you still have that costume? What happened to it?"

She shot an odd look. "Um, I was ten, so no. It's long gone. Probably got tossed when we moved out."

"From the house on Route Thirty-Eight?"

"Sure, whatever."

Simon pulled the frame from the wall.

"Hey! What are you—"

"It's important," he snapped. And whether it was something in his voice, something Jeanne Gillis knew, or simply all the years of shrinking under the barrage of an unfriendly world, she didn't argue with him.

"I want it back when you're done," she grumbled, and he nodded, holding the frame and photo tight against his coat.

Now, at least, he knew exactly what the monster had looked like.

24

Benjamin Gillis lounged in his nasty chair like the wicked king of some dark fairy tale. Elbows propped on both armrests, lanky bone-white fingers dangling over the edges, nicotine stained, twitching against the worn cloth. He sat hunched low, chin dipped beneath his shoulders. His face was mostly forehead, what hair he had left gone gray, needing a cut and a good wash.

Simon had expected the black-pebbled eyes of a cornered rat, but in this, at least, Gillis surprised him. The sockets under his wrinkled skin were too pronounced, perhaps, but within, the man's wide eyes were a shockingly disarming blue gray.

"What's this about?" Gillis asked. His voice grumbled, barely a whisper. "You need money?" He glared over at his daughter. "I don't got any."

"Mr. Gillis," Simon spoke for the first time since they'd entered the cramped apartment. He'd decided to stay as focused and peaceful as possible, for all that he wanted to attack, guns blazing. Had to play this smart, though. Especially without the police yet informed. Jeanne had gotten them in the door, both of them seated on the couch opposite Gillis. She was as slope shouldered and sour as her old man, but Simon felt energized, almost electric.

He knew he was in the right place. Knew it. Now all he had to do was tweak Gillis in exactly the right way.

The man turned his blue-gray eyes slowly back to Simon. The eyes were almost smiling, nudging Simon to *not* stay focused and peaceful.

To lash out, screw up. But Simon wasn't going to take that bait.

"Mr. Gillis," he began again. "I need to ask you a few questions about your house. The one up on Thirty-Eight."

He twitched, scratched at his face. "What about it?"

"I was out there. Tonight."

"So? I still don't even know who *you* are."

Simon straightened, lifted his chin. "I was out there with Mary Rose Morland."

The fairy-tale king stared ahead, looking through Simon. Then he turned to his daughter. "Who's that?" he asked.

Jeanne Osterby looked away.

"I think you know exactly who she is," Simon continued. "The little girl who vanished twenty years ago."

"I remember that, I think."

"Well, she remembers where she vanished to."

"Good," he grumbled. "God's blessing to her, then."

"How did you get her off the island?" Simon asked.

There was a tremor then, the barest flicker of reaction, and Simon felt the same surge of victory as when he got a jury member to shift uncomfortably in her seat, to sharpen his glance. Gillis was trapped, now. It was a matter of time.

The old man curled his wet lips. "Don't know what you're talking about, boy. And I think it's best for you both"—he paused to glare at his daughter—"to get the fuck out of here."

"Answer him, Da," Jeanne half groaned.

Simon leaned toward Gillis, gently tapped his leg. "Her DNA *will* be in the basement," he said.

"From tonight?" Gillis shot back, his grin displaying crooked yellowed teeth and a sudden cunning Simon hadn't expected. "Well, so what's that mean?"

Simon hid, he hoped, his dismay. Had he sabotaged the whole case against Gillis? Had bringing Mary Rose to the house truly ruined that whole DNA angle? Surely, forensics would be able to tell the difference.

"How did you get her to the house from the island?" he asked again.

The man shook his head, reached out for one of the beer cans that littered the table beside his chair. Shook several cans, muttering.

"Mary Rose Morland," Simon prompted.

The sly grin was back. "I think . . . I think maybe I do remember that name now."

Simon felt his energy ebb, the surge of victory wavering. He was losing control of this interview. Maybe he'd never had it. "You knew the Morlands."

Gillis nodded, then paused, frowning absently. "Oh, no . . . I don't recall."

"Sure you did. You used to sell the British tourist kids weed. Get 'em free booze and hit on the teenaged girls."

Gillis laughed at that, apparently enjoying the memory. "Okay, bawbag. So?"

"So, I bet you remember the Morlands. James Morland. His wife, Francine Hughes. Surely, David Morland, the older one."

Gillis pointed a protracted finger at his daughter. "Him," he grunted. "Aye, that's the one they should have looked into. Funny business there, I tell you."

"So you do remember what happened. That summer."

He shrugged. "Vaguely. Tourist problems."

"You remember their daughter: Mary Rose."

Another grin. This one almost a leer.

"Was she painting when you took her? Or had she gone to the woods?"

"You don't—" He peered at Simon. "Who are you?"

"I'm her husband."

Gillis blinked, but his chuckle, when it came, was forced. "No, no. She don't have a husband."

"Indeed she does." Simon held up the back of his hand to show the ring. "Three months now. And we've come here on our honeymoon."

The man squirmed in his chair. "You're talking rubbish."

"And," Simon continued, "now she's remembering all sorts of things, like being blindfolded and taken by boat to your house, being kept in your basement for thirty-three days."

"It's a lie," Gillis growled.

"You deny all of it?"

"She isn't married."

"*That's* your concern?" Simon looked up at Jeanne and held out his hands, confused. "Mr. Gillis, in the UK, there are no statutes of limitations for kidnapping, assault, rape . . ." His voice had broken when he'd said the last, and Simon locked his teeth together, composing himself. The idea that this—this man . . . Simon steepled his fingers, breathed deeply. He wanted to hurt the man. Maybe even to kill. But face-to-face with the possibility of such violence, he found himself clinging instead to some, any, manner of . . . normalcy.

"I never touched her." Gillis focused his hooded eyes on Simon, staring flatly. "Never once."

His denial had come out as a confession. Admitting to everything *but* that. It was in his face, his defiant tone. Simon was sure of it.

"Da?" Jeanne's voice croaked out, and Simon glanced her way, taking in her horrified, nearly sick expression. She thought he'd done it, too. Or she feared as much, anyway, which was almost worse. To not know the limits of your own father—to suspect him of the unthinkable . . .

"Mr. Gillis," Simon rallied, repeating the name like a mantra as he turned back. He had no idea what to say next. He needed to keep Gillis talking. The man clearly *wanted* to. To talk about her . . .

Benjamin Gillis had waited twenty years to talk about her.

The same as the psychiatrist had. The same as Mr. Amy.

But any confession would be inadmissible, even if he started recording with his phone. Now Simon only wanted enough information to cull together the truth, to fortify his call to the cops, convince them to arrest Gillis immediately. Justice would surely follow after. It had to.

"What happened that day?"

"You're not her husband." Gillis shook his head rhythmically, and the certainty in his voice stopped Simon's churning thoughts. "That . . . She'd never belong to any man."

Simon forced himself to slow down again, refocus. Gillis had given a thread to pull. "What do you mean by that?"

But Gillis shifted to the side again, muttered incomprehensible words.

"Mr. Gillis . . ." Nothing. Simon shifted back to the main line of questioning. "Benjamin, why Mary Rose? Did you see her in town?" He hated using her name but saw the response in Gillis's eyes every time he did. "Was it just opportunity? How—"

The cunning gaze swung back, lit again with sly interest. "Ask her."

"She's not here. I'm asking you."

"Not the girl." Gillis grinned. "You're not as clever as you think, are you? Ask Franny."

Simon stiffened. "Francine Morland?"

Gillis nodded.

"What's she got to do with it?"

"That's for her to explain."

"I'd prefer to hear it from you."

"No one cares what you prefer. No one."

"Okay." Simon stood. "We're good. I think it's far past the time for the police to get involved." He looked at Jeanne when he'd said it.

Tears welled in her eyes as she nodded.

"She paid me," Gillis said abruptly.

Simon looked down at him. "What?"

"Franny paid me to take her. Four thousand pounds. She—"

"Bullshit." Simon turned his back on the man. "Fucking bullshit."

But Gillis kept talking, more quickly now. "It was supposed to be at the lake. Or maybe at sea. But . . ." He shook his head, as if still mystified over the event after all these years. "Couldn't do it. So I took her back to the house."

Simon stopped and looked back. Something in the man's words rang so real, so true, there was no room for doubt. That quickly, Simon tensed with feral purpose, ready to jump the distance between them and simply beat Gillis to death. He'd never before known such anger. He tried focusing on the last spoken words instead, tried processing what Gillis was claiming, barely holding on to the edge of civility.

"You were supposed to kidnap her?"

"To *kill* her," he said. "That's . . ."

"I don't believe it. You're a fucking liar."

Gillis waved Simon's words away. "Okay, go off, then."

"Francine offered you money."

"Aye. And more."

Despite the circumstances, Simon still laughed. "Now I *know* you're lying. Francine Morland's not the type to offer much else but money."

"Yeah, well, the Francine Hughes I know use to fuck in the moonlight. Even let us watch a couple times. She and David. Pretended it was all magick, but I think they liked being watched. And so, she knew she could trust me. And I knew she wouldn't really put out for me, not even if I did this, but I'd always wanted to do something for her. For a proper girl like her. Another little rich cunt."

"*You*, motherfucker"—Simon stabbed his finger—"are going to jail. And, I hope—"

"You're not big enough for this, son. Not for this. For her. Mary Rose." It was the first time Gillis had said her name, and Simon felt nauseous. "I tried to kill her the first day," he confessed a second time. "I did. But I couldn't."

"Why?"

He stared, terrified. "The island wouldn't let me."

Simon froze. "The island . . . ?"

Gillis gripped the armrests of his chair again, as if drawing strength from its shabby bulk. "She was *protected*. Every day, I'd tell myself '*this* is the day' I'm gonna get this over with. But, it took me a month to get up the nerve to try again. And by then I prized her. By then . . ." His ugly lips twisted in his florid face. "But even when I killed her—and, I did, finally—she remained . . . protected."

Gillis was talking madness now, for all of his conviction. Simon forced his own response. "I don't understand."

"She was *dead*. I know she was. . . ." Gillis shuddered. "As sure as I know you're standing there right now. Then I came back an hour later and she was sitting in her chair, waiting for her dinner. Like nothing ever happened."

Simon realized he'd taken a seat on the couch again, steadying his legs.

"Brought her back early the very next morning," Gillis went on, his gaze no longer on Simon but off to the right, staring at the wall that separated his dirt-brown apartment from the street, the village, probably the sea. "Before the sun even. Brought her back to where she belongs. Even so, she wouldn't go away. For years, she'd stomp around the basement and shake the walls and scream. Sometimes, I suspect, she went and did it elsewhere."

Simon ignored the ghost stories. Had to. Kept focused on what the rest of the world would understand. "You're admitting to trying to kill a six-year-old girl?"

Gillis snorted, the spell on him as quickly broken as it had been set. "No," he said flatly, facing Simon again. "I'm admitting to *killing* one. But she came back anyway. That's the island done that. That's what you don't understand. It'll never let her go. She's not to be had by any man. She's not your wife, young man. I don't know what you married. But Mary Rose Morland *died* twenty years ago."

"Da! For Chrissakes!" Jeanne sprang from the couch, Simon standing with her almost automatically, ready for anything. She took a menacing step toward her father, but the old man simply stared back at her like she was nothing, as meaningless as a worn sheet. And Jeanne saw that in his look, saw it and recognized it on some primal level. A sob squeaked from her, and she raised her hand to her mouth. Then wordlessly, she turned and rushed from the room, bursting through the front door.

Simon started to go after her, then spun back on Gillis.

"You'll tell all this to the police? Everything you just told me."

It was the confession that could put Gillis away for the rest of his life, one that could end all the speculation, would answer all of Mary Rose's questions. Simon had not yet even begun to process the claims about Franny Morland—but he would, he would. The pathetic bid of a cornered man, already laying down the groundwork of slanderous claims for a future jury? Simon imagined that such a case, without a straightforward confession, would last several years. Mary Rose would be called upon to testify and—Francine *Morland*? Seriously?

And yet . . .

Simon couldn't shake the woman's name, her face, so like Mary Rose's, from his mind. He replayed her behavior, things she'd said, her treatment of Mary Rose, in all the time he'd known her. That any mother would do that to her own daughter was absurd. It wasn't unheard of, though. That, it certainly wasn't.

Gillis didn't reply. Instead, he watched Simon as if he could track Simon's thoughts, follow them down into the rabbit hole he'd opened up.

Simon checked his phone, then dialed 911, keeping a watch of Gillis. The call failed, no signal perhaps. He glared down at his mobile.

"Nine-nine-nine," Gillis said.

Simon looked over. "What?"

"To call the police." Gillis smirked from his throne. "It's nine-nine-nine here."

Simon punched the digits into his phone, but he couldn't pull his eyes away from Gillis. The old man sat there like some sort of troll, the nightmare under the bridge. The nightmare who'd stolen Mary Rose and tried to kill her—twice—an experience so harrowing that it had haunted her for decades. Would haunt her forever, Simon realized now, his hands beginning to shake. And only now, perhaps, beginning to truly guess or recognize the real terror: her near murder. That her own mother . . .

The room's stink suddenly overpowered him, beer and grease and unwashed clothes. Worse, the call wasn't going through. Couldn't go through, he realized, with only one fucking bar on his phone, as if the squalid apartment kept even the cell connection from going in and out, the way it seemed to block the air from flowing.

Simon swung toward the door without speaking, Gillis never moving, and stepped into the hallway for a second or even third bar. Before the police, he should call James Morland at the cottage. Make sure Mary Rose was okay.

Mary Rose. Good God, even imagining her in the hands of the decrepit creature sunk in his easy chair. Probably hadn't moved from it for days, and he'd taken her and . . . He'd . . .

Simon scowled, fumbling with his phone. He didn't know the number, wasn't sure he had Morland's cell anyway. But surely, he'd called the man once regarding the wedding and whatnot, right? He knew he had. Just needed to find a familiar exchange—Britain country code. He scrolled through, forcing himself to read each number, think about what he'd even say to Morland, to the police— my God, to Mary Rose—

Blackness dropped past Simon's eyes.

Not the blackness of a sudden dark space, like the lights going out or falling into a hole. This blackness had form, substance. It was flat and slick and heavy and it was pressing—*pressing* against him, pulling him back with an impossible force as he sucked in a startled breath, a breath that was no longer air but something wet and thick and full, pushing into his mouth, swelling out, slapping against his tongue and the top of his throat.

No!

His head jerked back, his body falling with it, disorientation swamping him as his hands automatically came up, the phone clattering against the wall as his fingers grabbed and tore.

Panic spiked with a sickening surge, his heart pounding. Pounding in a deafening roar as he crashed hard on the wooden floor, his head still twisting, fingers digging into the slick slippery plastic—plastic!

A plastic bag over his face.

One bought in a box with nineteen identical bags for a couple of dollars, *that* was what was going to end his life.

Lights exploded behind his eyes. He couldn't see otherwise, couldn't seem to reach the hands—but there had to be hands, holding the mass of plastic so tight—too tight.

More dimly now, he felt his shoes kicking out at the walls. He twisted and tore, his fingers connecting now—connecting with something that wasn't plastic—and his heart surged again as he heard bestial sounds, inhuman snarling.

A sudden burst of outrage scored through him and his legs kicked harder now, bucking him backward into his attacker. How fucking dare he—how dare he! Reducing Simon to a victim, all the air gone, knowing that his life, all that had come before, meant . . . nothing. Nothing! Fuck Gillis and his strength—how was he so strong?—But Simon was stronger, damn it, stronger, and he ripped away at the hands that he realized finally *were* hands, panic fueling his own attack.

"*This* is how she died," Gillis said. The voice was distorted. It filled Simon's whole world. Simon shouted back, the bag sucking farther back into his mouth as he gagged on the intrusion. "Like this."

The terror racing through his entire body made each movement even more difficult. A tiny shift and there was breath—but not enough, not enough! He pushed back again, using his weight to drive the weight behind him away. It only grew closer.

"Her hands tied," the relentless voice said. "Kicking and squawking. And after five minutes . . ."

Simon thrashed to break free. Gillis only clutched more tightly.

"After five minutes," the voice shouted through the bag. "I stepped back! An' looked down at her. For an hour I watched her. Dead. Unmoving. An hour . . ."

"No!" another voice shattered through Gillis's monotone. "Oh God, no!"

Simon slammed forward, shoved, the bag whipping his head around as he sprawled against the side of the hallway. He rolled away, ripping the released plastic from his face. Gasped. Scrabbled back away before the nausea overwhelmed him. Retched, wobbling on his hands and knees, the air in his throat a searing pain.

Finally, the sound of hysterical sobbing broke through his daze. Simon turned his head. Saw Jeanne, far down the hallway. Saw something else, too. Something insane.

Gillis had been wearing the mask.

An enormous dog-faced creature slumped against the wall, sitting with one leg outstretched. Resting almost casually, head tilted. Watching Simon with wide, flat beaded eyes, larger and more glassy than Simon had imagined. The dog's ears hung down to Gillis's shoulders, comical and wrong as the costume head had been knocked askew, the entire image swimming in Simon's vision as he collapsed back against the wall and struggled to draw deep, broken breaths.

"I wore this so she wouldn't be scared," the doggie man said. The voice was muffled, a gruff perversion of sound emanating from the mask. "When I brought her dinner. I thought she'd . . . I found this in Jeanne's things. I didn't want her to be afraid of me. Not her. Not my Mary Rose."

Simon shivered, his own moan sounding closer to an animal's than human. Still, he couldn't look away.

"I loved her," the dog thing said.

And stared back at Simon like a reflection in a mirror.

25

Francine Morland stood over her only child, looking down at her as she slept. Hands folded tightly at her waist, the cross on her covered neck lifting with each deep breath, she gazed at Mary Rose as if it were the first time she'd truly ever looked at her. As if she were in her cradle. Or coffin.

"How is she?"

She didn't turn to Simon's voice. "She's slept the whole time."

"That's good."

"Did you find him?" she asked.

"Yes."

She smiled.

"Why don't we talk in the next room," Simon said. He kept his voice steady despite the feeling of nausea that'd followed him since Gillis's attack. In fact, the aftereffects were striking him harder than the actual assault. Some combination of the brutal violence, a kind of force Simon had never encountered, overshadowed by an even greater force: the man's words.

He walked back into the front room where James Morland stood eagerly, Morland's eyes sad and tired despite his pent-up energy. It'd been a long day and night for everyone, Simon understood. A long *life*, perhaps.

Simon collapsed into one of the cushioned wicker chairs.

Francine followed him into the room. She and her husband stood waiting for him to speak. *Let them wait*, he thought and closed his eyes, embracing the silence.

It'd been twenty years. What was another few minutes?

"Benjamin Gillis has been arrested," he began with eyes still closed.

"What in Heavens for?" James Morland's outburst was sharp, querulous. This hadn't been what he'd expected. *Join the club, old man.*

"Well, he tried to kill me."

There was a short, horrified silence, and Simon drank it in, reveling in it. After all he'd heard tonight, silence was a luxury he craved more than he realized. It couldn't last, of course.

"My . . . God." Morland again. Stiff. British. The inevitable accusation following. "What have you done?"

Simon laughed, opened his eyes. "Exactly what I was just thinking about, myself." Then he waited to speak again, watching them both. Two actors complicit in the atrocity against Mary Rose. How many others were there, he wondered. Was he, as well? He pushed the thought away. "Actually, I think he was only trying to scare me," he said, considering Gillis dispassionately for the first time. "Or rather, to teach me a lesson of some kind."

"You truly believe he had something to—"

"He did." Simon interrupted James's question. "And he confessed. To all of it." He looked between Mary Rose's parents. James Morland had put his hands on the kitchen counter to steady himself. Francine stared out the front windows into the continuing darkness. "Seizing her on the island, taking her to his house . . . keeping her there. For thirty-three days."

James Morland drummed fingertips on the counter, trying to hold his reaction, his composure.

Simon tensed, his own eyes welling despite himself. "And he claims he tried to kill her," he said. "Put a bag of some kind over her face and . . ." His voice had cracked, when he thought he could do this straight. "Tried to . . . to suffocate her."

"No, my God, no." James Morland stepped away sharply from the counter and, with the deliberation of a man who'd chosen his path long ago, crossed the room to his wife. "Our sweet, precious Mary Rose. Dear God . . ."

Simon watched as Francine pulled away from him, and he kept talking. "Seems he wore a Halloween dog mask of some kind when he was keeping her. An old costume lying around that'd belonged to one of his daughters. Said he wore it so Mary Rose wouldn't be afraid. Can you imagine? Coming down the steps to her in the dark, wearing such a thing. She was six." He shuddered. Even at thirty-three, in the light, it was horrifying. "He evidently kept it in a special box for twenty years with some other stuff. A couple of pictures she'd drawn on her stump that day. Shells she'd gathered and had in her little pockets. I think, in his way, he . . ." Simon couldn't bring himself to say the word. "He 'cared' for her. Wanted to protect her, even. Claimed it'd had something to do with the island. I don't know."

"Did he—"

"No. I don't think it was about that." Simon leaned forward, stretching. The adrenaline wearing off, finally, leaving the bitter, caustic taste in his mouth along with the still curiously delicious stir of *air*. "We should get some sleep. All of us. Tonight was only the beginning."

"What do you mean?" Morland asked, confusion deepening the wrinkles of his forehead. "It's solved. After all these years, we finally know what happened to her."

"Yes, but there will be a long legal process now. You know that better than I. And this whole family will be under the microscope again. It could get ugly. Names in the papers once more, and maybe worse than before. It's going to be a rough couple of years."

James stiffened, paling, then he put the pieces together himself, his proper and stalwart demeanor once more masking the chaos within. "I understand," he said. "If gossip and publicity is the price we pay again for the end to all of this, it's very well worth it."

Simon nodded, agreed, brought his hands to rest on his knees, his mind already on to the logistics of what would come. Set aside the horror, the outrage, and the sick truth of what had happened all those years ago, and what was left was a legal case. He understood well how to manage that. "Know that I will do everything I can to support this family. You're Mary Rose's parents, and I will work hard to make this right again. We're in this together. I told you when I first visited, I'll do whatever I can for her. Always. I love your daughter more than anything, James." He turned. "Francine. And I'll do everything necessary to make sure she never knows another day of pain." He'd stood.

"What else did he say, Simon?" Francine asked.

Simon shook his head, even as something dark curled inside him, something hard and cold and better left alone. "In the morning."

"Simon."

"Save it for the morning," he said, looking directly at her. The possibilities, the genuine misery, of what might have happened were too large for tonight. It could wait another twelve hours. It had to. "It'll help, maybe. All of us. Good night. I need to see Mary Rose."

"Mary Rose . . ." Francine's voice cut sharply between them. "Yes, go running to poor Mary Rose. Why would *you* be any different?"

"Francine," Morland warned. "Simon's right. Let's get some sleep and we'll talk again in the morning."

"What did Gillis tell you?" she asked again.

Simon looked away, genuine anger returning for the first time in hours. He'd wanted to avoid the accusations, the truth, as long as he could. Not so different from the Morlands after all, it seemed. "I don't want to talk about it right now."

"No," she snapped. "I'm not going to be swept aside again for you to discuss in the morning."

"Who's 'sweeping' anyone?" James Morland sounded truly panicked. "I don't understand."

"He told you it was my idea," Francine said. "Didn't he?"

Simon breathed deeply. *Air.* He could still taste the plastic bag in his mouth. Responding to Francine became almost an afterthought. "Yes."

James Morland looked between them, his hard-earned mask slipping once more. "Franny?"

"I want to know what he told you," she demanded, still glaring at Simon. "What he'll no doubt tell the police."

"*Told*," Simon corrected. "But there's time before anyone takes an old drunk child abductor seriously. That's for *his* lawyers to worry about."

Francine straightened at that, a curious mix of indignation and piety on her face. "I'm a respectable woman; he's a wasted soul. Accusations and gossip from twenty years ago. No jury will ever believe him."

Simon nodded. It was only the truth. "You're probably right, *Franny.*" God, he hated the bitch. But loved Mary Rose more. "And, if we're really lucky—for Mary Rose's sake—it won't even get to that. Play this right, I suspect no one will even glance at you twice."

And that, it seemed, was the breaking point. He should have recognized it sooner. That everything had led to this. This one crossroads, and he'd blundered into the moment as if he knew nothing about people, nothing about their pain. Nothing about betrayal.

But, he *did* know these. Had learned them both in his own life and on the job. Just foolishly hadn't expected to find them here.

Because of their age, their money. Their manners.

When, at the end of it all, they were just other broken people.

"I paid him four thousand pounds," Francine said abruptly. The words were like a shot of steam from a boiling pressure cooker, and once begun, what followed came in a hissing rush. "Four thousand pounds, and I wasn't sorry. For six long years I'd carried the burden of my sins and for what? For nothing."

"Francine!"

But Morland's voice seemed a haunted echo to his wife's outrage.

"He didn't love me, and you know what was worse? Even after I confirmed to him that Mary Rose was his daughter. So beautiful, so *precious.*" She spat the last words like a curse. "He still wouldn't love me again. He loved only *her.*" Her gaze shifted to her husband. "As you did, always more than me. How you *saw* her, in a way you never saw me. He never saw me . . ."

James didn't speak. He, like Simon, stood spellbound by the woman before them. A woman who'd been as ordinary as wallpaper and teaspoons, pearls and starched skirts, but who'd now become something else. Leaving both men no choice but to see her at last.

"You've always suspected, I know." Francine's lips twisted in a faint, almost nostalgic smile. "That I slept with your brother for almost a year *after* you and I were married. How could you not? I left the love letters and journals and trinkets lying about the house for years. But, I suppose we're both to pretend you never found them. And still, you didn't see me."

James Morland's face grew redder, even as it slackened in surprise. Surprise at what, Simon didn't know. That his wife had finally found her voice? Or what she was saying with it? "Francine, please . . . We'll discuss this later. Not in front of Simon."

She laughed. "But Simon is 'family' now, dear. Didn't you hear him? He's part of the Morland team tonight. Isn't that right, Simon?"

Simon couldn't speak. All he wanted anymore was Mary Rose. The rest, all of it, had become unimportant.

"Well, *I* loved someone other than Mary Rose," she went on bitterly, almost triumphantly, as if reading his thoughts. "I loved David before I was married, *and* after. Loved him in ways I could never love you, James. But, that, at least, I *know* you've always understood." She touched her chest and the fragile cross that hung there. "Our treasured Mary Rose was conceived in a sacred ritual during the summer solstice. In front of a dozen others."

"On the island." Simon heard the voice, was surprised it was his own.

"Yes." Her eyes gleamed. "'On the island.' In the moonlight. Revealed and embraced before the first gods. Born of *love*."

"So much for the 'forever beloved' part though, huh?" Simon said coldly. "And I thought Gillis was the monster. You paid someone to *kill* your only child? I can't even begin to understand that."

"No," she agreed. Her eyes showed an age and knowing that terrified him. "You can't."

"Why?" James asked. His face had morphed to that of a supplicant in the midst of a devastating storm, confused and dazed and willing it all to stop—simply stop. "I'm listening to you now, Francine. Tell me why."

She stared back. "To punish him."

"My brother?"

"For not taking me from you. For not wanting me enough. If he wouldn't claim me from you . . . I waited six years." She flicked her glance away, staring at the wall. "Said he wouldn't do that to you. That it wasn't the right thing. That we were stronger and had obligations to those . . ." She looked at James. "*Not* as strong. You ridiculous men. Half of you are still little boys. The rest . . ." She looked at Simon. "Marching around with your chests puffed out, tilting at windmills . . . Always trying to fix and solve things that can't be fixed or solved. Always trying to be 'men.' Instead of simply accepting reality, real consequences, real passions. I wanted to tell him what I'd done. After. I knew doing that would make him finally understand. That he'd see what he'd caused."

"But she came back." Simon challenged her designs from twenty years before.

Francine had turned at the crack of his voice. And then she straightened, smiled again. "She did." Piety once more shone in her face. "And for that, I thanked God." Her voice no longer held the outrage of the woman damned but the fervor of a convicted zealot. The transformation was so quick, so absolute, that Simon backed up a step.

"God?" he said.

Francine continued, however, as if he hadn't spoken. "I knew that first night I'd made a terrible mistake. One that had damned me to hell for eternity. The first night. As I know it now." She grasped her cross again, completely transported by her own tale. "And so I prayed. All day, *every* day. I purchased that tombstone, yes, but I also prayed for God to take it all back. For her to return to us. To me. And he heard my prayer." Her eyes sought and held Simon's gaze. "Heard and answered me. And from that moment on, I knew that *He* could see me. He could hear me."

She sagged a little then, the fervor of her conviction turning sour as realization settled more firmly against her bones. "But you've taken even that from me, haven't you, Simon. It wasn't God that brought her back to us. It was Benjamin Gillis. Because *he* loved her. Or, rather, it was the island. That it had . . ." She sighed, her mouth flattening into an awful, self-pitying grimace. "All this time I prayed for my soul to be delivered, and, though I know I will likely end in hellfire, I still wanted to believe someone was listening. That someone truly ever loved . . . me."

"I love you, Mother."

Simon turned.

Mary Rose stood in the hallway behind him, a snowy blanket swathed around her shoulders. Her face had never been more beautiful—or, eerily, more serene. It was as if she was once again seeming to dance for all that she was standing still.

Simon knew she'd heard everything.

Or enough.

"Everything's all right now," Mary Rose said.

Simon exchanged puzzled looks with James Morland.

"There's nothing to fear," she continued. "Or cause hurt anymore. She knows where she belongs."

"Who?" Simon crossed the room to her. "Mary Rose . . ."

"The dead girl." She tilted her head, remembering. "She . . ."

Simon embraced her. Despite the glow in her eyes, the blanket, her whole body felt chilled through.

"I remember looking down at her," she said, her voice somehow even more brittle and cold than her body.

Simon pulled back, still holding on to both her arms.

"She had no face. I looked down and . . ." Mary Rose shivered. "All it was . . ." Her eyes darkened, the pupils absorbing the white. Her fingers wriggled beneath him, as if drawing. "Nothing but black."

The plastic bag. Simon understood.

The dead girl she'd drawn for twenty years.

Herself.

Some kind of out-of-body experience. A near-death vision.

I don't know what you married.

Mary Rose Morland died twenty years ago.

Gillis's words echoed in Simon's memory, and he fought to keep sturdy. She needed his support. All those years thinking of herself as something incomplete, something not fully human.

Something escaped from its grave.

"Mary . . ." Simon began to speak, yet hadn't any notion what he might say. How could he ever—

"Simon's right."

Simon had barely heard James Morland's voice but turned.

Morland regarded his wife with weary eyes. Francine sat on the couch, crumpled over, hands together in prayer. "We should all get some sleep," Morland said. "We'll find a room in town."

Simon started a weak protest, but Morland stopped him.

"Good night, Simon," he said, and extended a trembling hand to his wife.

Francine gazed up at him as if in a trance, but took it.

A lifeline that somehow lifted her from the couch and away.

"Mary Rose." Morland turned back. "Until tomorrow, my dear flower."

She smiled. "Good night, Daddy."

Francine Morland, slouched and facing the door, also looked back at her daughter from over her shoulder. "Mary Rose . . ."

"Come along, Franny." Morland led her from the cottage.

The cottage door shut.

Simon couldn't think beyond the same milestone of sleep.

Darkness. Nothing.

"Come on," he said to Mary Rose. "Let's get you back to bed." He winced at the sound of the Morlands' car starting outside. "We'll talk more tomorrow." Everything could wait until then. All of it.

He led Mary Rose into the bedroom again, covered her, kicked off his shoes to join her.

"Dear Simon," she said again, looking up at him as if already lost to a dream. "My beautiful man."

He drew her into the sanctuary of his arms. Safe.

She would always be safe now, with him.

"I love you," he said.

She closed her eyes, smiled, nuzzled against him.

Simon reached out to switch off the lamp. A couple hours' rest was all they needed. In the morning . . .

Something. Anything.

He'd think of it then.

And then keep doing that for the rest of their lives.

When he woke, it was almost daybreak. Seabirds cawed in the distance. The windows stood open, letting in the fresh air he could still not quite get enough of.

And Mary Rose was gone.

On her side of the bed, where she'd slept only hours before, was a flat oval rock and a sprig of rowan leaves.

The rock was smooth to the touch and a perfect piece for any cairn. The rowan retained its musty scent.

And the blanket was still warm from where her body had rested.

"Mary Rose?" he whispered into the gloom, but there was no response.

His hand closed around the rock. "Mary Rose," he said again, but softer, not louder as he'd expected, the first inkling of dread snaking along his veins.

Through the open window, he could hear the soft murmuring of the tide lapping against the shore.

Simon ran for the front door.

Outside, the gulls started screaming.

26

The morning of the thirty-third day since Mary Rose's disappearance—her second—came and went with little fanfare.

Simon stood at the edge of the cairn field, his hands shoved into the pockets of his khakis, cinched another two holes deep on his belt, but he hadn't much noticed missing meals.

The cairn he'd built a month ago loomed above the rest.

The lone rock she'd left behind balanced at the very top. A beacon for her to find again. A promise kept, he hoped.

The last bit of magic he could maybe cling to.

He wasn't alone in that desire.

They all were keeping the watch now.

James Morland, the druid Brodie, even Cameron.

Simon turned as the wind picked up again, skiffing off the water's edge in the distance. It was a beautiful day, promising enough. Cameron's fishing boat bobbed offshore, anchored against the turning of the tide. The captain had disappeared into the grassy hillocks without speaking, the same as he'd done the first several days of the search.

Simon couldn't believe it at first. The man wanted to help find her, he'd said. To do something—anything. Said he felt responsible. After the first few days, he'd left them to search on their own for a week. But in the end, he couldn't stay away. Simon grimaced. *Responsible.* Cameron had no reason to feel that. But he was a good man, for all that he'd spent his whole life passing an island that had alternately frightened and embarrassed him for twenty years. He'd still wanted to help find Mary Rose.

They'd done it once before, hadn't they? They could do it again.

And as the end of the month came closer, the wind-chapped captain had held on to the same hope that Simon fostered, the same possibility her father had held tightly again behind his doleful mask.

That first morning, they'd found the speedboat—the hotel's, the same he'd once taken her on—drifting gently against the island's shore, half beached by the waves. But she was gone.

Many of the locals who'd come out to search were old enough to remember the first time, old enough to give knowing looks. Cameron had been one of them, had even brought Simon out that first morning.

Thirty-three days ago, today.

Today, she'd come back, and it all would be okay. Once more.

Brodie Rothes had slipped off again. The Scottish druid had also eagerly joined the search from the beginning, consulting his rune stones, praying to his rich and varied gods, spirits and ancestors, dutifully counting each of them off on his long rope of colored beads. He hadn't come for attention or to play magician, either. This perfect stranger had genuinely come to help in whatever way he could. And he'd never even met her.

Simon had walked the island with the man a dozen times by now. Rothes had scoffed at the circle of standing stones from the beginning, considering it far too sullied by generations of curious teens for the ancients to heed its call anymore. Instead he'd spent most of his time at the little lake on the far side of the island. Simon had watched him, secretly adding his own prayers to those Brodie offered up. He had no other choice, really, than to hope the magic of the island that Brodie hinted at was real.

He wanted it to be—needed it, really. The alternative was too terrible. The thought of Mary Rose somehow falling overboard, or maybe losing her way in the current as she went ashore, fighting for her life in the icy waters before finally slipping away.

Simon shuddered.

They'd discussed dredging the small lake, but the idea had been quickly abandoned. Mary Rose wasn't there, they all knew. And a full-scale dredging operation would attract more attention than they wanted. Bad enough the locals knew about the disappearance, but they wouldn't noise it around. People disappeared every day, after all.

Most of them never came back.

And given the Gillis arrest and the obvious truth they'd mucked up the investigation of Mary Rose all those years ago, the constable's office sure as hell didn't want the press involved with yet another disappearance of the same poor woman. This time, Simon agreed with them.

And what did that say about him?

He grimaced, turning his face into the wind.

They'd come every day, rarely only him alone. They'd all felt the supernatural pull of the island—he wasn't making that up. There was definitely something here, something beyond common tragedy. Beyond the memories of a little girl's laughter or the knowing smile of a young woman.

He wanted that woman beside him again.

Above all else. To love. To cherish. To hold.

The island wanted her more.

He suspected it could turn on them again soon, too. That it would drive Cameron away as it had years before. Find ways even to chase Simon off, now that she wasn't there to protect him. How long before the streams ran crimson and rotted things stumbled out from the woods or the phantom image of a tree and two teens dangling together forever in the ocean wind?

Soon, he knew. He'd felt the forewarning creeping under his skin, growing stronger each day. This month, it had tolerated them. It had gotten what it wanted. The rest, all of it, had become unimportant. It had protected a little girl once twenty years before and finally come to collect. A promise, a debt from decades ago. Finally fulfilled.

Or, maybe, Mary Rose had returned solely of her own desires. She'd returned freely. Joyfully.

An idea he was not yet willing to contemplate in the daylight.

"Never did truly understand the meaning of this field."

Simon didn't turn to the voice.

James Morland had come upon him silently, but the man seemed to do that more and more these days. Moving like a wraith in corduroy and tweed.

Francine had moved out of their house two weeks before.

Morland gestured. "It's always been like this, even when we were kids. All these little piles of rocks. Some of them new, sure. But so many more look like they'd been here for generations. No one seems to disturb them, either. Which always seemed to make it more eerie, every time we came out. Franny and I even built one together . . . once."

Simon nodded. Knew he should say something—anything, about Francine. Still couldn't find the words.

As if he'd spoken, though, James shuffled forward, squatting down to the nearest of the towers. He reached out, his palm barely an inch from the precarious pile. "She's lost to me, Francine," he said, matter-of-factly. He moved his hand around the cairn, as if sensing its primal, preserving order. "She's already filed for divorce."

Simon's throat was dry as he forced the words out. "I'm sorry." It seemed woefully inadequate to the moment, but he had nothing else.

"Yes, well." James stood again. His mournful gaze remained on the cairn field before he turned to Simon, the hollows in his cheeks more pronounced, weighed down by the dark circles now beneath his eyes. He twisted his lips into a wry, devastating smile. "Funny thing, really."

"What's that?" asked Simon.

"If you'd only left it alone—left it all alone, from the very beginning, we'd still all be where we were."

"James . . ."

"Not entirely happy, perhaps. There was too much gone past for that. But peaceful enough. Mary Rose had you, she had her life in the States. She never needed to come back here, not really. But you couldn't leave it alone."

Simon wanted to respond, he did. Couldn't. James's voice cut through whatever shreds of any justification or apology he could give, slicing up his defense syllable by syllable.

"It was a selfish thing you did," Morland continued calmly, without emotion. The most damning indictments didn't need emotion. "Careless, even. Needing to push, to prod. To find answers when the questions really weren't yours to ask."

No, Simon implored silently. *No, that's not it at all.* Mary Rose had been getting worse. The nightmares, the nervous tics. The strange laughter at odd times. *We were losing her.* He'd had to find out what was wrong—had to help her.

"We might not have done everything right by Mary Rose," Morland said. "But she deserved to hold on to what happiness she'd carved out for herself, didn't she? We all did what best we could." He gave a soft, mirthless laugh. "Until you came and decided you could do it better."

With a swift, vicious kick, her father lashed out at the nearest cairn, toppling it. The rocks spun and skipped off their fellows, the long-standing talisman destroyed with a single movement, never to be rebuilt in this strange desolate place.

"I thought . . ." Simon didn't know who uttered the words. Not him, certainly. It didn't sound like his voice at all.

"You thought," Morland said. "You thought so much that now we're here together. And we've *both* lost our wives, haven't we?"

Before the question had fully faded away, Cameron emerged again from the woods, angling toward them. The sun inched higher in the sky. Brodie too stepped out of the shadows, his gaze on the far water, the sky, the rocks and sand. He walked too slowly for a man with any news.

They all walked like that now, as if conserving their energy, drawing inside themselves like sea things skulking on the dark ocean floor, hauling along the shells of their expectations, unable to fully move forward.

They couldn't break free.

They were waiting for Mary Rose to return.

She didn't.

He stared at the circle of rocks. They never changed, no matter what evidence of activity he found within their loose embrace. This year, it was again the scuffed earth and charred embers of a campfire, probably three days old. The wind had whisked away any shoe prints, but he'd seen the telltale marks often enough by now. Another group of kids, dancing and howling at the moon. Smoking pot, risking a kiss or more. Being kids . . .

He turned, made his way back through the overgrown brush, the spotty forest. Though nearly soundless, there *was* life here, he thought. Buds still coming out on some of the trees despite the lateness of the season, leaves a soft green. The color of spring, renewal, of hope.

It was the work of ten minutes to reach the stump at the top of the hill again. The same as it always was. Reassuringly so, after so many years.

Winded him more each year, he admitted.

Though it never seemed that anything could disturb it, no matter how much time passed. Wind-scoured smooth, its thick roots plunged into the ground, it was strangely inviting, almost homey. As if it was waiting for someone—a little girl, perhaps—to return, to sit, and draw, and dream.

The first few years, Simon had done exactly that. Sat on her stump, staring everywhere, alert to every sigh of the wind, every crash of far-off waves. Sat and dreamed and waited. Traced his fingers over initials grown ever more faded. Mary Rose hadn't appeared, of course. Foolish to think that she would, and yet—

And yet.

He stood for a long time with his hands in his pockets, staring down. Catching his breath. Feeling the tug of being closer to sixty than forty.

He'd lied when he told that minister in England—couldn't remember his name now—about knowing when his father was truly gone. It hadn't been when they'd gotten home that afternoon. It'd come much later. When Inky, the family dog, had stopped running to the door to greet her master at the end of the day. It'd taken more than four months. But, eventually, she'd stopped.

"The Broadhurst case went well," Simon said.

The words startled him, for all they were his. He hadn't spoken aloud on the island for years. It hadn't seemed right, since James Morland had passed. But now, once begun, he couldn't help but continue. "Phillips—you remember him, right? Said it was a turning point for the city, that it would ice my legacy. Ha, some legacy. Says it's the right time for me to run for city council again. Can you imagine? Always says things like that. Anyhow, what else? The new kid, Gianni, just tried his first case. Straight out of college, scared as shit. Reminds me of . . ."

Simon grimaced and looked away, letting the sharp breeze dry the unexpected dampness on his cheeks. The wind had picked up, and he pulled his hands free of his pockets, zipped up his windbreaker. Sometimes the island was warm, inviting him to stay. Sometimes, like today, it hustled him through the visit, nudging him back down to the shoreline, back toward his waiting boat, and sometimes, like today, he didn't fight that nudge.

He picked his way back down the scrubby ridge, his hands drifting together, right thumb and forefinger twisting the wedding band on his left ring finger. He'd never removed it. Hadn't seemed right, for all that he knew that Mary Rose would have wanted him to move on, to laugh, to enjoy life.

The way she'd never been able to, for all she'd tried. As she'd never enjoyed anything so much as she'd loved being on this island, standing here in the wind, her smile wide and open, her eyes flashing with excitement. So real. So alive. As she looked in the self-portrait she'd painted once.

The one which hung on the wall in his office, since he spent more time at work than at home, and it was nice having her there. With him. Funny, on the opposite wall, hung a mirror and—with him looking in the mirror just so, standing with the painting behind him—he'd long ago discovered it was almost impossible to tell where the island ended and his own reflection began.

A particularly sharp gust of wind blew up off the water and Simon turned his shoulder into it, turtling into the stiff, upright collar of his coat, the move unconscious after so many years visiting the Scottish shore. Sand kicked up and battered his jacket, peppered his hair, but the wind dropped again as quickly, as if already tired of the game.

A scent familiar and sweet lingered behind.

He turned back to the shore, squinting in the strange light reflecting off the ocean in a vibrant haze. Its blue an almost neon color. And there was something—

Someone there. Now, on the shore with him.

Another adventuresome tourist, his mind categorized immediately.

Her clothes too bright, too new for a local. The vivid blue of her jacket drawn tight across her slender frame, the jaunty bill of her sunhat almost daring the wind to knock it off.

He hadn't seen anyone on the island in years, roaming the beach like this. But it happened. It was, after all, the Little Island That Likes to Be Visited. He'd wave, maybe stop to say hello. He was long done with warnings.

The woman swayed a little in the breeze, seeming to dance for all that she was standing still.

Simon's hands clenched. His heart sped up. Surely—no. Even from a distance, the woman was too young, far too young, pliant with the languid carelessness of youth. Barely thirty, he would guess.

He moved toward her, trying not to rush. Certain she'd seen him already. She didn't move but seemed almost to wait for him as he stepped deliberately across the shifting sands. The strange miasma of shimmering light held above the long stretch of sand, a trick of the sunshine and sea.

He'd seen it before on the island.

But he hadn't seen this. Hadn't seen anyone quite like this.

Even as he walked, he turned his reactions over and around like a child's puzzle, one of those cubes, studying, storing them, knowing the disappointment would come, but before that—before that, there was this moment. This hope, this thought. And what would he do, he wondered, if he ever did happen upon the girl he'd loved and lost and who held him still. He studied his reactions the way he studied juries or thick, rambling dossiers pulled out of musty files, searching out weaknesses, leverage points. His heart quickened further, his hands sweaty now, his breathing tight. Good to know he could still feel something. To know the wind and sea of this island hadn't eroded everything from him. He still could touch the frayed edges of the excitement, the hope, that crushing, all-consuming love he hadn't even fully understood until he'd lost it. Until the memory of it was all he had.

He approached her more quickly now, the figure on the sand. Too quickly. Short of breath, even. *Slow down, slow down!* He should savor this moment, revel in its fleeting lost hope, not caring for what would come next. The awkward smile, the confusion in eyes he did not know, had never known, the wrenching disappointment. He should—

The woman turned, a flash of deep red searing Simon's vision.

Rowan berries, tucked behind her ear.

He froze, throat closing up even as his mouth worked. No sound escaped. His hands were down in front of him, palms out, and he could only stare.

She was partially turned, but he could see the woman before him was young, impossibly young.

Her hair the color of ebony beneath her broad brim, the side of her face smooth, radiant. Untouched by time. So *young*. And, also, so real. So alive.

"Hi—hi," he managed. "I don't . . ."

Simon stopped, breathed deeply. He could even smell her now.

Vanilla. And sandalwood.

"Is it . . ." His voice faded. He lowered his head.

Reaching up, she brushed a cool, light hand through his hair, then pausing, almost as an afterthought, to settle a tuft of graying hair.

Her words were almost lost beneath the gentle break of dark water against hidden shorelines. "Isn't it just perfect," she'd said.

AFTERWORD

An Old Master's Unheard *Cri de Coeur*: Alfred Hitchcock's *Mary Rose*

by Joseph McBride

Alfred Hitchcock wryly described the subject matter of his 1958 masterpiece *Vertigo* as "a form of necrophilia." While that ultimate sexual taboo proves only an illusion in *Vertigo*, sexual congress with a dead woman is an actual plot element in the most intriguing unfilmed project of Hitchcock's career, *Mary Rose*. A darker version of Sir James M. Barrie's whimsically haunting 1920 play, this ghost story would have taken Hitchcock's characteristic mingling of eroticism and death into dimensions beyond any he had explored on-screen.

Hitchcock's dream project for more than half a century, *Mary Rose* ultimately proved too troubling for Universal Pictures, which forbade him to make it. The poetic meditation on death and eternal youth that Hitchcock wanted to direct from Barrie's play, drawing on his own obsessions about women and sexuality, might have become the director's most deeply personal work. His failure to realize it was, according to biographer Donald Spoto, "perhaps the single greatest disappointment of his creative life."

Hitchcock's most intense creative involvement with *Mary Rose* was undertaken in 1963–64, while he was preparing and filming *Marnie*. He worked on an adaptation of Barrie's play with *Marnie* screenwriter Jay Presson Allen. *Mary Rose* would have been part of Hitchcock's powerful cycle of early sixties films dealing with extreme forms of psychological and social disturbance (*Psycho*, *The Birds*, *Marnie*). The filmmaker's long-repressed sexuality was pushing its way violently to the surface of his personal life, and sexually based trauma became the dominant theme of his work. Camille Paglia, in her monograph on *The Birds*, aptly calls that period Hitchcock's time of "existential crisis."

Not unnaturally for a man of advancing years and failing health, Hitchcock's late films also reflected his increasingly urgent preoccupation with mortality, a risky subject for any Hollywood filmmaker. Hitchcock took advantage of the new license given filmmakers to deal with previously taboo subjects and imagery. Though his late films are of uneven quality, and sometimes were rejected by audiences or critics because of their graphic violence and frequent misogyny, it cannot be denied that Hitchcock's closing years took him boldly into uncharted artistic territory. The boldest exploration of all was his trip into what Shakespeare called "the undiscover'd country from whose bourn/ No traveler returns."

No traveler, that is, except Mary Rose.

Like Barrie's earlier *Peter Pan*, *Mary Rose* deals with an enchanted island that serves as "a safe place" for lost children. The Scottish playwright drew his inspiration for both plays from Celtic mythology about children abducted by fairies. To *Mary Rose* he added his own melancholy preoccupations with interrupted childhood and disrupted motherhood. Barrie adumbrated the central theme of *Mary Rose* in his 1902 novel *The Little White Bird*: "The only ghosts, I believe, who creep into this world are dead young mothers, returned to see how their children fare. . . . What is saddest about ghosts is that they may not know their child. They expect him to be just as he was when they left him, and they are easily bewildered, and search for him from room to room, and hate the unknown boy he has become. Poor, passionate souls, they may even do him an injury."

Mary Rose Morland disappears at the age of eleven (seven in the screenplay) while on holiday with her parents on an island in Scotland's Outer Hebrides. She returns after twenty days, knowing nothing of where she has been. At age eighteen, she marries a middle-aged man named Simon Blake, with whom her parents conspire to keep her in the dark about the childhood incident. Her mother warns Simon that there is "something she doesn't know of herself, and it makes her a little different from other girls." Mary Rose bears a child, but on a belated honeymoon to the same island, she vanishes again. This time she is gone for many years, returning when her parents are old and her son is fully grown. But she herself is unchanged, still an ingenuous young woman, seemingly uncorrupted by age or marked by sexual awareness, despite having been a wife and mother.

In one of the play's most beautiful passages, Mrs. Morland tells Simon, "I have sometimes thought that our girl is curiously young for her age—as if—you know how just a touch of frost may stop the growth of a plant and yet leave it blooming—it has sometimes seemed to me as if a cold finger had once touched my Mary Rose." Simon responds uncomprehendingly, "What you are worrying about is just her innocence—which seems a holy thing to me."

Barrie's style is charmingly fey. But something sinister about Mary Rose's reason for disappearing is briefly suggested by her cryptic response to her father when he asks what frightens her. She replies, "I am most afraid of my daddy." Perversely, this revelation leaves Mr. Morland "rather flattered." It implies that her escape to her "safe place"— safe from growth, sexuality, and the adult responsibilities of marriage and motherhood—is motivated by fear of being dominated or even sexually violated by her father, and perhaps also by fear of her future with her equally paternalistic husband. Along with its overtones of incest, her anxiety suggests the dangerous futility of attempting to preserve childhood innocence beyond natural limits.

The play's great success with British audiences in 1920 has been attributed in part to its psychological timing. *Mary Rose* opened less than eighteen months after the end of World War I. In the stage version, Mary Rose's son, who has run off to sea at the age of twelve, returns from the war as an Australian soldier. Patrick Chalmers observed that Barrie's "lovely and spiritual conception was staged in the ugly and uneasy period that followed immediately upon" the Armistice, bringing "joy and peace and a tear or two to thousands, weary of the War and the War's aftermath, during the years of its run." Audiences took from the play a mystical answer to Rudyard Kipling's cry of national bereavement, "But who shall return us the children?"

As a twenty-year-old theater buff attending the original production at London's Haymarket Theatre, Hitchcock was enraptured by

Fay Compton's performance as Mary Rose. He later cast Compton as the countess in his only feature-length musical, *Waltzes from Vienna* (1933). A note in the director's papers at the Margaret Herrick Library of the Academy of Motion Picture Arts and Sciences indicates that in October 1963, around the time he started planning in earnest to film *Mary Rose*, Hitchcock inquired into Compton's availability. He may have wanted her to play Mrs. Otery, the elderly woman who tends the English country house haunted by Mary Rose.

Hitchcock was so impressed by Norman O'Neill's ethereal music for the London stage production that, while making *Vertigo*, he had the only surviving recording brought from England to play for composer Bernard Herrmann. The "call" prompting Mary Rose's disappearance was created with bagpipes and "wordless voices" played on a musical saw. Hitchcock described the sound as "celestial voices, like Debussy's *Sirènes*." Anyone who has heard Herrmann's chilling *Vertigo* music and his lovely score for Joseph L. Mankiewicz's *The Ghost and Mrs. Muir* can imagine what he might have done with *Mary Rose*. Bill Krohn points out in his fascinating book *Hitchcock at Work* that "hints of *Mary Rose* appear in *Vertigo*: After Scottie [James Stewart] pulls Madeleine [Kim Novak] out of the Bay, she can barely be heard saying 'Where is my child' in her sleep." That is one of the phrases Novak's Madeleine/Judy uses to persuade Scottie that she is possessed by the spirit of a dead woman, Carlotta Valdes, who went mad when her child was taken away by her rich and powerful husband.

Mary Rose offers a virtual catalog of Hitchcock's ambivalent views toward women. In her book *The Women Who Knew Too Much: Hitchcock and Feminist Theory*, Tania Modleski writes that Hitchcock's films "seek with equal vehemence both to appropriate femininity and to destroy it—hence that curious mixture of 'sympathy and misogyny' found in these films."

Mrs. Morland tells her husband in Barrie's play, "It is as if Mary Rose was just something beautiful that you and I and Simon had dreamt together." This observation is a key to understanding Hitchcock's attraction to the project: the romantic heroines in his films tend to be alluring but insubstantial, more tantalizing than pleasing. Mary Rose flees from her father because she wants to remain young and innocent, but she does so at the cost of remaining in an unnatural state of dreamlike stasis. Perhaps her father subconsciously wants her to stay that way as well; Simon certainly does. Like *Vertigo*, *Mary Rose* deals with neurotic male possessiveness brought on by sexual anxiety and carried to the point of preserving the beloved dead in a state of romantic perfection. *Mary Rose* can be seen as a reflection of Hitchcock's Catholicism and its myth of the Virgin Mary, who bears a child yet remains untouched and later is assumed bodily into Heaven.

Hitchcock's *Mary Rose* would have been more nightmarish than dreamlike, intensifying the anguish felt by the title character and her aged family members. The director and his female screenwriter intended to make the audience feel the full horror of a woman being treated as a child. When Mary Rose sits on the knee of her grown son (called Harry in the play, Kenneth in the screenplay), it's a grotesque twist on Norman Bates's line in *Psycho*, "A boy's best friend is his mother." Perhaps that sentiment explains why, in the closing scene of both play and film, Harry/Kenneth is not upset by the ghostly reappearance of his dead mother but instead seems happy to play with her, as if she were his child or puppet.

What causes Mary Rose to return from the dead and haunt the living is her guilt over abandoning her child so she can live in self-sufficient tranquility on the island. Hitchcock and Allen greatly heighten the intensity of the play's final scenes. In their version, Mary Rose's discovery that Kenneth, who joined the United States Army in World War I, may be a prisoner of war provokes a harrowing sequence using subjective camera and sound techniques to convey her overwhelming anguish. The realization of this loss literally kills her (again). But worse is yet to come.

In the screenplay's updated denouement (set in 1939), Kenneth returns to his boyhood home, still an army officer, and encounters the ghostly Mary Rose. She thinks he must be the person who stole her child. Facing him menacingly with his army knife, she demands, "Give him back." Kenneth sadly admits that, in a way, he *is* the one who took her child. Then he offers the forgiveness she seeks for having abandoned him. Her hand falls to her side and she gives back the knife, finally freed to accept her death. Barrie, too, flirted with this disturbing situation of a mother contemplating her own son's murder, but the playwright's Mary Rose, unlike Hitchcock's, never took the knife from behind her back.

The poignant, blissful ending of the screenplay—Mary Rose bidding her son farewell, hearing the call of her heavenly voices, and returning to her island forever—can be seen as Hitchcock's final absolution of his own mother.

Among the monstrously domineering mothers in his films of the early 1960s are the mummified Mrs. Bates in *Psycho*, Jessica Tandy's Lydia Brenner in *The Birds*, and Louise Latham's Bernice Edgar in *Marnie*. Asked why mothers in his films are often such sinister figures, Hitchcock replied, "Well, I suppose, generally speaking, Mother can be a bloody nuisance. . . . Sometimes she can be all-pervading. She can hang around and interfere with everybody's life."

The most famous story about Hitchcock's childhood is about the time when he was five or six and his father sent him to the local police station with a note about some childish transgression. The officer who read the note locked little Alfred in a cell for five minutes, telling him, "This is what we do to naughty boys." Although the frightening father appears in *Mary Rose*, the influence of Hitchcock's mother seems to have been even more baleful. Emma Hitchcock was a strict Irish Catholic. Well into Alfred's young manhood, she made him stand at the foot of her bed each evening and tell her everything he had done that day— "the evening confession," he called it. That feeling of stifling scrutiny by a mother who would not let him grow up was mingled, paradoxically, with an acute feeling of abandonment. Hitchcock's emotionally cold parents sent him away to boarding school when he was nine.

"Fear? It has influenced my life and my career," Hitchcock acknowledged. "I remember when I was five or six. It was a Sunday evening, the only time my parents did not have to work. They put me to bed and went to Hyde Park for a stroll. They were sure I would be asleep until their return. But I woke up, called out, and no one answered. Nothing but night all around me. Shaking, I got up, wandered around the empty, dark house and, finally arriving in the kitchen, found a piece of cold meat which I ate while drying my tears."

Hitchcock would have agreed with Barrie's observation "To be born is to be wrecked on an island." In both the play and the screenplay of *Mary Rose*, there is a brief mention of another child who disappeared on the island, a lost boy who may be "on the island still." Perhaps in that lost boy Alfred Hitchcock recognized himself. Among the touching lines he contributed to the screenplay was Mary Rose's remark to her husband "If you plan to be bald and fat, I daresay I shan't mind!" Hitchcock also wanted Mary Rose's grown son to tell her that he too had been searching: "For you—or for something you might have been."

The barriers Hitchcock encountered in trying to bring *Mary Rose* to the screen were an outgrowth of the powerful impulses that drew him to the material. In the 1950s, the director considered making the picture with Grace Kelly, the epitome of the cool, elegant blondes he favored. But Kelly escaped Hitchcock's grasp by becoming the princess of her own doomed fairy tale. The catalyst to move *Mary Rose* into active preproduction was the emergence in the early sixties of the inexperienced young blond actress and former model Tippi Hedren as Hitchcock's new personal obsession. Ultimately, both Hedren and *Mary Rose* fell victim to the director's desperate attempt to replicate his vanished feminine ideal represented by the Grace Kelly of *Rear Window* and *To Catch a Thief*.

With Kelly, Hitchcock could keep his fantasizing within the bounds of decorum, but he had difficulty doing so with Hedren. François Truffaut told me with amusement about the time he went to visit Hitchcock at Universal and found him alone in his private screening room, where he had been watching, over and over as if in a masturbatory reverie, a television commercial featuring Tippi Hedren. That black-and-white spot for the diet drink Sego, the commercial in which Hitchcock had first discovered her, shows Hedren walking down a street and hearing a wolf whistle. She turns to see that the whistler is an impish eight-year-old boy. Hitchcock was so fond of that commercial that he recreated it in the opening scene of *The Birds*, filmed at San Francisco's Union Square.

Once Hitchcock had Hedren bound to him by an exclusive seven-year contract, he closely supervised her wardrobe and appearance and tried to assert control over every aspect of her life, personal and professional. He treated her much the same way Stewart's deranged Scottie treats Novak's Judy while transforming her into the spectral blond vision of Madeleine in *Vertigo*. But like the earthy Judy, Hedren remained intractably real. Hitchcock seemed both stimulated and frustrated by her emotional and sexual unattainability, finding her tantalizing yet maddeningly distant.

The real-life anguish of a man longing for the unattainable contributed greatly to the heartrending portrait of *Mary Rose* in Allen's screenplay, on which she worked closely with Hitchcock. "I think there was always something of that in what Hitch did—that was a part of his power," Allen told me in an interview for this article. "He lived very much in fantasy. But at the same time he was terribly grounded, he was a very funny guy."

In August 1963, Hitchcock directed his agent, Herman Citron, to acquire the film rights to *Mary Rose* and to register its title with the Motion Picture Association of America along with an alternate title, *The Island That Likes to Be Visited*. Allen signed her contract to write the screenplay in January 1964. At the time, she was finishing her work on *Marnie*. Based on a novel by Winston Graham, *Marnie* deals with a kleptomaniac dominated by a disturbed mother who keeps her at a childlike stage of emotional development, pathologically terrified of sex. A former television writer, Allen later became best known for her stage and screen adaptations of Muriel Spark's novel *The Prime of Miss Jean Brodie*. Hitchcock hired her to replace another screenwriter on *Marnie*, novelist Evan Hunter, after somehow obtaining a copy of the still-unproduced *Jean Brodie* play script (the director never told Allen how he had managed to do so).

Allen willingly assumed the role of the master's apprentice, helping him realize his artistic conceptions. "I had a marvelous relationship with Hitch," she recalled. "He was wonderful to me. I had never done a film before *Marnie*, and he was a sensational teacher. He just couldn't teach me fast enough for me to write a great script." On both *Marnie* and *Mary Rose*, she said, "We would sit and discuss something for ages before I would go to work. Hitch loved to play, and I never knew where the playing left off and the input started. He was very skillful; he made everything seem fun for me. I probably wouldn't have stayed in the business if I had started out with anybody else."

Allen wrote two drafts of *Mary Rose*, the second dated February 15, 1964. She smoothly solved most of the structural problems of adapting the play and embellished Barrie's dialogue with natural elegance. But the script still presents some problems. Overly wordy in spots and bogged down by its theatrical origins, it tends to vocalize the play's subtexts, dissipating some of the mystery. Furthermore, the visual schema of this cinematic fantasy is only sketchily indicated on paper and would have had to be elaborately imagined by Hitchcock during the production process.

Matte artist Albert Whitlock, whom Hitchcock described in the late 1970s as "by far the finest technician that we have in our business today," had trouble grasping what the director had in mind for *Mary Rose*. Whitlock remembered doing "a lot of sketches" for the project, calling it "a very moody thing. And I said to him, because he was always very strong on the selling point, 'What's the selling point, Hitch?'" Revealing his need to claim Barrie's story as his own, Hitchcock replied that the film would be sold not as "Hitchcock's *Mary Rose*" but as "A Ghost Story by Alfred Hitchcock: *Mary Rose*." "That'll get 'em," Hitchcock declared.

A somewhat more concrete sense of what Hitchcock visualized came in his discussion of the project with Truffaut in their 1966 interview book. Hitchcock described *Mary Rose* as "a little like a science-fiction story. I still haven't definitely dropped the idea of making it. A few years back it might have seemed that the story would be too irrational for the public. But since then the public's been exposed to these twilight-zone stories, especially on television. . . .

"If I were to make the film, I would put the girl in a dark-gray dress and I would put a neon tube of light inside, around the bottom of the dress, so that the light would only hit the heroine. Whenever she moved, there would be no shadow on the wall, only a blue light. You'd have to create the impression of photographing a presence rather than a body. At times she would appear very small in the image, at times very big. She wouldn't be a solid lump, you see, but rather like a sensation. In this way you lose the feeling of real space and time. You should be feeling that you are in the presence of an ephemeral thing, you see."

"It's a lovely subject," commented Truffaut. "Also a sad one."

"Yes, very sad," Hitchcock agreed. "Because the real theme is: If the dead were to come back, what would you do with them?"

Though Hedren gives an extraordinarily moving, underrated performance as Marnie, playing Mary Rose probably would have been too much of a stretch. She was too mature and soignée to step believably into the part of a childlike eighteen-year-old girl. But that did not matter to the obsessed Hitchcock. Donald Spoto's *The Dark Side of Genius: The Life of Alfred Hitchcock* reports that Hitchcock came to Hedren's dressing room during the making of *Marnie* to tell her of a recurring dream he was having. The dream seemed straight out of *Mary Rose*: "You were in the living room of my house in Santa Cruz, and there was a rainbow, a glow around you. You came right up to me and said, 'Hitch, I love you—I'll always love you,' and we embraced. Don't you understand that you're everything I've ever dreamed about?"

"But it was a dream, Hitch," objected Hedren. "Just a dream."

Hitchcock's relationship with the actress was tense throughout the filming of *The Birds* and *Marnie*, partly because he put her through such grueling physical and psychological experiences. After *Marnie* finished shooting, Hitchcock cryptically told Peter Bogdanovich, "Svengali has a few more gray hairs." Spoto revealed that Hitchcock made an "overt sexual proposition" to Hedren near the end of shooting. That was in late February 1964, shortly after Allen finished scripting *Mary Rose*. Hedren's rejection was a shattering experience for the emotionally fragile old man. All Hitchcock would say of it was, "She did what no one is permitted to do. She referred to my weight."

"I am convinced that Hitchcock was never the same after *Marnie*, and that its failure cost him a considerable amount of his self-confidence," Truffaut observed. "This was not so much due to the financial failure of the film (he had had others), but rather to the failure of his professional and personal relationship with Tippi Hedren."

"I was agonizingly sorry for both of them," Allen told Spoto. "It was an old man's *cri de coeur*. She had her own life, and everyone was telling her not to make Hitchcock unhappy. But she couldn't help making him unhappy! By the end of the film he was very angry with her."

That spelled doom for *Mary Rose*. Lew Wasserman, president of Universal's parent company, MCA, and Hitchcock's former agent, "didn't like *Marnie*," the screenwriter added. "It was made at a time of career crisis for Hitch. And they didn't like the first drafts of *Mary Rose*. They knew it would make him fall back into the Tippi trap."

Wasserman's lack of enthusiasm for the material predated the crisis over Tippi Hedren. Allen told me: "I don't know whether it was because it was period, whether it was because it was costume stuff, maybe marginally intellectual, I have no idea, but Lew Wasserman was on record as not being interested in it to begin with. Hitch never had a green light for the project, never. He just went ahead on his own. By the time *Mary Rose* came up for green-lighting, Tippi was out of the picture, and I think that is possibly why Hitch didn't fight for it. He might have given up more quickly than otherwise because of the fact that he and Tippi came apart during the filming of *Marnie*."

However halfheartedly, Hitchcock did try to sell Universal on making *Mary Rose* with another actress. For a while, Claire Griswold, the young wife of director Sydney Pollack, became another of Hitchcock's intended Grace Kelly clones. He signed her to a seven-year contract when she played a small role in a 1962 TV show he directed, "I Saw the Whole Thing." Griswold subsequently starred in an elaborate screen test Hitchcock directed, playing not only a scene of Ingrid Bergman's from *Anastasia* (opposite the distinguished British actress Cathleen Nesbitt) but also a scene from Hitchcock's own *To Catch a Thief* in which Griswold uncomfortably was forced to re-create Kelly's performance with slavish exactitude.

For Universal, it was a case of *déjà vu* all over again when Hitchcock suggested casting Griswold as Mary Rose. She eventually rebelled against Hitchcock's attempts to dominate her life, leaving the business after becoming pregnant with her second child. Hitchcock agreed to dissolve her contract. Today she is best remembered for playing the Doll opposite Robert Duvall in the classic 1963 *Twilight Zone* show "Miniature."

In a telegram to production manager C. O. (Doc) Erickson on May 31, 1964, Hitchcock outlined his plans for the months ahead, already referring to *Mary Rose* partly in the past tense: "I have a script ready for a short scheduled feature of Sir James Barrie's play *Mary Rose*, which I intended shooting before Christmas." On August 31 of that year, MCA acquired all outstanding stock in Hitchcock's production company, Shamley Productions. The deal made him and his wife, Alma, MCA's third-largest stockholders, but it involved the surrender of a certain degree of his creative freedom.

Albert Whitlock recalled, "I used to ask him what happened with the front office and their acceptance of the [*Mary Rose*] idea, and he said, 'They believe it isn't what audiences expect of me. Not the kind of picture they expect of me.'" While this may have been partly a rationalization by Universal executives wanting to avoid a direct confrontation with Hitchcock over the "Tippi trap," even Hitchcock, with all his success, never had carte blanche in Hollywood. In the late 1970s, he wrote Truffaut that he was "completely desperate for a subject. Now, as you realize, you are a free person to make whatever you want. I, on the other hand, can only make what is expected of me; that is, a thriller, or a suspense story."

Hitchcock attempted to resuscitate *Mary Rose* after the commercial success of *Frenzy* in 1972, but once again Universal's Black Tower refused. He controlled the film rights to Barrie's play through 1987, but died in 1980, four years after the release of his last film, *Family Plot*. Perhaps Hitchcock could have persuaded Universal to free him from his contract temporarily to make *Mary Rose* as a low-budget independent production. "That would have been a cheap movie to make," Allen noted. "Simple, no big locations or anything like that, just a little island," even though Hitchcock toyed with the idea of shooting partly on location in Scotland.

While talking with Truffaut during the seventies, I lamented the forced inactivity of directors in the Hitchcock-Howard Hawks generation. Truffaut surprised me by saying he had little sympathy for wealthy old filmmakers who could afford to finance their own work but did not do so because they would have found it too humiliating.

In any case, Allen doubted that Universal would have let Hitchcock make *Mary Rose* independently because "he was on a pretty tight contract."

When I visited Hitchcock on the set of *Family Plot* at Universal in 1975, I told him I hoped he was still planning to make *Mary Rose*. He said Wasserman actually had put a clause in his contract stipulating that he could not make *Mary Rose*. I have not been able to verify that statement, since Hitchcock's contract is not among his papers at the Academy of Motion Picture Arts and Sciences' Margaret Herrick Library. But like a sly little boy delightedly getting away with a prank, Hitchcock told me how he had outwitted Wasserman by sneaking some elements of *Mary Rose* into the opening scene of *Family Plot*.

That film begins with Julia Rainbird, a wealthy old woman played by Cathleen Nesbitt, holding a séance with a phony spiritualist, Madame Blanche (Barbara Harris). Tormented with guilt, Julia is seeking absolution for her action forty years earlier in forcing her sister Harriet to abandon her illegitimate baby for fear of scandal. Julia tells her sister's ghost, in words that could have been addressed to Mary Rose, "If he's still alive, I'll find your son, and I'll take him in my arms and love him as if I were you, poor Harriet." Pretending to speak through the dead, Madame Blanche reassures the distraught Julia, "In the end there will be happiness. From the tears of the past, the desert of the heart will bloom."

Jay Allen, who had not known about that borrowing until I told her, responded, "Oh, God, how funny! Well, that's very *Mary Rose*ian. He was very mischievous." The scene in *Family Plot*, with its moving performance by Nesbitt, is much sadder than the rest of Hitchcock's final film. Hitchcock largely was content to treat the subject of occultism as an oddball *jeu d'esprit* rather than as the artistic testament *Mary Rose* might have been.

Perhaps another director may yet bring to the screen something resembling Hitchcock's vision for *Mary Rose*. "You should make the picture," Hitchcock told Truffaut rather despondently. "You would do it better. It's not really Hitchcock material." The French filmmaker did not take Hitchcock up on the suggestion, even though his own fascination with morbid love stories might have suited him to the subject. In 1986, Steven Spielberg's Universal Television/NBC series *Amazing Stories* ran a blatant imitation of *Mary Rose* titled "Without Diana." Written by Mick Garris and directed by Lesli Linka Glatter, it involves a troubled eight-year-old child (Gennie James) who vanishes on a country excursion with her war veteran father (Billy Green Bush). She returns unchanged forty years later to take her dying mother (Dianne Hull) to heaven. Although more prosaically handled than in Barrie's play, the situation remains affecting in this Americanized borrowing.

If anything, *Mary Rose* would speak more clearly to audiences today than it might have in Hitchcock's time. It would address our contemporary obsession with youth and our fascination with childlike women, which suggests a misogynistic aversion to mature womanhood. Spielberg might be the director best suited to make *Mary Rose* now, if the failure of his 1989 film *Always* has not soured him entirely on fantasy love stories. For Mary Rose, he could cast the ethereal, waifish, and elegant blonde Gwyneth Paltrow, who appeared as Young Wendy in *Hook*, his 1991 gloss on Barrie's *Peter Pan*. [This essay was published in spring 2001, when Paltrow was twenty-eight.]

Perhaps the most melancholy fact about Hitchcock's failure to make *Mary Rose* is that Universal forbade him to make it precisely because it was such a personal and idiosyncratic project. The depth of Hitchcock's emotional involvement is indicated in the closing narration for the film, which he wrote himself. The narrator is the island's boatman turned clergyman, Cameron, whose sibilant Scottish Highlander dialect is indicated in the script, as well as underlining for emphasis:

Once more THE ISLAND as we saw it first, a sweet solitary place, a promising place. And now again, we hear CAMERON's voice.

CAMERON (o.s.):
The Island. The Island That Likes To Be Fisited. Surely we all know at least one such tempting place . . . such an island

. . . where we may not go. Or if we do dare to fisit such an island . . . we cannot come away again without . . .

(there is bitter humor in his voice)

. . . without <u>embarrassment</u>. And it takes more than a bit of searching to find someone who will forgife us <u>that</u>.

(CAMERON's voice changes now, becomes louder, matter-of-fact, and final)

Well, that iss it. Let's go back home now.

(ironically)

<u>There</u> of course it's raining . . .

THE CAMERA begins to retreat.

The Island grows smaller, mistier.

CAMERON (cont'd, o.s.)

. . . as usual. And there's a naughty boy waiting for punishment and an old villager who had the fatal combination of weak heart and bad temper. <u>He</u>'ss waiting to be buried. All the usual, <u>dependable</u>, un-islandy things.

(he sighs deeply)

You understand.

As the Island becomes no more than a distant vision, CAMERON's voice diminishes as well, until at last we have lost them both.

FADE OUT.